The rawhide ties of her loosely laced long sleeved shirt held his attention, as did the snug jeans skimming her petite frame. Heavy hiking boots completed her attire.

"Jacob Sutherland?" she asked as she briskly mounted the four shallow steps leading to the porch.

Limping forward, he inclined his head. "Call me Jake."

"I'm Hannah Montgomery." After she shook his hand, she shoved her hands into her pockets. "How do you manage this mountainous terrain with a cane?"

The concern in her tone irritated him. He didn't want her sympathy. His stupid leg injury was the reason her father was dead. Every ache, every twinge, reminded him of his unfinished business.

Unfinished business that he meant to finish.

He shrugged. "It isn't a problem."

"I'm sorry for only giving you a few hours notice, but I had an unexpected opening in my schedule. My job has a tendency to take over my life."

Her words glossed over her three-month delay, making it appear that she was glad to finally be here. But he knew otherwise. Her closed body language and that flicker of annoyance in her eyes suggested she didn't want to be here at all. Too bad.

House Of Lies

by

Maggie Toussaint

House Of Lies

Contact Information: info@thewildrosepress.com

Cover Art by *R.J.Morris*

The Wild Rose Press
PO Box 706
Adams Basin, NY 14410-0706
Visit us at www.thewildrosepress.com

Publishing History
Crimson Rose Edition, January 2007
ISBN 1-60154-031-0

Published in the United States of America

Dedication

This book is dedicated to my husband.

Acknowledgements

Thanks to Marcia Balestri, president of the Maryland Ornithological Society, for providing information on birding, to Harold Domer, former City Police Chief of Frederick, Maryland, for bringing me up to speed on law enforcement matters, and to Erica Osmann Trexler, yoga instructor, for sharing her life's work. Thanks also to Wally Lind, retired senior crime scene analyst, and all the gang at Crimescenewriters for help with the car chase scenes. Any errors on these technical matters are mine and mine alone.

Many writers have supported me on this journey. Marilyn Trent has been there with me from the beginning. John Rubincam, Gail Barrett, Barbara Cummings, Susan Donovan, Karen Smith, Susan Dudics-Dean, Rebecca McTavish, Ellen Dye, and Julie Halperson read the story in its rawest form and provided input. My online critique partners Diana Cosby, JL Wilson, Judi Fennell, Donna Caubarreaux, Angela Jefferson, and Lynne Connolly have provided encouragement more recently. Thanks to Terri Ridgell who bridged the gap for me between Washington Romance Writers and First Coast Romance Writers and introduced me to writers in the Jacksonville area.

Thanks to family and friends for providing moral support and good advice. Your unflagging belief empowered me to reach into the mist and beyond.

Chapter 1

Loud static crackled on the car radio.

Hannah Montgomery punched the off button. She had enough internal static to fuel three radio stations. And what was with those headlights in her rearview mirror?

Was someone actually following her?

Don't be ridiculous. There was no reason for anyone to follow her. Whoever was back there just happened to be heading this way. Sheer coincidence.

She peered through the swiftly moving windshield wipers to read the road signs she passed. At Moxley Road, she turned right and reset her odometer. She held her breath as the car behind her also turned right. Creepy.

Thank goodness her father's elderly friend awaited her at the cottage. She'd called him this morning to let him know she was coming. His grumpy old man voice mail had gotten right to the point: "Leave a message," so she'd told him she was on her way.

Her father's cottage. She'd avoided coming up here for three months, but she'd finally decided to tackle this obligation as a prelude to her California vacation with her mother. So here she was in the Catoctin Mountains in Maryland on a Wednesday afternoon, a workday when she would normally be snowed under reviewing laboratory notebooks.

At one point five miles, she signaled a left turn onto a gravel lane. Relief slid down her back as the car behind her sped past. Nerves. She had a bad case of them all right.

She was alone, truly alone for the first time in a long time. Her co-workers were back in Bethesda, her mother already in California. Her father was—no she wouldn't think about him right now. Though this darkly shaded lane looked like the type of forest he loved to explore.

With the rain, the woods were too dark and dreary for her. Some vacation this was going to be. But coming here had been necessary. This house was a loose end she needed to tie up.

The house she'd inherited from her late father.

She hunched forward, squinting into the April shower. It had taken her two hours to reach the mountains from Bethesda, and it looked like it might take another two hours to inch up this gravel lane.

This deluge had come out of nowhere after she'd turned off the main highway. If she believed in omens or portents or the new age stuff her mother parroted, she should have turned around at the first raindrop. But Hannah wouldn't let a torrential downpour deter her. Not now.

Not when she'd finally decided to go through her late father's things. She'd postponed this trip repeatedly because coming here meant accepting he was dead. Acknowledging that her father would never again unexpectedly call out of the blue. Hannah groaned miserably and brushed her wispy bangs back from her forehead.

As if that would help her to see better. Fat chance. Between the heavy rain obscuring her vision and the irrational dread mushrooming inside of her, she couldn't see or think worth a darn.

But she wasn't turning back now. She wasn't a quitter. She had never quit on her father, even though he'd quit on her twenty-two years ago.

Long ago, on the night before he left, he'd pretended nothing was wrong as he read aloud her favorite bedtime story. Every detail of those last few minutes together was etched in her childhood memory.

He'd smelled "Daddy" perfect and his nighttime whiskers had tickled her face. She'd burrowed into his lap, delighting in his dramatic rendition of the fairy tale.

The very next day, she'd learned that "happily ever after" was a myth. Happily never after was more like it.

She hated this blinding rain. She hated her faltering courage. But most of all, she hated the onerous duty waiting at the end of this steep incline.

The rain eased and then stopped altogether. Slender fingers of sunshine penetrated the moisture-laden tree canopy, reaching down to the earth in shafts of wavering light. The dark overhead branches finally gave way to brilliant blue sky. Hannah summoned her resolve and drove out of the shadowy forest. Then she slammed on the brakes.

Her mouth gaped. She didn't believe it. Like a gleaming mirage, her late father's home sparkled in a dreamy pool of sunlight. As if the cozy cottage had been lifted intact from the pages of *Little Red Riding Hood*.

Every detail was as she remembered it, from the crisp white Victorian trim to the gingerbread brown stain on the wooden siding to the weathered rockers lining the rustic front porch. She drew in a long shaky breath, filling the empty space in her gut, blinking back hot tears. She could almost smell the cinnamon.

Would the big bad wolf be inside?

The hair on the back of her neck stirred at the thought of her childhood nemesis. At twenty-nine she was too old to believe in fairy tales. Even so, what were the chances this house existed outside of an illustrator's imagination?

Hannah massaged her overly tight jaw, understanding her unease. Going through her secretive father's personal effects was her worst nightmare. Far more unsettling than big bad wolves.

As she slid from her car, a large shadow passed over the clearing.

****

Finally.

Jake Sutherland had wondered when Hannah

Montgomery would show up. By his estimation, she was three months late. What kind of daughter waited three entire months to claim her inheritance?

She'd had him cooling his heels the whole time. He itched to get out of here, even though his injured leg was still mending.

And damn D.C. Montgomery for not having any pictures of Hannah. His late partner had never mentioned that his daughter was a looker. In his mind, Hannah was a bookish school-marm type with organizing tendencies.

In reality, she was a knock-out. Her wind tousled brunette locks framed a heart-shaped face, covering her ears like an unruly cap. His heartbeat kicked up a notch at her grey-green eyes. A pert turned up nose, rosy cheeks, and a flawless complexion rounded out her facial features.

The rawhide ties of her loosely laced long sleeved shirt held his attention, as did the snug jeans skimming her petite frame. Heavy hiking boots completed her attire.

"Jacob Sutherland?" she asked as she briskly mounted the four shallow steps leading to the porch.

Limping forward, he inclined his head. "Call me Jake."

"I'm Hannah Montgomery." After she shook his hand, she shoved her hands into her pockets. "How do you manage this mountainous terrain with a cane?"

The concern in her tone irritated him. He didn't want her sympathy. His stupid leg injury was the reason her father was dead. Every ache, every twinge, reminded him of his unfinished business.

Unfinished business that he meant to finish.

He shrugged. "It isn't a problem."

"I'm sorry for only giving you a few hours notice, but I had an unexpected opening in my schedule. My job has a tendency to take over my life."

Her words glossed over her three month delay, making it appear that she was glad to finally be here. But he knew otherwise. Her closed body language and that flicker of annoyance in her eyes suggested she didn't want to be here at all. Too bad.

Her scent, faintly floral and distinctively female, invaded his head as he studied her. She had an interesting way of cocking her head when she listened, and her eyes, damned if she didn't have D.C.'s intelligent eyes.

Though hers weren't jaded or world-weary like her father's had been. Hers sparkled with vitality and trust.

Trust. The word soured in his mouth. His passion for women had cost him dearly. Because he'd let down his guard, his leg was busted, his partner dead.

He limped towards the door. "Come in."

"Let me get that door for you." Hannah scooted around him and manned the door. "Are you sure you should be up and around on that leg? You don't look too steady on your feet."

"I'm fine," Jake growled. He navigated carefully. Why had she honed in on his physical weakness at the first possible moment? Behind him he heard her rapid intake of breath as she entered the living room.

Not his fault.

He'd given up on checking his voice mail messages after three months of waiting, so he'd missed her call this morning. Thanks to D.C.'s driveway pressure sensor, he'd known a vehicle was coming up the mountain when she started up the drive. That's when he'd accessed his voice mail and heard her message.

If he'd had more than ten minutes warning, he would have picked the place up. As it was, he'd been lucky to retrieve his gun and tuck it inside his T-shirt and under the back waistband of his jeans before she arrived.

He wasn't expecting trouble in this wooded hideaway, but old habits died hard.

"This place needs a good cleaning," she said in a critical tone.

She knew exactly where to stick the knife in his ribs and turn it. There wouldn't be a mess in the house if she hadn't taken so damn long to get here. Neatness and order were greatly over rated anyway.

Jake eased himself into the brown chenille recliner and engaged the foot rest, grimacing at the mechanical jarring of his left thigh. Greeting her on the porch had left him drained. If he'd known she was coming today, he wouldn't have pushed himself to walk the property perimeter this morning. "I didn't get hurt yesterday."

Hannah appeared to consider his words for a moment. Then she frowned at the cluttered living room again. "I apologize. That didn't come out right. I didn't mean to offend you. I'm nervous about being here. My father and I weren't close."

She hesitated for a moment. "How long ago did you hurt your leg?"

Twelve weeks and two days, the exact length of time her father had been dead. "About three months ago," he replied casually, waiting to see if she would make the connection. He was half afraid she would, even more afraid she wouldn't connect the two events.

"Oh." She immediately started tidying up, stacking his computer magazines into a pile, collecting the empty soda cans he'd left lying around. "How well did you know my father?"

"We worked together."

She paused momentarily. "You're in the import business?"

He and D.C. Montgomery had worked in an elite group of professional liars. "We were partners."

"Partners." Her faltering voice tugged at his cold heart. She cocked her head, studying him again, her look intense. "His Will didn't have any provision for his business interests."

Jake fought off the urge to squirm in his seat. He didn't like lying to her. So he stuck as close to the truth as possible. "Your father and I made arrangements concerning his business interests before he died. I bought him out."

Hannah stopped at the bookshelf. Her delicate fingers trailed the length of the dusty book spines from *Moby Dick* to *Mark Twain*. He noticed her fingers were conspicuously devoid of rings. Not that her potential availability meant anything to him. He'd sworn off women.

"My mother inherited his life insurance money and his investment accounts," Hannah said, moving on to touch the ugly brown lamp. She wiped a streak of dust off the plain wooden coffee table. "I got this house. My father's house. You know what? I never knew this place existed until he died. My father didn't think enough of me to invite me to his home."

Damn D. C. for being such a jerk. Now he felt sorry for her. He didn't want to feel anything for her. Helping her dispense with D.C.'s belongings was a job, and as soon as they finished, he could get on with his unfinished business.

Seeing her touch everything in that exploring way she had was making his blood thrum with anticipation. Feelings were trouble, but they also made him feel alive for the first time in months. Silent longing had him gripping the armrests, wishing he'd removed the gun from his tight jeans before he sat down.

"How long did you work with my father?" she asked from the coffee stained island separating the kitchen from the living room.

"Five years."

She circled past him and stopped in front of the window overlooking the front yard. In a soft voice she asked, "Did you travel together?"

"Yes." That wasn't a lie either. He and D.C. Montgomery had circled the globe more than once.

Hannah turned to face him, her eyes bright with wonder. "The things you must have seen. My father's travel stories bordered on the incredible. Do you plan to travel abroad in the future?"

"I've got one trip on the horizon." That was true. He

had unfinished business in the Middle East.

Her tidying movements annoyed him. He didn't need a maid. "Why don't you sit down and relax?"

She shook her head stubbornly and returned to the bookshelf, aligning the book spines on the top shelf. "My father never told me about this place. Now to be standing here in his house, touching his things, it's too much. I suppose you think I was a bad daughter for never visiting him, but all I had for him in the way of an address was a phone number. He was a very private man."

No kidding. Not many secret agents went around blabbing about what they did and stayed active in the field. D.C. Montgomery had been one of the best field operatives in the agency's history.

Hannah carried four dirty glasses to the kitchen sink. "These drinking glasses are storm blue. The living room carpet is the same shade. I never even knew Dad liked my favorite color. What kind of daughter doesn't know what her father's favorite color is?"

The chiding tone of her voice hinted of unresolved issues with her father. He bristled, mentally leaping to an offensive position. But this wasn't a battle where he had to take sides. "D.C. wasn't much for explanations."

As a rule, Jake didn't get emotional about his work, but he thought the world of D.C. Years of learned caution tempered his tongue. Caution and honor. He'd learned both from D.C.

He wouldn't betray D.C.'s trust, but it would be a long visit if Hannah pestered him about his late partner.

Hannah's head disappeared beneath the counter as she found the trashcan and discarded the empty soda cans. "I don't even know if he had a woman in his life."

"D.C. used to say there were only two women in his life, his wife and his daughter." Oops. Jake winced inwardly. That wasn't supposed to slip out. What was it about this woman that had him volunteering information? He knew better than that.

Damn if her eyes didn't brim with moisture as her

head popped back up. Her chin wobbled. "He did?" Her voice faded into dreamy softness.

Jake shrugged. He wouldn't let those tears sway him. He had been trained to repress his emotions. But he owed her father. He couldn't let her believe her father was a complete jerk, even if he was dead.

What would it hurt if he hinted at D.C.'s accomplishments? "Your father was well respected. The best in the business."

She gave a tremulous smile as she rummaged through the kitchen cabinets. "Thank you for that. Let me repay you by cooking us dinner before I find a motel."

"No point in staying in a motel. There's plenty of room here."

"I wouldn't want to put you out."

"It's your house. You should stay here. If you want me to leave, I will."

"No. That isn't necessary. Why don't I work on dinner, and we'll decide on the other later."

Jake nodded towards the refrigerator. "The freezer is stocked with frozen dinners. Take your pick."

She chewed her lip. "No, I meant, let me cook us dinner. A real meal. I brought groceries with me."

Jake couldn't remember the last time he'd had a home-cooked meal. "Sounds good."

"Great. I'll bring the groceries in and get started."

She was pretty. She cooked. And there was a chance she'd sleep under his roof. In the past he hadn't been very selective about women he slept with, but he'd had a great deal of time on his hands lately. She was his ideal woman, and he couldn't touch her.

No problem, unless he admitted he'd been successful at swearing off women because none were available. Having one in close proximity would test his resolve. "How long do you plan to be up here?"

She scowled down at a pot. "A day or two. My vacation was supposed to start next Monday, but I took off early to come up here."

"Where are you headed?"

"I'm catching a flight to California on Sunday to join my mother." Hannah leaned across the island countertop separating the two rooms. Through the open laces of her shirt he saw the deep shadow outlining her ample cleavage. "But, before I do that, I'm taking advantage of you."

He hadn't expected a sexual invitation. Desire roared to life. The dull throbbing in his leg faded in prominence as he envisioned a seduction scenario. His rumpled bedroom wasn't up to her uncluttered standards. But out here would work.

What were the odds? He'd been out of circulation for three months and the first female he saw threw herself at him. He must be imagining this. He stared at her, noticing the bright red flags on her cheeks.

Her hand clapped over her mouth. "I can't believe I said that. I should've been clearer about my intent. I plan to take advantage of your desire to stay here."

"You'll need to be clearer still. I don't understand."

"Oh. Sorry. I want your signature on a property lease."

Jake thanked his lucky stars he hadn't loped over there and jumped her. His resolve to stay away from her wasn't firm at all. This is D.C.'s daughter, he told himself. You're supposed to take care of her, not jump her.

He owed D.C., but how could he fulfill a deathbed promise to his mentor when he was attracted to Hannah? Sweat beaded on his brow as the sharp pain in his left thigh made itself achingly apparent.

The doctors had told him to stay in bed for a month and then to gradually increase his activity over the next six months, but he'd followed his own course of accelerated physical therapy.

"Jake? What's wrong? Won't that arrangement suit you?"

Her floral fragrance tickled his nose, her compassionate voice wormed into his subconscious. His eyes snapped shut defensively. Heat rose from his shirt collar. Thank God there was no earthly penalty for lusting after a woman in his thoughts.

He swore under his breath. This was exactly why the agency had let him go. Not his bum leg or his blown cover. But his marshmallow soft spot for women.

At thirty-three, he had no job, no prospects on the horizon, and no career. In short, he had nothing to offer a domesticated female like Hannah.

One thing was certain.

He wasn't going to rusticate out here in the woods one second longer than he had to. He was a wanderer. It was unnatural for him to stay put for this long. And it was past time for him to set the record straight with his dead partner's daughter.

"I thought you knew." He spoke in a slow measured tone. "I've been watching over this place for you as a favor to D.C. I don't plan to stay."

"Oh dear."

Her response puzzled him. He expanded his answer. "I told the lawyer I would stay until you arrived, but I never intended to live here permanently."

Hannah's chin jutted forward. "Why not?"

"I move around a lot. I'm here because I promised D.C. I would help you. Living in this particular house isn't easy for me either."

Her huge eyes filled with sympathy, damn them. Jake didn't want her pity. He didn't need anyone to coddle him. Self-sufficiency was his way.

"I'm being selfish," she said, clutching her hands together against the hollow of her breasts. "You've lost a close friend. I'm so sorry."

Jake forced himself to let go of the chair armrests. He was a man, not a wimp. "Don't feel sorry for me. I made a mistake, and I'm paying for it."

Hannah moved closer. "It's obvious both of us have issues about being here," she said, her voice soothing and conciliatory. "But I have to do something with this house.

If you don't want it, I'll have to rent it out. I'll whip this place into shape, and you can help me screen rental applicants."

Her words washed over him like a series of powerful ocean waves. He thrashed about in the swift current of her words. "You're not going to live here?"

She shook her head. "I'm heading to California for two weeks and then back to my job. Now that my mother has pots of money, she's decided to bring yoga to the masses through a series of instructional videos. I got stuck tying up the loose ends here in Maryland. Living in this woodland fairy tale cottage isn't part of the long-range plan."

That wasn't what his partner intended. "D.C. believed you would live here."

Hannah scowled. "Why would he think a darn fool thing like that?"

He shrugged, but his conscious gesture was an out and out lie. Immediate assessment of a situation had always been his tactical strength.

From the moment he saw Hannah, he knew she belonged here. She belonged to this storybook place in a way that made his heart ache. He'd never belonged, not even in his foster family.

"Nothing has to be settled right now," Hannah said. "You get some rest, and I'll start dinner."

Jake eased his legs down. "I'll help unload your car."

"No thanks." She pushed against the top of his chair, reclining him. "I can manage two bags of groceries on my own."

"Fine." If she wanted to be stubborn, he'd let her win this battle. It was a small price to pay for a hot meal.

Chapter 2

When Hannah had shopped for this meal, she'd chosen easy to chew foods out of deference to her father's elderly boarder. But the joke had been on her.

Jake Sutherland wasn't an old geezer. Jake had all his teeth and wouldn't have any trouble chewing through a side of beef.

The phrase about big teeth from the *Little Red Riding Hood* story came to mind. "The better to eat you with, my dear." A chill snaked down her spine as she imagined Jake's sensuous mouth touching her. She sucked in a quick breath.

This wasn't the time to drift away in one of her daydreams. Jake would eat her up if she let him. She wasn't going to let him.

Hannah turned down the heat beneath the boiling water and picked up the pasta box, but before she could get it opened, her cell phone rang. She answered the call.

"Hannah, its Mom. You busy?"

She suppressed the irritation she felt at being checked up on. "Hi, Mom. I'm cooking dinner. Why?"

"I just had to share with you that I'm having the most marvelous time in California. There are so many yoga studios and so many movie producers out here. It will take me a year to meet them all."

Searing pain shot up the right side of her face, radiating over to her ear. Tension caused her to clench her teeth, in turn putting pressure on her jaw, yielding pain and discomfort and more stress. She massaged her aching jaw. "I don't have a year to help you get your yoga video launched, Mom."

Cradling the phone between her shoulder and her ear, Hannah ripped the cardboard top off the pasta box. Half a box would normally feed her for a few days, but how much would Jake eat? Better to have too much than not enough. She dumped the entire package of noodles in the boiling water. "I've got two weeks off from my job, and then I have to get back to work."

"I wish you'd quit that job," her mother said. "It takes up all your time and makes your shoulders tense."

A lot of things made her tense. Arguing with her mother for one. "Lucky for me my mother's a yoga instructor. You help me work that shoulder tension out of my system." Hannah dumped croutons on her tossed salad greens, and then arranged them so that no two croutons were touching.

"Seriously, Hannah. We have plenty of money now. You don't have to work anymore."

Technically the money was her mother's. This house was Hannah's. Becoming financially beholden to her mother was a step back in Hannah's independence, a step she wouldn't take. "I want to work, Mom. I'm good at my job. I like organizing data into useful information blocks that people can understand."

"But your job keeps you out of the main stream of life. How am I ever going to get any grandchildren if you spend your time fixing other people's mistakes?"

Hannah could practically hear violins playing as her mother warmed up to her favorite theme. She didn't need this lecture right now, not with such a willing sperm donor so close at hand. She'd seen the lust that had flared in Jake's eyes when she'd inadvertently propositioned him.

Thank God Jake had retreated to his room to rest while she cooked. With an eye towards the closed door of Jake's bedroom, Hannah dropped her voice to answer. "I'm not in any rush to have children."

"Exactly my point. I'm going to be too old to enjoy my grandchildren, if I ever get any. You're not getting any younger either."

"We've been over this before, Mom. I am not threatened by my biological clock. Is there anything else you wanted to talk to me about?"

"Actually, yes. The producer I met today, Doug Nichols, a charming man by the way, is interested in seeing my art portfolio. I told him all about the murals in our house and he said he wanted to see them. How much trouble would it be to run home tomorrow, wrap up my portfolio, and ship it out here to me?"

Hannah groaned aloud. "I just got here, Mom. This weekend is supposed to be my time to deal with Dad's house."

"I wouldn't ask if it wasn't important." Her mother's insistent voice grated on Hannah's nerves. "Maybe your father's boarder would join you for the car ride. Then the trip wouldn't seem so long."

She cupped her hand around her mouth so that her words wouldn't travel much beyond the phone. "Dad's boarder is a temporary situation. He's been hanging out here until I arrived, apparently. He doesn't plan on staying."

"Oh dear. Does this change your plan for coming out here?"

"No. I'm still flying out there on Sunday. I already purchased my airline ticket. If I don't have the house rented by then, I'll hire an agency to do it."

There was a slight pause before her mother responded. "You're keeping the house?"

"Did you know about this place, Mom?"

"No."

"So, you haven't ever seen Dad's house?"

"What's wrong, Hannah?"

Why was her mother's voice so sharp? She wasn't here. She had no right to be upset. Hannah had plenty to be upset about. "What's wrong is that this house is the spitting image of grandmother's house from my *Little Red Riding Hood* book. Are you sure you don't know anything about this house?"

"How odd. But then your father always was a little secretive."

Hannah precisely halved fresh strawberries into a small bowl. They'd go nicely with the angel food cake she'd bought for dessert. "Try a lot secretive."

"Don't blame me for your father's squirrelly behavior. He deceived me into thinking he was normal when we met, but he was already full of secrets."

"The energy flow in this house feels off." Hannah inhaled deeply, opening her senses until she could discern what was bothering her. "The living room and the kitchen are sparsely furnished like an efficiency motel room, but the master bedroom is furnished nicely. There are no pictures anywhere, just books. Shelves and shelves of books. He chose storm blue for the walls and the carpet. My favorite color."

Hannah's mother sighed. "Sneaky of him to do that."

"But why? Why would he want me to like this place? The location is miles from anywhere. It's not like I could live here and keep my quality assurance job at Potomac River Labs."

"If I knew how your father's mind worked, I would have saved myself years of agony. Let's get back to why I called. Will you ship me my portfolio tomorrow?"

Hannah stirred the fettuccini noodles and visually verified that the bottoms of the silverware were aligned on the paper napkins. "It's inconvenient, but I don't see any reason why I can't run back home and get it. I don't mind waiting another day before I pack up Dad's clothes and books."

"Your father's boarder will probably be thrilled to have an outing. Ask him to ride along."

If her mother knew how close Jake had come to jumping her earlier this evening, she'd probably call out the National Guard. Best not to mention Jake's age either. "We'll see. I've gotta run. Bye, Mom."

****

With one ear to the muffled conversation beyond his closed bedroom door, Jake cruised through computer screens, checking each window for traces of his elusive quarry. Now that Hannah had finally arrived, it was time for him to put his offensive plan into action.

He'd been methodically searching for information about Ursula Gruber for months. Last week he discovered activity on another identity she occasionally used, Joan Andress. He'd been cross-referencing her aliases through several data banks to pinpoint her location when the driveway alarm had notified him of Hannah's approach.

The dull ache in his thigh reminded him of his need to complete this last mission. He had been put out to pasture by the government, but this unfinished business with Ursula pulled at him. He wasn't ready to retire.

His need for vengeance drove him through each day. D.C.'s murder would not go unavenged. Justice would be served.

He'd screwed up, he freely admitted that, but his oversight of leaving a phone number in his billfold shouldn't have been fatal. He'd been wracking his brain going over the events just prior to the ambush, but he'd drawn a blank. Ursula was all he had, so she was the focus of his investigation.

D.C. had kept information close to his chest for the last few months of his life. Had D.C. known that something strange was in the works? Had his legendary sixth sense warned him that their last mission was headed for disaster?

"Dinner's ready," Hannah called from the kitchen.

Jake cleared the screen at the sound of her cheerful voice. "Be right there." He closed his laptop. Should he hide the computer in his duffel bag?

D.C.'s daughter wasn't a spy. She didn't have any idea of what her father did for a living, and Jake planned to keep her in the dark. Besides, his machine was password protected. She'd have to be a computer genius to hack into his files, and nothing he'd read about her suggested that was within her capability.

Jake limped to the kitchen. He hoped for lots of meat and mashed potatoes. If he'd been a blind man, he could have easily followed the appetizing vapor trail. His empty stomach rumbled. "Smells good."

It had been a long time since he'd had home cooking. He hadn't been to visit his foster parents in six months. From the threshold he took in the soldier straight lines of silverware guarding the plates. This woman had serious organizing tendencies. At this rate, she'd have this place categorized and filed away before the sun set.

Where would she file him?

"I hope you like fettuccini," Hannah said.

"I like anything I don't have to cook." He scanned the bowl of steaming noodles on the table. No meat. Not a good sign. "Are you a vegetarian?"

"Mostly."

"Mostly?" What kind of an answer was that? Jake waited for her to sit down, then eased himself into the other chair and watched her surreptitiously. Women like Hannah always had unwritten rules about eating.

Hannah unfolded her napkin and placed it in her lap. "I've been known to eat meat, on occasion. I draw the line at touching raw meat. Not happening."

Jake did the napkin thing, sliding his silverware into a jumbled heap. "So you're an occasional carnivore?"

A delightful blush warmed Hannah's face as she transferred white noodles on her plate. "The way you say that makes me feel like I'm cheating on a diet. I'm not against meat or meat-eaters, I just chose not to prepare meat. Did you have a nice rest?"

"Sure." Jake accepted the tongs for the noodles and helped himself. Hunting down a cold-blooded killer on the Internet soothed him like nothing else. He downed a bite of noodles as he tore off a hunk of bread. "This tastes great, thanks."

Her delicious meal steadily filled the gnawing hole in his middle. He was used to eating without talking, but he didn't want her to feel ill at ease. He searched for something to talk about. "When do you want to get started on the house? Tonight?"

"I'd planned to start in the morning, but my mother called. I have to spend most of tomorrow running an errand for her."

"Oh?" Jake ripped his bread apart and sopped up the creamy white sauce on his plate.

"She needs her portfolio overnighted to California."

Jake arched an eyebrow and helped himself to seconds on the salad. Not many of those crunchy croutons were left.

"She's lining up movie people to do a yoga video," Hannah said in a breathy rush. "A producer she met expressed an interest in her work. That's why she needs it."

"Your mother's an artist? What does she paint?"

"Everything. Once she ran out of wall space in our house, she started in on our clothes." Hannah fingered the collar of her shirt. "She painted this shirt."

Jake noticed the faint swirls down Hannah's sleeves and her torso. Bold folk art edged the neckline. He'd assumed those details were dyed into the fabric.

"Wow." Hannah's shirt was a work of art, and he hadn't noticed how unique the design was until she'd pointed it out to him. He must be slipping.

If that was so, then his obliqueness was entirely her fault. Having a woman underfoot was a torment and a joy. "I'll go with you tomorrow."

"I appreciate the offer, but you don't have to."

Her gentle rebuff stung. Now that she was here, he was anxious to fulfill his obligation to her father. Once Hannah was settled, then he could fully concentrate on his revenge.

"You'd be doing me a favor," he said, emptying the remaining noodles on his plate. "I'm ready to venture out into the world again."

Alarm flared briefly in Hannah's tropical green eyes,

but she covered by quickly flashing him a smile. "Suit yourself."

She didn't want him tagging along. Why was that? His curiosity about her grew. "Tell me about your work. What is it that you do?"

She pursed her lips. "My ordinary work in quality assurance would bore you to tears. You've led such an exciting life with all that travel."

Jake lounged back in his chair. Interesting. Once again she had deflected the conversation away from herself. "Traveling isn't all it's cracked up to be. Even before my injury I thought about switching jobs. My foster mother always said to be careful what I wished for because I just might get it, and she was right."

"You're closing the import business?"

"Way ahead of you. I've been unemployed for a few months."

Hannah took a long drink of water. "Was it wise to quit one job before you had another lined up?"

Did she think he was a bum because he didn't have a regular job? It bothered him that her approval mattered. "I didn't really have much choice. Without D.C., the business wasn't going anywhere."

"I see."

Her comment irritated him worse than his throbbing leg. She couldn't see a darn thing because she had no idea what business her father had been in. Her father's savvy smarts and thorough methodology had set the standard in the intelligence field. No one was better at getting the job done than D.C. Montgomery. No one.

****

The next morning Jake still felt irritated. It hadn't been easy sleeping one bedroom away from Hannah. He'd heard her tossing and turning in there for most of the night.

Then, just as he finally drifted off to sleep, his computer woke him up with a series of distinctive chirps. He'd programmed an electronic interface between the external house security system and his laptop. That series of chirps meant someone had just crossed the front yard.

Jake yanked his gun out from under his pillow and limped over to his window. He raised the vinyl shade to see a familiar brunette head disappear into the forest which ringed the house. His gut tightened. What was Hannah doing in the woods at daybreak?

He slipped on a pair of jeans and followed her out into the yard. The dewy grass felt cold on his bare feet. He rubbed the sleep from his eyes and listened intently to the sounds of the forest.

As long as Hannah stuck to the trails around the house, she wouldn't be in any danger. Over the past three months, he'd traversed all the trails on the property as he strengthened the muscles in his leg. Nothing out there but woods, a spring-fed meadow, and more woods.

He'd put the coffee on and get a shower. No point in going back to bed if she was up and about. Not that he could sleep with her out there.

He was on his second cup when she returned. Her cheeks were brightly flushed, and she walked with purpose across the tiled floor. She had on another hand-painted shirt, this one with various shore birds outlined on the butter colored fabric. Her green twill slacks had strands of intertwined tone on tone ivy running the length of the outer leg seams. Jake felt rather plain in his blue jeans and the black T-shirt he'd thrown on.

"Did I wake you?" she asked, placing her binoculars next to the coffee pot. She poured herself a cup of coffee and wiped the counter clean. Binoculars. The deluxe brand D.C. had favored. "Best in the business for long distance vision," D.C. had claimed. Jake's heart missed a beat. Who had Hannah been spying on out in the woods?

He didn't like that she wasn't what she was supposed to be. This was supposed to be a routine assignment. "I had to get up anyway."

"I could have sworn I was as quiet as a church mouse. I'm sorry to have interrupted your sleep."

Did she know about the house alarm? She said she'd never been here, but what if she was playing him about that too? "Not a problem. What time would you like to leave this morning?"

Hannah glanced at her watch. "We need time for breakfast and showers. How does an hour and a half sound?"

It sounded like she was going to feed him again. His belly rumbled in anticipation. There was no harm in enjoying her cooking. "Sounds good."

Hannah bustled about the kitchen, taking eggs and bread out of the refrigerator. "How's that leg this morning?"

Jake shifted in his chair and a flash of pain knifed through him. "Fine."

"You never did get around to telling me what happened to you."

And he wasn't going to either. "You know that old saying that two objects can't occupy the same space at the same time?" She nodded. "My leg got in the way of a sharp object."

Hannah cracked eggs into the frying pan. "Ouch. I bet you'll never do that again."

Jake's cheek twitched. "Not if I can help it." He brooded over his coffee as the eggs sizzled in the frying pan. He wouldn't try to stop a bullet again with his leg.

The toast popped up out of the toaster. Hannah slid the fried eggs on the toast and joined him at the table. Breakfast. It smelled great. It tasted even better.

Those binoculars sitting on the counter bothered him. Time to ask a few subtle questions. "Do you always take early morning walks in the woods?"

"Every chance I get." Hannah beamed a brilliant smile at him and his hormones revved in response.

Jake groaned inwardly and ducked his head back down to his plate. This was D.C.'s daughter. He had already let D.C. down once. He wouldn't do it again.

A wanderer like him had no business with someone

as settled as Hannah. Best to remember that. "How come? You a fitness buff?"

"Birder."

"Hmm." When Jake thought of bird watchers, he envisioned grizzled matrons standing on wooden platforms, with dainty binoculars trained on distant treetops. That image didn't jive with the active, vibrant woman who hiked across mountaintops at daybreak.

Her head tilted to the side, her eyes brilliant with daylight. "Aren't you going to ask?"

He was aware birds were in the woods. He'd used them at times to learn if someone was approaching, but he didn't care about the particulars. But she looked so hopeful. "Ask what?"

"What I saw."

"You told me. Birds."

Hannah whipped out a small pad of paper from her back pocket and reviewed the neatly written list. "That doesn't do the "Dawn Chorus" justice. This morning I saw Carolina wrens, white breasted nuthatches, doves, cardinals, Eastern phoebes, and chickadees. There was a downy woodpecker not far from the cute little meadow I found. And the warblers are here."

"Interesting," Jake said, his eyes glazing over. She had a distracted gleam in her eye as if she could talk about those damn birds for hours. Better not to give her any additional encouragement. No telling how many pages of bird names she had in that pad. He lurched to his feet and carried the dishes to the sink. "I'll get my shower now."

He thought he heard her laugh, but when he turned back, her expression seemed very carefully schooled. He scowled at her.

"Was there something else?" she asked.

"Never mind," he said.

****

Jake parked his pickup on the long, sweeping drive in front of the two story Colonial style brick home. The football field sized yard was neatly mowed. The evergreens ringing the foundation were geometric marvels. In every way, the pricey dwelling looked upscale but disappointingly ordinary, not what he expected after seeing Hannah's hand-painted clothes.

The house was located in a more expensive neighborhood than his foster family's home in Philadelphia. Even if he wasn't already on his best behavior because of his promise to D.C., one thing was clear. Hannah was way out of his league.

He rubbed his aching temples.

"If you'd let me drive, you wouldn't be so tired," Hannah said.

Jake wasn't about to let her drive him anywhere. He wouldn't feel safe until Ursula was behind bars. If evasive maneuvers were called for, he needed to be in the driver's seat. "I'm not tired so much as stiff."

Hannah opened her door. "Come on in. Moving around will help work that stiffness out of your leg."

Jake hobbled behind her. While the house exterior looked like upscale suburbia, the interior looked like he'd stepped into another century. The two-story foyer walls were covered in an intense Joan of Arc battle scene. There was something very familiar about the defiant tilt of Joan's chin. He couldn't resist touching the velvety muzzle of her armored steed.

"She's good, isn't she?" Hannah asked, noticing his hand resting reverently on the wall.

Speechless, Jake nodded his agreement.

Hannah stowed her small purse on the graciously curving staircase. "Make yourself at home. Who knows how long it will take to assemble Mom's portfolio. All she could tell me was that her collection of prints was in the office."

He nodded, uncomfortably aware that the three cups of coffee he'd had for breakfast now wanted to come out. "Bathroom?"

"Under the staircase."

Jake's heels rang out on the gleaming ceramic tile floor. He headed for the space under the stairs and refreshed himself in a room painted to resemble an Irish countryside. The verdant grasses and soaring sky were peppered with four leaf clovers and leprechauns. A rainbow arched over the sink, ending at the golden toilet. He'd been to Ireland, but this special room made him long to return.

His leg seemed better after a few more steps, and he didn't lean so heavily on his cane. In the living room, two huge fire breathing dragons were permanently frozen in attack mode. A gentle glade of unicorns peacefully grazed beside a flowing stream in the dining room, and transparent water sprites danced across the stream surface as if they were ballerinas in toe shoes. Woodland fairies graced the wooden chairs surrounding the delicate tree of life painted on the table surface. The ethereal artwork charmed him, making him wish he were part of this fantasy.

In the kitchen, southwest colors and canyons dominated the copper-punch covered cabinets. Beside the arched doorway, a mythical phoenix rose from the ashes of the desert floor. Off to the side of the kitchen was a mirror lined studio with an elegant Chinese pagoda painted on the red floor. Dinosaurs ruled in the office off the dining room where Hannah was searching through stacks of paper.

Hannah looked up. "I'll be at this for a while. Might as well sit down and relax."

He tried not to think about the sharp ache in his leg. "I'll be in the living room."

He wandered back through the house and sat down in the corner seat of the black leather sofa. Automatically, his hand reached down for the recliner handle, and he was pleasantly surprised when a foot rest sprang from the chair seat. He'd never admit it to Hannah, but the drive here had taken a lot out of him. A few minutes with his feet elevated should help.

His gaze stalled on the dueling dragons opposite him. Hannah's mother had what most artists would kill to have. Her vivid subjects leapt off the walls at him. This place was very different from the modest home he'd been raised in.

He and Hannah were nothing alike. Worse, he had nothing to offer a woman who wore original hand-painted clothing and could travel across the world in her own home.

Chapter 3

The creepy sensation of icy fingers brushing across the back of Hannah's neck returned. Someone was watching her. She was sure of it. The weight of their gaze followed her in and out of the Post Office. The first thing she did after mailing the art portfolio was to lock the doors of her mother's Mercedes.

Her pulse drummed in her ears. As she pulled out, she checked her mirrors. Two other vehicles exited the lot behind her, a gray pickup and a dark sedan. Was someone following her? She circled the block the wrong way to see if she was alone.

The dark sedan stayed behind her.

Her fingers gripped the steering wheel. Wasn't the car last night dark in color?

Fear quivered through her at the possibility. Though it was entirely possible, it wasn't very probable. Why would anyone follow her? She was the queen of ordinary.

But what if it was the same person today as yesterday afternoon? Did she have a stalker? She shook her head again as the sedan fell back in traffic. She lived in the analytical world of data streams and standardized procedures.

Her job wasn't sexy. Her life wasn't sexy. Depressing thought, that.

It was Jake's fault. She hadn't known how sterile her life was until she'd met him. In less than twenty-four hours he'd turned her orderly perceptions upside down. She hadn't thought about the lack of zip in her job as being boring. She loved having a set routine. But there was something to be said for spontaneity too.

It made her feel alive.

She didn't kid herself. If not for the circumstance of Jake being the caretaker of her father's cottage, she never would've met him. And she was ninety-nine point nine percent certain that once this weekend was done, they'd go their separate ways.

In the meantime, she had to learn how to deal with these erratic emotional swings she was experiencing. They weren't at all ordinary. In fact, she'd never been this unsettled when a man was around. The serious side of her wanted to take notes and compare the results with other experimental data. The 'data' being her tepid personal life.

She'd found it hard to get close to anyone at work because it was her job to police their work. And she knew that liars didn't change their stripes. If a co-worker lied about his research, he wouldn't hesitate to lie in a personal relationship. She was very good at her job. So good they called her the ice queen behind her back.

Which only went to show how boring and sterile her life was. Boring people didn't have stalkers. What was going on?

She turned on the winding approach road to her neighborhood, tapping her thumbs rhythmically on the steering wheel in time with the oldies music on the radio. She let out a deep sigh when the road behind her stayed clear. That whole worry about the sedan had been for nothing. Hormonal hysteria. That was the only logical explanation.

She sighed heavily.

As she prepared to round the first curve, she thought she caught sight of a car behind her, but then she was turning and there was only scenery in her rearview mirror. She relaxed, slowing to enjoy the large estate homes that flanked the road. Everything looked just the way it was supposed to.

Familiar.

Ordinary.

Sunshine bathed the world in strong, vibrant light. A red car passed her going downhill towards the shopping center. Daffodils bloomed beside the miles of white vinyl fence. One more warm spring day and the forsythia would pop.

Without warning, the black sedan loomed large in her rear view mirror. Her fingers tightened around the steering wheel. Not now. There was no place to hide. Worse, there was a bad turn right in front of her. She decelerated into the curve.

But the black sedan kept on coming, as if she wasn't even there, as if the sharp curve wasn't dangerous.

As the sedan closed on her, she noted the front license tag was missing. Virginia, Maryland, and D.C. required front plates. The hair on the back of her neck electrified.

Suddenly, the sedan swerved over in the oncoming traffic lane, alarming Hannah further. What was the driver thinking? If someone approached from the other direction, there'd be a three car pile up.

Hannah glanced anxiously in her side mirror. The windows of the sedan were tinted so dark she couldn't tell if the driver was male or female. It was a nameless faceless menace.

Like the trolls under her childhood bed.

Her gut told her this was a bad situation. Her father had warned her time and again to listen to her gut when faced with danger. Her gut said to get the heck out of here.

She stomped on the accelerator just as the sedan whipped towards where her rear bumper had been. Tires squealed as the sedan veered off the road and then back. Hannah didn't wait around to find out if they crashed. She hurried home.

She flew through the brick fence posts surrounding her neighborhood, roaring up the quiet streets, and the sedan faded from sight. Inside the locked garage, she shut off the car. Her heart hammered wildly.

She pried her fingers off the steering wheel, slowly flexing her stiff joints. God. What had just happened? Had someone tried to run her off the road?

The sedan's maneuvers had been deliberate. No amount of hormonal hysteria on her part would account for the other driver trying to ram her rear end. If she hadn't listened to her gut, the cars would've collided. There on that curve, at that speed, it was likely an inexperienced driver would've lost control of the car and spun off into the ravine.

The data was easy to interpret. Someone wanted to harm her.

But who?

And why?

****

Jake woke to the melodious sound of chanting monks and cozy warmth. He tensed at the unfamiliar homey sensations. Where was he? Bright sunbeams illuminated the room. Above him on the walls, dragons dueled.

Dragons. Vivid art work. He was in Hannah's house. The house she grew up in. His fingers stroked the smooth fleece blanket covering him. Hannah must have covered him. How long had he been out? How long did it take to assemble an art portfolio anyway?

He lowered the recliner's footrest and searched for her. He followed the serene music past the kitchen and out to the yoga studio. Under muted lights, Hannah's slim figure reflected off floor to ceiling wall mirrors. Curiosity kept him rooted in the doorway as she held an impossible looking position.

As if she sensed his presence, Hannah opened her compelling eyes and beckoned him forward. "Join me."

Jake blew out a long breath, acutely conscious of his maleness and her femaleness. His yang wanted her yin, which he couldn't allow while he was responsible for her. He shook his head. "My body doesn't bend like a pretzel."

Hannah crossed to the sound system, punched a button, and the monks ceased chanting. "Yoga can help you rebuild your flexibility. It can also heal you physically, mentally, emotionally, and spiritually."

Jake bared his arms across his chest as she approached. Was she commenting on his lack of fitness again? "I've gotten used to who I am. Don't plan to change at this late stage of the game."

"Yoga teaches us to listen to our bodies. Don't be afraid of it."

Was it the dim lighting or did her color seem a bit off? "I don't need yoga to know that I'm hungry. How long was I out?"

She glanced at the clock mounted above the door. "About two hours."

His stomach rumbled. Lunch was an immediate necessity. "Is there a restaurant near here that you'd recommend?"

The corners of her lips tugged up briefly. "There's a great Thai restaurant near the highway. While you were resting, I returned a call from an old family friend I haven't seen in a while. Graham Grafton wants to join us for lunch, if you don't mind."

Jake's only external response was his shallow respirations. Inside was a different story. Inside, he was sweating bullets. Grafton was CIA. What did he want with Hannah?

Jake didn't want to share Hannah with the Giraffe, but what choice did he have? He had no reasonable basis for a protest. "Sure, whatever you want. What about the portfolio?"

"Found it. Mailed it already."

His hand closed over the warm metal keys in his pocket. Had she borrowed his keys as he slept? The thought of her touching him so intimately interested him. "Did you take my truck?"

Alarm flared in Hannah's expressive eyes. She shook her head so fast it looked like a shudder. "I borrowed Mom's new Mercedes."

It didn't take a highly trained secret agent to realize

she was upset. "Did something happen?"

"What happened," Hannah stated flatly, bringing her narrowed gaze up to meet his, "is that a moron tried to run me off the road."

Adrenaline surged into Jake's bloodstream filling him with infinite energy. He wanted to pound Hannah's unknown pursuer into the ground. His thoughts honed in on the worst case scenario. Was it Ursula? Was Hannah a target by proximity to Jake? He tried not to show his alarm. "Did you get a description of the car? Did you call the cops?"

Hannah's hands fluttered through the air. "The car was a black sedan. No front license tag. Tinted windows. It was like the car was being operated by a robot with one objective—to take me out. And no, I didn't call the cops. Mom's car has a lot under the hood. I broke every speed limit between here and there."

He could barely hear himself think over the staccato beat of his heart. "Did the other car hit you?"

A muscle in Hannah's porcelain cheek twitched. "It tried. When the sedan veered out into the oncoming traffic lane on the curve, I got scared. So I floored it."

He was such a loser. Standing here with his hands in his pockets. He'd been asleep on the job while she was in danger. He tugged his hands free, gesturing with one hand. "You should've called me."

Hannah shrank away from him. "There's nothing anyone could've done at that point. I had the feeling someone was watching me at the Post Office, but I didn't see anybody overtly spying on me."

That's because a spy would blend into the scenery. If the driver of the sedan was a pro, they'd wanted Hannah to see them. They'd counted on her fear and nervousness causing her to make a fatal driving error.

His fists tightened in useless fury. She'd been in danger, and he'd slept through the whole thing. Some protector he was.

Two scenarios occurred to him. Either an

acquaintance from Hannah's life had a grudge against her. Or Hannah's trip to the cottage had triggered an international chain of events. If they were dealing with Ursula and her associates, this could be very ugly. Hell, it was already ugly. Someone had tried to run Hannah off the road.

He wasn't good at beating around the bush. "Has this ever happened before?"

Fresh alarm flared in her eyes. "I lead an ordinary life. I can say with absolute certainty that no one has ever tried to run me off the road before."

She seemed very extra-ordinary to him, but he let her remark pass. "What about enemies? Have you had any death threats?"

"Most of the people I know in my personal life are my yoga buddies. They believe in nonviolence. My associates at work are always threatening to kill me, but I've never taken them seriously before."

"Explain."

"No one likes getting their data audited. When the principal investigators turn their lab notebooks in, there are always discrepancies and variances from their protocols. I do my job, which is identifying the inconsistencies, and they get mad at me. The researchers call my reports 'Killer Audits.' Last week, a PI said he'd kill me if I shut down his study."

Jake let out the breath he'd been holding. Maybe Ursula wasn't fixing to swoop down on them in a lethal rage. A disgruntled scientist would be a piece of cake to handle. "What's his name?"

"Dr. Jerry Esteban. He's always playing fast and loose with his research protocols. His grant money is at risk if he flunks his next data audit." Her hand covered her mouth. "You don't believe he'd really try to hurt me, do you? I've worked with him for years. His wife takes yoga from my mother."

He wasn't ruling anyone out. He'd snoop around and see what trouble Esteban had been in. "Anyone else threaten you?"

"No." Hannah thrust her feet in a pair of sandals near the door. "Not exactly."

His irritation level rose. She wasn't taking this seriously. "Either you were threatened or you weren't."

"Something odd happened yesterday. It wasn't a threat, but when that dark car started following me today, I remembered about the other car."

"What car?"

"The one that followed me from the highway through the back roads of Frederick County until I turned up the driveway to the cottage."

God, if it was Ursula, they were screwed. He'd left his pistol back at the cottage, though he had a small Chief's Special and two knives hidden in his pickup. "Was it the same car?"

She shrugged. "I couldn't tell."

"You should call the police."

"I've got nothing to show the police. There's no damage to me or the car. And I'm not staying here in their jurisdiction. I'm headed back to the mountains for a few days and then I'm off to California. It was probably some nut with a case of road rage."

"Doesn't sound like you cut anybody off. I'm not buying the road rage story. This could be serious. You should stay close to me until you get on that plane to California."

She frowned at him. "I don't like the sound of that. I'm not your responsibility. I took care of myself just fine today."

He knew better than that. D.C. expected him to keep Hannah safe. And he would. She'd be safest at the cottage. "Why don't we see about lunch with your friend? That is, if you feel up to it."

Hannah's smile was fleeting. "Never been better."

Stubborn. Just like D.C. That brought a heaviness to his heart. He'd failed his partner. He wouldn't fail Hannah.

Her head tilted to the side as she studied him. "Want me to drive to the restaurant?"

"I can manage."

"You sound like my Dad. Pig-headed stubborn. I couldn't talk him out of a chosen course for love or money." She stared down at the comfy sandals she'd just donned. After a moment, her gaze lifted. "Asking for help isn't an admission of weakness. You've had a serious injury. You don't have to pretend you're fit."

Jake gripped his cane tighter. "I'm fine."

Hannah's chin jutted out. "Suit yourself."

He generally did.

There wasn't a lot of depth to the man he'd become, but honor was pretty much all he had left. He'd be damned if he'd allow his past or his active libido to ruin the present and the future. He'd deal with this threat to Hannah's safety.

The more time he spent with her, the more protective he felt about her. His desire for her wasn't waning with time. But he wasn't a slave to his biological urges. He could control his desire to taste Hannah's rosy lips, to run his fingers down her supple body, to feel the power in those long legs of hers as they wrapped around him.

Used to be his best dreams were at night while he was sleeping. But since Hannah's arrival, his daydreams were fairly spectacular. D.C.'s daughter was a dream all right, and he'd do well to remember she had no permanent place in his life.

But in his dreams, that was a different story.

****

Graham Grafton was seated in the corner booth when they arrived at the Thai restaurant. He rose to his lanky height, towering over everyone in the red and gold trimmed room. "Hannah, how good to see you."

Through hooded eyes, Jake watched his former colleague embrace Hannah. Grafton seemed very comfortable around Hannah, and his hand rested easily on her shoulder. Jake didn't like that very much, but he had to keep his cool. Hannah introduced Jake to the Giraffe and they pretended not to know each other.

Another lie. One of an endless stream he was forced to tell Hannah. But the Giraffe didn't seem to have any trouble with lying. He told lie after lie to D.C.'s pretty daughter, lies about his life in Boston, about his recent trip to Rome.

Jake brooded during the entire lunch, envying the attention Hannah paid to the man. He couldn't wait to leave Grafton behind.

After the waitress took the check and Jake's credit card, Grafton waved Hannah closer with his hand. "I have something for you. Something your father gave me for safekeeping."

"You do?" Hannah frowned.

Grafton handed her a shopping bag. Hannah reached inside and pulled out a black case. Jake stilled. He knew that case. Knew it like the back of his hand. Those were D.C.'s field glasses. Had Grafton recovered them from the murder scene?

Hannah's eyes misted over. She stroked the case lovingly. "Thank you. This means a lot to me."

Grafton squeezed her hand. "He would have wanted you to have them. I'm sorry I was so long getting them to you. I've been swamped these last three months."

Jake wished he had something of D.C.'s to give her. It didn't sit well with him that Hannah looked at Grafton with stars in her eyes. Oh Grafton was all right, but Jake didn't like the man's smug attitude. After another nauseating round of hugs, lunch was done, and they hit the road.

During a not-so-quick stop at the supermarket and the long drive up to the cottage, Jake tried to curb his feelings of worthlessness. It annoyed him that Hannah seemed perpetually interested in something beyond her window. Though he didn't push her for conversation, he couldn't stop thinking about his beautiful passenger.

Hannah was the product of two extra-ordinary

people. Her father was known for his mental acumen, her mother an artistic genius. From what he'd observed, Hannah was organized and meticulous. She also had courage. Not many women could survive a harrowing ordeal like she had today and then lunch with an old friend.

He hadn't made it to the second floor of her home, but he was very curious about her bedroom. What powerful symbols graced its walls? Archangels? Pyramids?

The overriding theme in her home was the battle of good and evil. How much did Hannah's mother know of her husband's secret agent career?

Had Hannah's mother filled her house with mythology and magic to protect her daughter? The ordinary world was a dangerous place, and that could be all it was, but what if something else had inspired Libby Montgomery to paint of life and death? He would definitely like to speak to her.

But he wasn't planning a trip to California, and he doubted he'd still be in the country by the time Hannah's mother returned to Maryland. All he could do for now was to concentrate on Hannah.

His mouth tightened. Though he'd been forced out of the CIA, getting Hannah settled was his mission, and he'd be wise to remember that. Vigilance was the key to skirting danger.

But which was the bigger threat?

Ursula the killer?

Or Hannah the sleeping beauty?

Chapter 4

Hannah sipped her glass of Zinfandel. She rocked slowly on the deserted porch, enjoying the quiet bird calls and chipmunk chatter. Jake had gone to his bedroom when they returned. She'd come out here to be alone.

Blessedly alone.

Why had Jake been so tense and uncommunicative this afternoon? He'd practically growled at Grafton. Why was he mad at a man he barely knew?

And then Jake had dogged her through the supermarket. He'd made a ten minute tactical maneuver drag out into an hour-long campaign. She didn't need anyone watching over her. She'd been doing just fine for years.

Her neatly compartmentalized thoughts spilled out in a jumble. Seeing her father's binoculars today had been a shock. And this house, that had shocked her too. It was the location she'd always wanted for a bird sanctuary, but it was too far from her job and her home. She couldn't stay out here in the woods. It wasn't financially feasible.

Someone had tried to run her off the road today.

That thought came roaring back in her head. Either she had a powerful enemy or Dr. Jerry Esteban had gone off his rocker. Esteban she could check up on.

She glanced at her watch. Amanda Sinclair, her quality assurance associate, should be finishing up her day now. She could call Amanda and find out where Jerry had been at lunchtime today. Before she lost her nerve, she punched up the number on her cell phone.

"Amanda?"

"Hannah? You're already checking up on me? You've

got to let go of the reins, girlfriend."

Amanda's perky voice was a welcome slice of normalness. "I'm sure you're getting along fine. You are, aren't you?"

"Yeah. I even had your good pal, Dr. Jerry Esteban, in here this afternoon."

"Funny you should mention him. He's the reason I called. Is he giving you any trouble?"

"He tried to bribe me. He walked in here with a Genardi's pizza just after one and tried to sweet talk me into signing off on his paperwork without doing the audit."

Genardi's pizza was near the Post Office. The timing was right. Hannah shivered. It could have been Esteban chasing her in that dark sedan. "You didn't agree, did you?"

"Nope. But I ate my fill of pizza first."

Hannah heard the smile in Amanda's voice. She needed to warn Amanda, but how could she say anything without proof? Libel was a slippery slope. "Were you alone with Esteban?"

"Nope. He brought along his hottie research assistant, Arturio."

Everyone in the building knew Amanda was smitten with Arturio. Esteban was no fool. "This may seem like an odd question, but what kind of car does Esteban drive?"

"A sweet cherry red convertible. Why?"

Hannah remembered seeing that flashy car in the Potomac Labs parking lot before. She allowed herself a breath of fresh air. "I thought I saw him in Bethesda today. But the car was a dark sedan."

"Bethesda? I thought you were up in the mountains."

"I am. Mom needed me to run home and mail something to her. I'm back in the mountains again." There was no guarantee that Esteban hadn't borrowed the sedan to terrorize her. She needed to protect Amanda in any event. "Change the line-up of the audits on your schedule. Bump the Coolidge project up to the top of the list."

"You sure? I thought we were sticking it to Esteban. I thought I was gonna join the big leagues by exposing him for the slimeball he is."

"I've reconsidered. The Coolidge project will give you more than enough to do. We'll collaborate on Esteban when I return from vacation." And if he threatened either of them in any way, they'd call the police.

"Well. If you say so."

Hannah ignored the disappointment in Amanda's voice. "Everything else okay?"

"Yeah. I'm fine. How about you and the old geezer?"

"The old geezer isn't old, and he's annoying the crap out of me."

"Be still my beating heart. Tell me, is he cute?"

Hannah curled into the phone. "He scowls all the time, and he insists everything be done his way. The only thing he doesn't gripe about is my cooking."

"Ah."

"Ah?"

"You've seduced him, and you don't even know it."

Hannah stiffened. "That's outrageous. I haven't seduced anyone. The man's been subsisting on frozen dinners for three months. Anyone's cooking would taste great to him."

"What's wrong with him?"

"For starters, he's much too secretive. I can't read him. He's unlike anyone I've ever known."

"How hot is he? On a one to ten scale?"

Jake was easily a twelve. But, if she admitted that to Amanda, she'd never hear the end of it. "He's quite aware of his charm. I'm sure women drool over him all the time."

"Bummer. Men that are stuck on themselves never let their hair all the way down. Speaking of his hair, what does it look like?"

"Short. Very short."

"Is he one of those guys that shave their heads because they're already losing their hair?"

Disappointment rang in Amanda's voice.

"No. He's got hair in all the right places." Hannah quickly clapped her hand over her mouth to keep anything else from spilling out.

Amanda giggled. "You're so gone on him. What color are his eyes?"

"Brown."

"Plain old brown? What fun is that? What good are crummy brown eyes?"

Hannah leaned back and began to rock slowly in her chair. "They're not crummy brown. They're dreamy, like melted chocolate."

"You go, girl." Amanda whistled appreciably. "Now we're talking. What's the master schedule for this conquest look like? Seduction at dusk? Romantic candlelight dinner at midnight. Evening together? Satin sheets until dawn?"

"You're enjoying this, aren't you? My peace of mind is hanging by a thread. I'm supposed to be sorting through my father's effects. Only, I can't concentrate. Have you ever known me to obsess about a man? Have you?"

"Can't say I have."

"You don't have to sound so cheerful about it," Hannah griped. "I'm in over my head here. Twenty-four hours alone with a virile male and I discover I'm still a teenage girl at heart. Argh. Not fair."

Amanda cleared her throat delicately, twice. "You could always come back to the office where everyone thinks you are the ice queen."

Hannah groaned. "Let's see, which would I rather be, the sex kitten or the ice queen? Both sound scary as all get out."

"You'll be fine, boss lady. Let that sex kitten out of the bag. You deserve a good romp."

****

Jake gazed longingly at the almost empty bowl. "Mind if I finish this off?"

Hannah shrugged. "Help yourself."

Jake devoured the last of the tasty steamed vegetables. Hannah cooked like a dream. She was beautiful. Why hadn't some guy tucked her in a little three bedroom down there in suburbia? "I heard you talking on the phone this afternoon. Do we need to return to Bethesda?"

Hannah's fork stilled. "You heard me talking on the phone?"

"I heard your voice, but I didn't listen to your conversation."

Her cheeks flushed. "I called my associate at work."

He hoped like hell she hadn't been checking up on Esteban. Protecting her was his job. He'd spent the afternoon running background checks on every employee at Potomac River Labs. They all checked out. "Tell me more about your job."

"Research studies have critical events that have to be audited. I look at what the principals say should be done and compare it to the study records."

"You're a fact checker?"

"Sort of. The monitored parameters vary for each research project."

"And how many projects do you oversee?"

"About two dozen active researchers. It's been crazy lately. That's why we hired Amanda. So that the quality assurance wouldn't lag so far behind the research." She cleared her throat and looked straight at him. "I asked Amanda where Dr. Esteban was at lunch time. He was out of the office. But he drives a red car."

According to his online research, Esteban had a few problems. None that seemed big enough to motivate him to harm Hannah. "Did she see him driving the red car?"

"No. And I told her to delay his audit until I return. I don't want to worry about him going after her. She's just a kid."

He'd run all sorts of probabilities today. If Esteban was the sedan's driver, odds were he wouldn't leave his home territory. And he'd emailed Grafton and asked him to put a tail on Esteban. Until he knew something definite, all he could do was reassure Hannah. "No one followed us out here today. I checked. You're safe here. I promise."

She blinked and blinked some more. "How can you promise such a thing?"

Easy. Both his hands and his feet were lethal weapons. And he was good with knives and guns too. Plus this remote cottage had a top-of-the-line security system. "Just relax. I promised D.C. I'd get you settled, and that's what I'll do."

"I'm not staying here."

"So you've said."

She sighed heavily. "I'm sorry I snapped at you. I've had a hellacious day." She pushed a stem of broccoli around on her plate. "Let's talk about something else. What sort of work did you do for my father?"

"Anything he told me to do." Technically that wasn't a lie. But it wasn't entirely truthful either. He respected the oath of secrecy that came with his job.

"Can't you be more specific that that?"

"Not really. Each acquisition was a separate transaction. Like your job, my work varied by size and location." He was pleased they had that in common.

"What did my father do for the company?"

"D.C. managed everything. Sometimes he helped me with my part. Other times he ran things from behind his desk."

"His desk? Do you still have it?"

He winced at the hopeful tone in her voice. D.C.'s desk was in Langley. Neither Jake nor Hannah had access to that hallowed ground. "No. I don't."

"I would've given anything to see where my Dad worked."

At the wistful look in her eyes, Jake's gut twisted. He wanted to tell her the truth about her father, but he couldn't. He just couldn't.

****

Hannah stared at the pale moonlight filtering through the bedroom window and wished sleep would come. The deep yogic breathing hadn't helped, nor had the guided relaxation she'd tried. She'd tossed and turned until her white cotton nightgown was as wrinkled as an elephant's skin.

Thoughts kept circling in her head. Jake's pointed questions after her morning walk. Jake's aggressive driving and the cloying confinement of his pickup. Jake sprawled in the recliner. Jake acting edgy around Graham Grafton. Jake following her down every aisle in the grocery store. Jake inhaling dinner.

No matter where she turned, Jake was there. In just one day, he'd winged into her life, filling the empty places in her heart with unfamiliar flutterings.

His sudden invasion reminded her of Cape May, New Jersey, during the fall bird migration. One minute the sky would be clear and then hundreds of squawking birds would darken the sky.

Birders described the descending flocks of birds as awesome, loud, and exhilarating. No matter how you felt about birds before you experienced fall migration in the Atlantic Flyway, you were changed after seeing it. That's how she felt after spending the day with Jake.

She'd caught herself staring at him, wondering what it would be like to be in a personal relationship with him. Courtship, mating, and reproduction were known behaviors in the animal kingdom, but foreign to Hannah's everyday world. She'd dated a bit, but her interest level in furthering courtship rituals with her dates hadn't been as high as her personal standards.

Jake was the first man she'd ever wanted in such a yearning, deep seated way.

It was extremely irritating that he should affect her like that. This weekend together was a singular event, brought about through their mutual connection to her father.

Once she leased this house to a third party, Jake

would leave and she'd never see him again. He'd be off somewhere, and there'd be a woman in his arms.

She had a feeling Jake always had women.

That irritated her too. In fact the whole physical attraction was darned inconvenient. She wasn't a one-night stand kind of woman. Sighing, she flicked on the bedside lamp.

Maybe she'd feel better if she drank a glass of warm milk. But would her moving about the house disturb Jake? She wasn't up to dealing with him right now, not when her thoughts were on courtship and mating. She slumped back on the pillow and stared at the ceiling.

Hannah drew the covers tighter around her neck and then rubbed her sore jaw. She had to stop clenching her teeth. Ever since her father's death, she'd felt like one of those old timey dolls with a too tight rubber band holding her head on.

After the day she'd had, she should be exhausted.

She needed her rest because tomorrow was bound to be emotional as she packed up her father's personal items. She tried deep Tantric breathing to slow her thoughts.

No good. She shut her eyes and tried to focus using her inner eye. No good. Her eyes popped open again as a submerged memory surfaced.

As a girl, she'd been organizing her toy cabinet when her father had suddenly appeared in her pink and white bedroom. "Daddy!" she'd squealed in delight, running to him.

"Hannah-banana!" her father had said, scooping her up in his arms. He'd twirled them both in circles until they were dizzy with laughter.

Memories like that one baffled her. How could that fun-loving man have become her distant father? Why did everything about him seem so inconsistent?

Staring at the ceiling was boring. She turned on her side, facing the lamp to see if changing her position would help her relax. She scrunched the pillow to better accommodate her altered position, but her racing thoughts refused to slow down.

Maybe there were some cards in the bedside table. She leaned over and opened the wooden drawer. Inside was one item. A dog-eared copy of *Little Red Riding Hood*.

"Oh!" Her breath stalled as she gingerly lifted it out of the drawer.

Glancing closer, she saw the small tooth impressions in the upper right hand front corner. She'd made those marks on the cover when she had shown her father what big teeth she'd had.

In a timeless void, she leafed through the familiar pages, touching the beloved characters, reading the precious memorized words. No wonder this house looked like the one in her childhood story book. He'd used the book's cover illustration as his blueprint.

Hannah flipped through the colorful pages, crying fat, silent tears. She'd learned her first life lessons from this story. Little Red Riding Hood went astray by veering from the safe path and by talking to strangers. Hannah had taken the lesson to heart and to this day kept close to the well beaten path.

It wasn't until she finished the book that she noticed the plain white envelope glued to the back page, like a pocket for holding a library card. Odd. That hadn't been there before.

Hannah looked closer and saw something inside the envelope. Reaching in, she pulled out a lined piece of notebook paper filled with her father's familiar scrawl.

Hannah-banana, I'm so sorry you've come to be reading this letter. It can only mean one thing. My job finally caught up to me, the way your mother always swore it would. Being good at your work is a blessing and a curse. I became my job. Libby said I was seduced by my success. All I can say in my defense is that I have always passionately believed in my work. To keep you and your mother safe, I stayed away, but you were always first in my heart. I built this place to keep you safe from the "Big

Bad Wolves" of the world. I know how you love puzzles, so I've hidden two other letters regarding your inheritance in places that have special meaning to you. Humor an old man and find them both. Love, Dad

Hannah's lips mouthed each word. She stumbled on the last line. Strong emotions crashed through her until she shook from their excesses. Howling loss over her father's untimely death. Seething anger at her father for choosing his career over her. Overwhelming grief at the loss of a loved one she barely knew.

Great gasping sobs stole her breath, clouded her vision. Her heart felt like it had been ripped in two by territorial hawks.

Her father had stayed away because he loved her? What nonsense. If he loved her, he should have wanted to be with her, to see her grow up, to attend her first piano recital.

Suddenly, the door to her bedroom slammed open and Jake rushed in, shoulders squared. His fierce eyes scouted the room and settled on her. "What's wrong?" he demanded harshly.

She tried to tell him, but no sound emitted from her mouth. Her voice had been stolen by her father's jarring words.

Hannah fumbled for the letter she'd dropped onto the patchwork quilt. Before taking the paper from her trembling hands, Jake scanned the room again.

Jake's heart pounded in his throat, and his leg ached like a son-of-a-gun. He never should have overworked his leg yesterday, and he certainly shouldn't have walked so much on it today. He'd probably undone a month's worth of healing.

He visibly started at the familiar handwriting on the paper. D.C.'s handwriting. His mind reeled as his pulse pounded in his ears. No wonder Hannah was upset.

This was a message from a dead man.

Jake skimmed the words in silence. He'd been pulled from a light dreamless sleep by the sound of the lamp clicking on and a drawer opening.

An intruder was his first thought. Then he remembered Hannah was here. Then he worried someone was hurting Hannah.

Adrenaline pumped furiously through his veins. It wasn't possible for anyone to be in there upsetting her. His laptop was linked to the house security system, and the perimeter hadn't been breached. His head knew this, but he had to see for himself. When he'd heard her crying, he'd run to her room.

Damn women for crying anyway.

When he moved in three months ago, he'd done a cursory search of this room and the rest of the house. He'd been looking for weapons, bombs, listening devices, and booby traps. It had never occurred to him that D.C. might have left a letter in his bedroom for his daughter.

But his late partner had always thought outside the box. Usually Jake was privy to his motivations. Not this time. What did D.C. have in mind for his grieving daughter? A scavenger hunt? Not his normal style. Was it a father-daughter tradition? What was the point of the cryptic letter?

He wasn't sure Hannah could take finding anymore letters. This one had hit her pretty hard. Her shoulders were bowed forward, her head in her hands.

Jake grabbed a handful of tissues from the bedside table and waved them at Hannah. "Here."

She pressed them to her face, but the great gasping sobs quickly soaked through the tissues. He moved the tissue box to her lap, wishing he could take this heartache from her.

The letter had gotten to Hannah. Her distress was painfully real. He couldn't leave her when she was like this but watching her heart break was awful.

He should do something.

The muscles of her face were contracted, her eyes scrunched shut. Her mouth gaped, keening silently. She was turning inward, shutting out the world.

Jake didn't want to be invisible. Not to Hannah. A tight band of pain constricted around his chest. He had to do something.

Ordinarily, he wouldn't have hesitated to take a woman in his arms, but this was D.C.'s daughter. And he had the hots for her.

Tricky.

But he knew how to behave. His foster mother had taught him manners, and those ingrained habits demanded he comfort Hannah. He understood the ground rules.

What he didn't know was if he was strong enough to leave it at that.

Jake respected Hannah. In the last twenty-four hours he'd learned she was a focused, determined, no nonsense kind of woman. A strong woman. One who wouldn't put up with a wimpy guy.

He prayed he didn't screw this up. He gently tugged her up off the bed. She moved towards him, and his arms closed around her.

Her dampened cheeks rested against his bare skin. Her deep gasping sobs wracked his body. He took on her sadness and grief, giving back warmth and comfort, hoping it was enough.

He'd cried when D.C. died but not like this. His tears had been for a life ruthlessly cut short, for the loss of a mentor, for the end of his agency career. Nothing like the ragged, coarse sobbing, or the great chest heaving breaths Hannah took.

He stroked his hand across the back of her head, from the crown of silky hair down her elegant neck to the long supple curve of her spine. Joy filled him as she leaned into his caress.

His leg throbbed but he didn't care. Hannah was in his arms.

"Damn him," Hannah whispered raggedly.

Jake seconded that sentiment.

He'd learned everything he knew about gathering

intelligence from D.C. Montgomery. But there was nothing masterful or intelligent about a letter from a dead man.

What kind of twisted game was D.C. playing with his fragile, beautiful daughter?

Hannah dabbed her face with a fresh wad of tissues. "I didn't cry at his funeral. I wouldn't let anyone know how much his death hurt me. And you want to know why? It was because I was so mad at him I could have spit on his funeral urn."

"But, being here, seeing how he lived, learning that he built this house for me, I'm overwhelmed. I don't want any of it. I'd trade it all in a heartbeat for the chance to know who my father was."

Jake wanted to tell her everything he knew about her father, but he couldn't. D.C. had purposefully kept his occupation from his daughter. It wasn't Jake's place to reveal her father's agency career.

A familiar saying in the agency had been the "need-to-know" basis. D.C. made it clear that his daughter didn't need to know about his career choice.

Jake had come close to telling her too much before. In spite of his professional training, he wasn't adequately guarding his feelings where she was concerned.

Truth was, Hannah Montgomery got to him. He could see why D.C. had gone to great lengths to protect her innocence. Her freshness and purity were rare treasures in this ugly world. Treasures were meant to be protected.

Hannah lurched out of his arms. "Aren't you going to say anything?" she asked.

"I'm sorry," Jake said and meant it. He was sorry for her pain, sorrier still that she wasn't tucked up against him absorbing the radiant heat pouring off his body.

"Don't feel sorry for me," Hannah said tersely. "I don't want your pity. I'm a grown woman. Childhood disappointments don't matter anymore."

By the dullness in her expressive eyes, Jake knew she was still hurting. Her shoulders trembled.

He couldn't draw her in his arms again, no matter how much he wanted to. He couldn't guarantee his continued good behavior, which added to his frustration and crankiness.

His leg throbbed, and his sleep had been disturbed. He said the first thing that popped into his head. "Do you think you're the only person in the world who never knew their father?"

Her spine stiffened.

He should have left it at that, but just saying those few words opened a tightly sealed door in his heart. "At least you had your mother. I had nobody. I never knew my father and my mother abandoned me when I was three. I bounced around through the foster care system for years, until I finally got placed with a decent family."

His words came faster now. "Thing is, I wasn't nice like them. I never forgot I came from the wrong side of town. When I said I was sorry for your loss, I meant it. I know exactly how it feels to have a big hole in your gut, to know you're different from everyone else."

Jake ran his hand across the back of his neck. Why had he told her all that? He didn't want her to feel sorry for him either. This woman had definitely messed with his head.

She hadn't invited him into her bedroom. He'd come running in here because he thought she was in danger. His blood hummed with surplus adrenaline.

He'd had it all wrong.

He was the one in danger. It wasn't natural to be standing in a cozy bedroom beside an alluring woman dressed in a thin white nightgown and not make love to her.

"I'm sorry. I shouldn't have unloaded my problems on you." Jake sighed deeply. He had to get out of here before he turned into a babbling idiot. "Why don't we both turn in? We can deal with this letter in the morning."

Hannah's bottom lip jutted out. "I'm not sleepy."

Jake's self-control slipped a notch, and his thoughts

spun back to the sensual realm. Her enticing fragrance perfumed the air he breathed, filling him with dangerous longings.

He well remembered the feel of her silky tousled hair, the creamy softness of her neck, the snug fit of her curves to his hollows. His head clouded with the image of her riding him like a wild tigress.

Lust bit him hard. He'd sworn off women, but God help him, he wanted this one. His passion warred against his conscience, seeking to justify him taking what he wanted.

Hannah had nothing to do with his former profession. Sleeping with her wouldn't be hazardous to his health, unlike sleeping with his previous lover.

The rumpled bed yawned large behind Hannah. He could have her on her back in seconds. He could be making love to her in minutes. She wouldn't have any trouble sleeping after what he had in mind.

His slumbering conscience raised its ugly head. This was D.C.'s daughter. He'd promised to look after her. Sleeping with her wasn't part of the deal. But then again, he'd never promised not to sleep with her. That spark of hope fought a losing battle with his conscience.

"Do you play cards?" Hannah asked, cocking her head to the side.

Cards.

Since his mind was already dwelling on things it shouldn't, Jake envisioned a quick game of strip poker. She had on one or two garments at most. He had on his jeans, boxers, and belt. Not that it mattered. Neither one of them would lose at the game he had in mind.

"I was looking for a deck of cards when I found the letter," she said. "I was thinking of playing solitaire, but we could play gin rummy."

A stabbing pain lanced his heart.

She would say gin rummy. Gin had been D.C.'s favorite game. They'd whiled away many an hour playing gin rummy. Hannah's inadvertent choice of card games silenced his carnal thoughts.

It would kill him to sit down and play cards with her right now. He was primed for sex and the sooner he withdrew from the thick sensual haze in here, the better. A cold shower was definitely in order.

"Some other time." Jake limped towards the door.

"How about some warm milk?" Hannah's breath branded his bare shoulder.

Jake's temper flared. He was doing his best to leave her alone. She had no idea of the danger she invited by following him so closely. "Hannah, I'm trying to do the right thing here. If you had any sense, you'd let me walk out of this bedroom."

"So you don't like warm milk. That's no reason to jump down my throat." Hannah's exasperation came through in the sharp tone of her voice. "What's wrong with you?"

Jake hobbled through the threshold into the fresh air of the dimly lit hallway. He turned slowly, pivoting on his good leg. "What's wrong with me is you. It's the middle of the night. I'm a man and you're a desirable woman."

Her rosy lips rounded into a breathless "Oh."

He'd finally gotten her attention.

Good.

Resisting temptation wasn't one of his strengths. "I've been living like a monk in this cloistered cabin for months. I'm not used to going without female companionship for that long, if you catch my drift."

The whites of Hannah's eyes showed. She backed away from him. "You want to sleep with me?" she squeaked.

"Sleep is the farthest thing from my mind." Frustration soured his response.

"You just met me yesterday."

"Any woman is the right woman for a man like me," Jake said. That wasn't much of a lie. If a woman caught his eye and he caught theirs right back, he made a play for her.

What was weird about this situation was that Hannah had definitely caught his eye, but she didn't seem to have any idea how this game played out.

Someone needed to take her in hand, someone who had her best interests at heart. Someone who wasn't lusting after her even as he drove her away.

Her bedroom door slammed in his face and he smiled ruefully. D.C.'s daughter had spunk. She may not know the rules of the game, but she caught on fast.

He thumped down the hall, back to his small twin bed, thankful that the ache in his leg dueled the ache in his groin for his attention. Had D.C. purposefully made the guest bed small so that Jake wanted to sleep in Hannah's spacious bed? Was his partner testing him from beyond the grave?

If Jake had any sense, he'd walk out the back door, get in his black pickup, and high tail it down this mountain. He couldn't, of course. He'd promised D.C. he'd get Hannah settled, and she was far from settling in here.

Besides, D.C. wasn't the only one who knew how to play games. Jake had learned a lot these last five years. He could take whatever D.C. threw at him and more.

The only wildcard in this game was Hannah.

Chapter 5

The tantalizing aroma of freshly brewed coffee seeped into Hannah's conscious and nudged her awake. Inhaling deeply, she stretched, gradually becoming aware of her surroundings.

A storm blue room bathed in the soft glow of iridescent sunrise. A cozy sleigh bed. Her father's house. A smile tugged at her lips. Her house.

From outside her unadorned window came the rich chatter of early morning bird calls. A distant veery trilled its ethereal flute-like welcome to the new day, a phoebe repeated its name over and over again. The morning show had begun without her. She'd better get moving.

Hannah slid out of bed, smoothed the bedcovers flat, and padded off for a quick shower in the adjoining master bathroom. The warm water sprayed over her head, energizing her. Today was Friday. She had two days left to remove her father's possessions from the house. Her heart panged at the idea, but she had no other choice. It wasn't practical to let his belongings stay here until the house got rented.

She had to stay focused to get the job done. But it was hard to focus on anything with Jake in the picture. Jake wasn't ignorable.

Heat steamed from her face as she remembered slamming her bedroom door in his face last night. It wasn't like her to be so rude, but she'd had no choice. Her feminine intuition had warned her Jake would make love to her if she didn't put a physical barrier between them.

Hannah toweled dry and then selected a green shirt, brown pants, and hiking boots. Jake knew how to use those expressive eyebrows, smoldering eyes, and poetic hands. There would be no fumbling or awkward moments when making love with Jake. He'd tune into a woman's sensual needs and he'd ensure mutual satisfaction.

She tugged on her clothes. Her spine tingled in remembrance of his gentle caress. Hannah frowned. Her thought processes were out of control. So how did she fix this mess? Wait out the unwanted attraction? Or send Jake away?

Sending him away would gain her the quickest relief.

As she walked to the kitchen she worked out her plan. First, she'd apologize for her rudeness. Second, she'd tell him to leave. Third, she'd take that morning walk to calm her frazzled nerves and give him time to vacate the premises. Fourth, she'd return to the empty house and hunt for the hidden letters. And finally, she'd drive herself down the mountain and secure a rental agent for this house.

"Good morning," she said casually.

Jake's gleaming eyes peered over the top of his newspaper. He wore another black tee shirt with his jeans and bare feet. His penetrating gaze held her, warming her like a slice of bread in the toaster.

Hannah sensed banked sexual heat and masculine amusement. Her defenses instantly went on red alert. She tore her gaze away and poured herself a cup of coffee.

"Morning," he replied.

"You're up early," she said, reaching for the sugar.

"I don't sleep much."

She heard the crinkling sound of his newspaper folding, felt the heat of his gaze sweep her length as she stirred in a generous dollop of milk. Her pulse quickened in response to his perusal.

She groaned inwardly. He wasn't courting her, but she was reacting as if he were. She had to extricate herself from this dangerous situation immediately. Time to tell him to hit the road.

"About last night," she began, summoning her

courage as she joined him at the tiny table for two. Out of habit, she placed a paper napkin under her coffee mug on the woven placement.

"I apologize for my outburst," Hannah continued. "Thank you for looking in on me. That letter caught me off guard, and I reacted far too emotionally. After thinking this over, I concluded that I would prefer to handle this family matter privately. I'm experienced at sorting, packing, and discarding as I recently moved out of my townhouse."

The air temperature in the room chilled. Hannah shivered, curving her fingers around her warm coffee cup.

"That's quite a change from our initial agreement," Jake said. "I thought it was all settled that I was staying. You said we would take this one day at a time."

She'd initially wanted him to stay to learn more about her father, but all indications suggested that the trade off wasn't worth it. Just hearing the gravelly sound of his morning voice had her heart doing somersaults.

Jake was a study in sharp contrasts, smooth and ragged edges, sexy and comforting, dangerous and safe. The mystery of him intrigued her, the secrets he guarded aggravated her. All things considered, it would be best for Hannah if Jake left immediately.

"I spent a lot of time on this last night," she said. "If you're not leasing this place, it's wrong for me to expect you to stay through the weekend."

He blinked several times. "What about the letters?"

Hannah shrugged. "I'll find them."

"I'm not leaving."

The steel in his voice irritated the heck out of Hannah. Her back teeth ground together as her focus narrowed to the implacable male in front of her. "I'm not helpless. I can pack up my father's belongings and contract with a rental company on my own."

He exhaled slowly, his eyes boring into her. He didn't seem relieved at all. More like, annoyed. Under the small kitchen table, Hannah's fingernails bit into her palms.

Jake bared his arms across his chest. “I promised D.C. I would help you. If you’re uncomfortable with me staying here, I’ll stay elsewhere. But I’ll come here every day to help you.”

He wasn’t giving an inch. He was determined to stay put. She wanted him to leave. Because it would be easier on her if he wasn’t around. But Jake’s sense of honor wouldn’t let him forget the promise he’d made to her father. A stalemate if she ever saw one.

If he was determined to drive back up here each day, then it wouldn’t be right to ask him to incur housing and travel expenses on her account. She wasn’t made of money either. No telling what expenses he might charge to his room if she offered to foot the bill for his hotel stay.

Hannah stared into her empty storm blue coffee cup. She hated being boxed in. “I’m stuck with you, no matter what?”

“That’s one way of putting it.”

Sighing heavily, she looked up and caught his gaze. “Then there’s no need for you to move out. I appreciate your offer of help, but I’m used to taking care of myself. I’m used to doing things my way.”

“Bossy, are you?”

“Stubborn. And, I don’t deal well with change.”

“You’re dealing pretty well from where I sit. I admire your spunk for trying to throw me out this morning.”

His compliment took her by surprise. Her mouth gaped. “You do?”

“Yeah.” He cleared his throat delicately. “So, what’s the plan for today?”

“Before we look for the other letters, I’m heading out for a walk. “The Dawn Chorus” is already underway.”

At his puzzled look, she gestured towards the kitchen window. “Birds. Singing. Dawn. I’m a birder, remember.”

His eyebrows drew together. “Be careful. Walking in unfamiliar territory can be dangerous. The paths out there are narrow, meandering deer trails.”

What was his problem? Hannah got the feeling he

wanted her to stay out of the woods. "I didn't have any trouble yesterday. Besides, I've tromped through much less civilized places than this."

"You don't know the area." His brows knitted together. "Black bears are common in these mountains."

"You can't scare me with tales of bears in the woods. I'm more likely to run across deer ticks than a small Maryland black bear."

His dark eyes hardened. "Lyme's Disease is wicked. If you find ticks on your clothing, I'm taking you to a doctor."

"You know the symptoms?"

"Sure do. D.C. came down with Lyme's Disease four years ago. It was touch and go for awhile."

Her father had been gravely ill and she hadn't known? "Where were you guys?"

Jake's expressive lips thinned. Hannah wasn't certain he would respond, but he did. "Central America."

Not a hot spot for imports. Hmm. "What were you doing there?"

"We had business in the area."

He avoided her gaze, focusing instead on the floor tiles. Obviously, he didn't want to talk about Central America. But she did. "Did you take any pictures while you were there? I didn't see any picture albums on the book cases."

Jake seemed to find the table top absolutely riveting. "The photos we took were business related. I got rid of them when I closed the business."

Hannah waited for him to say more, but he didn't. His reticence irritated her. "You took my dad to a Central American doctor?"

Jake appeared to be considering his words. "D.C. was flown to Texas for medical treatment. The hospital kept him on intravenous antibiotics for a week."

"Exactly when was this?"

"Four years ago this August. D.C. griped the whole time."

He'd missed her birthday that year. When he finally showed up in late August, she'd told herself she was too old to let his forgetfulness bother her. That it shouldn't be important to her that her father remembered her birthday.

But it had rankled. How hard was it for him to just pick up the phone wherever he was one day a year and say hello? "I remember that August."

Her father had been pale and thin. All he'd wanted to talk about was the seminar she'd taught at a recent Quality Assurance conference. She'd asked him if he'd been ill, he'd said that he'd spent a lot of time indoors recently. Nothing about being in the hospital. No excuses. No regrets. That's how her secretive father operated.

He'd brought her a bolt of brightly colored fabric. Her mother had helped Hannah make drapes for her townhouse out of it. Drapes that would suit this house beautifully.

"I wouldn't want you to end up as sick as D.C. was. It's a long way from here to a hospital."

"I'll manage just fine. All I need are my *Sibley's Field Guide to Birds* and binoculars, and I'll be ready to go."

Jake muttered something mostly inaudible.

"What was that?" she asked.

"If I didn't have this busted leg, I'd accompany you. Why don't you watch the birds in the back yard?"

Hannah's spine stiffened. She was a birder, not a birdwatcher. Birders went to different habitats to see birds. Birdwatchers watched birds that came to them. "And miss all the fun? Not hardly. Besides, the feeders are empty. Birds don't come to empty feeders."

"What if you turn an ankle or fall in a ravine? It's not like I can easily come get you."

Hannah forced a smile. "It's so sweet of you to be concerned. I'll be okay. I carry my cell phone for emergencies. Besides, there's nothing tougher than a Montgomery."

****

Ten minutes after Hannah melted soundlessly into the woods like a seasoned recon agent, Jake couldn't stop thinking about her unconscious style. In her hunter green tee and dark brown pants with her father's Zeiss binoculars slung over her shoulders bandolier style, she'd blended into the foliage immediately.

He absently massaged the stiff muscles in his leg. Had D.C. known of Hannah's covert talents? Was that why D.C. had isolated Hannah from his professional life?

If so, D.C. had been a fool. A tiger couldn't change its stripes. Being good at reconnaissance didn't mean Hannah would follow in her father's footsteps. All it meant was that she took after her father.

He'd see if she was as good as D.C. at puzzles when she returned. He'd known nothing about the hidden letters until last night. The contents of the hidden letters worried him.

D.C. might come clean with Hannah. How much would D.C. reveal about his fake import career? If D.C. told Hannah his real occupation, then she'd know Jake had been lying to her as well.

Hannah was a decent person. Someone he'd rather not lie to, but he was caught in this web of deception. All he could do was restate the lies he'd already told her.

What would Hannah's reaction be if she found out the truth? He imagined her expressive eyes filling with scorn and disgust. She would see him for what he was, a professional liar. Brainiacs didn't associate with losers. Thinking of her disapproval made him sad, as if letting her down had some real consequence.

Why did it matter to him what she thought? He was taking care of her like D.C. asked. His assistance was temporary. He'd make sure Hannah realized the full value of her inheritance. For starters, this fifty acre tract had to be worth a small fortune.

No telling what else D.C. had squirreled away. In spite of his injury, his hunter's instincts rose to the challenge. One thing was certain; taking care of Hannah wasn't boring.

He'd agonized over his callous threat to make love to her during the long sleepless night. He hadn't needed to be so purposefully crude with her, but something about her made him want to push her to notice him.

He'd wanted women before, but he had never had one dominate his thoughts the way Hannah did. Had getting shot in the line of duty changed him so much?

He couldn't afford to let her get to him. He had plans for the future, dangerous plans that didn't involve a domesticated female like Hannah. His plans involved traveling light and fast.

And hunting a known killer.

He headed for his computer. He'd use the security system to track Hannah's progress through the woods and to make sure no one else was out there. And he'd simultaneously work on finding Ursula.

Escorting Hannah yesterday had been a valuable lesson learned. Despite his aggressive physical therapy, he wasn't fit enough for a trip overseas. He needed full mobility before he dealt with the cold fire smoldering in his gut. But waiting didn't suit him.

****

Hannah kept the morning sun at her right shoulder as she briskly strode along the narrow deer track down the mountain. Chipmunks and squirrels scampered through the underbrush and darted across her path. Overhead, songbirds trilled their good mornings, from the cardinal's rich purty-purty-purty, to the towhee's cheerful drink-your-tea, and the chickadee's buzzy chickadee-dee-dee-dee.

The further she hiked from the house, the more Jake's strong *opinions* bothered her. She'd been on her own for years, without anyone telling her what to do, and she most certainly knew the hazards of nature. This was her element. She'd observed more about animal behavior than he could possibly imagine.

There weren't any berserk drivers out here to force

her off the road. The woods were her home away from home. She was completely safe out here. If someone came her way, she'd know by the change in the birdsong.

Her heels struck the ground hard, startling a small garter snake off the path. She noticed the forest understory was thin here. Probably grazed out by deer. The song sparrows and hooded warblers that should have been feeding on the floor of a mature forest weren't here. If this were a bird sanctuary, she'd install a deer barrier so the ground nesters would return.

She'd like to erect a Jake barrier in her head. He was a difficult man. Just like father.

Hannah ducked under a low hanging branch, slowing as the woodsy scent of the forest penetrated her thoughts. The fresh musty aroma and the earthy sharpness soothed her as much as the deep breathing exercises she'd learned in her mother's yoga classes.

She inhaled deeply, letting the wonder of the forest flood her being with joy and harmony. Rolling her neck to relieve the tightness, she spied an early warbler creeping along the trunk of a nearby oak.

She froze, stealthily raising her father's powerful binoculars, to gaze at the black and white striped bird. Black and white warbler. Black throat. A breeding male.

Hannah sighed at the coincidence. Breeding males were too much on her mind since she came here. Her response to that train of thought startled her. For the first time, she felt like a breeding female: gravid, in heat, ready to mate.

Jake's showy, bold swaggering attention flattered and bewildered her. But last night, he'd been considerate and compassionate, tender almost. She didn't know what to make of him.

She didn't want Jake to be solid and substantial. She much preferred him being shallow and self-serving. It was easier to ignore the strong undertow of sensual attraction when she didn't respect him.

Stepping over a fallen tree, she paused to finger the

soft green lichen thriving on the decaying wood. On Sunday she'd join her mother in California. Though it made financial sense to sell this place and invest the money, she didn't want to sell. Maybe one day she'd open a bird sanctuary up here. Until then, she needed the rental income to pay the property taxes.

She walked slower now, pausing in the dappled sunlight to bask in its encompassing warmth. Warmth like a father's love. How could she reconcile what she knew with his written declaration of love? There were years of missed birthdays, school programs, and graduations. Years of her thinking she wasn't special, that he didn't love her.

To have the facts of her life upturned by his posthumous letter wasn't fair. His hands-off parenting style didn't correlate with what she knew of devoted fathers. She'd studied their behavior through the years. Devoted dads attended important occasions, gave hugs, and encouraged their offspring.

But her father had never completely forgotten her birthdays. He had given her belated presents every year, presents that often astounded her. She'd gotten Madame Alexander dolls when other girls played with Malibu Barbie, *Treasure Island* and *The Jungle Book* when she'd wanted the popular stories where the reader chose the endings, and Zeiss binoculars when she'd had her heart set on a shiny new bike.

She'd accepted his odd choices, seeking his approval and love. No matter how good she'd been, no matter how many times she ostracized herself from the other kids by playing with his unusual gifts, it hadn't mattered.

He hadn't come home.

He'd continued living his merry life elsewhere. She had withdrawn to the safe world of facts, a world where liars were invalidated, a world where truth ruled.

Odd, she'd never thought of her career choice that way before. She'd spent her whole life trying to earn her father's love. Her strength and self-reliance had developed as a defense mechanism to overcome her father's absences and inconsistency. She was strong, but she'd paid a high price for that strength.

Her steps quickened at the sound of running water. The narrow path veered sharply around a large maple and emptied into a lush meadow hemmed in by blooming apple trees. The air was sweet with the promise of new life.

She stopped to take it all in. It was so lovely, so beautiful that it took her mind off her troubles. The bright blue vault of a sky overhead drew her spirits to new heights, away from her troubling thoughts. She spun in a circle, raising her face and her arms to the life-giving sun, standing tall.

The gently gurgling water drew her over to the flowing spring. Beside the spring was an unexpected bench that offered comfortable seating. Hannah perched on the rough hewn surface and pulled out her birding notebook. She scribbled down the date and location, then the shorthand that birders used. Noca for North American cardinal, sosp for song sparrow.

Here in this beautiful meadow, nature reigned with its maxim of survival of the fittest. The strong survived.

Hannah was strong, but her father was her greatest weakness. Her biggest failures in life had been because of her father. In first grade, she'd refused to be the third dancing sunflower in the school play because he wasn't there for the performance as he'd promised.

He'd blown into town weeks later, his face gray and lined, his mood withdrawn. Her parents had quarreled bitterly that night. At the time, she'd been delighted with her mother for standing up to him, but in later years, she'd wondered if her father would have continued coming home if she'd tolerated his erratic schedule.

She'd grown up overnight once he left for good. On the surface, she switched her primary allegiance to her mother, but deep inside, she yearned for the man who wasn't there.

Those tears she'd cried last night had been a long time in coming, but she'd cried enough. Her father couldn't hurt her now. She'd find those hidden letters, she'd even get along with his injured partner. Lust wasn't something she was used to dealing with, but she'd persevere.

Challenges didn't faze her. She'd overcome loneliness and isolation. Letters from a dead man paled beside the hurts she'd already survived. She was strong. She didn't need anyone.

Especially not an irritating, stubborn man like Jake Sutherland.

Chapter 6

Jake limped to the kitchen, catching the house phone on the fifth ring. "Hello."

"Oh dear. Did I get the wrong number? I'm trying to reach my daughter Hannah."

Jake leaned against the counter to ease weight from his hurt leg. "You've got the right number, but you just missed her."

"And you are?"

"I'm Jake Sutherland, ma'am. I assume you're Hannah's mother?"

"Guilty. I'm Libby Montgomery calling from California, and I desperately need to speak to Hannah. I tried her cell phone but she didn't answer. Do you know when she'll return?"

The woman spoke so fast it took Jake a few additional moments to sort through her words. Using the surveillance cameras wired into the security system, he'd tracked Hannah to the meadow. "She went out to catch the dawn chorus about half an hour ago."

"Her and those darn birds. I swear, she'd sprout wings and fly if it was up to her. I need to talk to her right away. A very time sensitive matter has come up out here. Will you give her my message right away?"

Jake checked his watch. It was almost seven o'clock. He subtracted three hours to get California time. Four in the morning. What had Hannah's mother stirred up so early? "Is there anything I can do to help?"

"No, I don't think so. Hannah is in charge of my money. There's a yoga studio for sale, and I've got to be very proactive on it."

"I'll make sure she returns your call right away."

"While I have you on the phone, tell me something Jack."

"It's Jake."

"Sorry. I'm a bit distracted. Is Hannah all right? I wasn't sure how she would bear up under the strain of settling her father's affairs."

Other than the letter, she'd been holding up just fine. Should he tell her mother about the letter? Probably Hannah would tell her if she needed to know. "I didn't know her before she came here, but she seems okay to me."

"What did she do when she came in the house?"

Jake scowled at the spotless kitchen. His annoyance at her tidiness crept into his voice. "She picked up, straightened up, and organized everything."

Hannah's mother laughed, deep and throaty. "That's my girl. She sounds fine. You know how mothers worry."

Jake didn't remember anyone worrying about him until he landed in his final foster family. Stuart and Gloria Brewer had worried about him. "Sure."

"May I ask you a personal question?" Libby asked.

Jake's grip tightened on the phone. Most personal questions were entirely too personal. "Why?"

"I know you were friends with D.C., but you sound like a young man. How old are you?"

"Older than Hannah, but not as old as D.C."

"That tells me more than you know. Worked with D.C., did ya?"

"Yes."

"Ahh." Her voice trailed off.

Jake pressed the phone tightly to his ear to hear the background noise. Someone else was in the room with Hannah's mother. A man.

"I'll be sure to give Hannah your message," Jake said.

"I'm counting on you. Bye now."

Jake ended the call. He believed Libby Montgomery knew exactly what her ex-husband had done for a living.

She knew that the import business was a cover story. His gut tightened. Would she tell Hannah?

He couldn't control what she told Hannah. There were a lot of things he couldn't control these days, and he was better off not worrying over them.

Right now he had two immediate goals. Get Hannah settled and bring Ursula to justice. Until Hannah returned, he would look for Ursula on his computer.

He hobbled into his bedroom and locked the door. In near darkness, he typed in his computer password. Seconds later, he was deep in official databases, scrolling through screens, looking for his elusive quarry. He intently regarded the sequential records on his monitor.

A patriotic flag appeared onscreen as he scored a hit in an international credit card database. "Gotcha." He took a moment to bask in his triumph. Ursula Gruber was on the move in Europe. She'd covered her tracks, but he recognized her Joan Andress alias.

Hope sparked in the cold place where his revenge festered, a brilliant flash of light on a vast artic plain. He lounged back in his chair, tapping his fingertips together, remembering.

Ursula's guise of museum curator fooled him once. He wouldn't be so easily duped by her again.

The clues had been there all along, but he'd been too preoccupied to notice. Ursula hadn't wanted to be seen in public with him. That should have tipped him off, but he'd been so caught up in the physical aspect of their relationship that he'd shrugged off his concerns.

His hunter's instincts had finally kicked in, but by then it was too late. Ursula had discovered his professional connection with D.C.

His fingers clenched into tight fists. There were ways to deal with double crossers. Slowly. Painfully. D.C.'s murder would not go unavenged.

His partner's death weighed heavily on his shoulders. He had to right this wrong. Soon.

A pop-up message appeared on his computer screen.

The south-facing motion detector at the lawn perimeter had been activated. Hannah was on her way back to the cottage. Quickly, he shut down his computer.

He had just hobbled back to the kitchen when Hannah breezed in, laden with a bulky stack of cardboard. Bright flags of color accented her pale cheeks, and her gray-green eyes bloomed with warmth. The pungent aromas of pine and oak wafted in with her, and he sniffed the fresh air until he found Hannah's subtle floral essence.

"Let me help you." Jake moved forward to help her, but with his bum leg he wasn't fast enough.

"I got it." She stacked the cardboard against the bookshelves. "I don't think I brought nearly enough boxes. I hope I can pick up some more in town later on today."

There was a finality about the cartons that depressed him. He'd gotten used to seeing D.C.'s books on the shelves. But his job was to help Hannah, and if she wanted to box things up and move on, that's what they'd do.

"Have a nice walk?" he asked, handing her a glass of water. Her fingers touched his as she accepted the glass from him.

A spark passed between them, buzzing through his arm and electrifying his senses. From the sudden, almost imperceptible narrowing of her beautiful eyes, Hannah must have felt it too.

"Thanks for the water," Hannah said, drinking deeply. "This area is teeming with birds. I could easily imagine a nature sanctuary or a meditation center located out here."

Jake caught the excitement in her voice, in the way her eyes sparkled as she talked. Her passion intrigued him, causing him to wonder if she was this passionate in a man's arms. "Does this mean you're going to move up here?"

"Not practical, I'm afraid. I have a good paying job two hours from here. The daily commute from here to

Washington, D.C. would be a real killer."

She belonged here, but it wasn't his place to insist that she live in this house. His mission was to get her settled. Whether that meant moved in or out, it didn't matter to him. It couldn't. He had other things to do and so did Hannah Montgomery.

"Your mother called while you were out," Jake said.

Hannah drained her glass of water. "Mom called? Is something wrong?"

Jake shrugged. "She wants you to call her back. Something about a time sensitive lead on a yoga studio."

Hannah chewed her lip as a coil of icy dread spiraled through her. Before her mother left, they had agreed Hannah would approve all major expenditures for the yoga video. Did she expect Hannah to approve something sight unseen?

She set the empty glass on the counter. "Excuse me. I need to call her back."

From the privacy of her bedroom, Hannah phoned her mother. She braced herself for her mother's latest scheme. "Mom? What's going on?"

"Thank goodness you called! I wasn't sure you would respond in time. I've got the greatest news. Doug says there's a yoga studio for sale near my hotel. If I buy the studio, we can film the video at our convenience."

"Doug?"

"Doug Nichols. The movie producer. I told you about him. He's very excited about doing my video. Doug says I have a good handle on the high concept."

His high concept was probably directly related to emptying her mother's bank account. Hannah ground her teeth together. There weren't supposed to be any Dougs in the picture. "What about our plan to work cooperatively with an existing studio and their students?"

"Doug says it's best to be open to all possibilities."

Hannah was having a hard time liking Doug. "Please don't be hasty. Let's explore every possible avenue before we commit to anything."

"That's why I called, dear. Can you come out right away? If you caught a red-eye tonight, we could submit an offer for the studio tomorrow. Doug recommended a really good realtor. The studio won't be on the market for long."

Hannah massaged her sore jaw. "Mom, I understand you're excited about this studio opportunity. And I know how much you love yoga, but we have to do this logically. We don't know anything about neighborhoods or locations out in California. There's a reason that studio is for sale. We need to know why."

"Don't be so rigid," her mother said in a huff. "The doorman's cousin is related to the property owner, and the doorman says the studio is a good deal. This feels right. Besides, Doug says it's under priced."

Her mother had once bought a Jeep because it had good karma. The fact that the purchase had been a good one, that the Jeep hadn't been a lemon, was incidental in Hannah's mind. Her mother had owned a perfectly good car at the time and hadn't needed another vehicle.

"Tell me more about Doug," Hannah said.

"He's a real sweetie. I've been seeing a lot of him."

Hannah hoped her mother meant that in the figurative sense. The last thing she needed was for her mother to get taken in by some smooth operator.

"Don't sign anything until I get out there," Hannah cautioned, pacing around her tidy sleigh bed. If her mother stayed busy, maybe she wouldn't obsess about this studio. "Contact the studios I located through the Internet and find out how much it would cost to use their facilities. Once we have enough information, we'll make a decision."

"You can't fly out today?"

Hannah blinked back a wave of guilt at her mother's disappointed tone. "No. There's too much to do here. Something unusual has come up here as well. Did you give Dad my copy of *Little Red Riding Hood*?"

"No."

Hannah exhaled slowly and sat down on the soft bed. "I found it in his bedside table last night. Along with a letter he wrote to me."

"A letter?"

She winced at her mother's sharp tone. "He says he hid two more letters in this house and that I'm supposed to find them."

Her mother groaned. "I finally have the means to do what I've always wanted to do and he has you tied up with his secrets. It isn't fair. You should be out here with me."

She took a deep breath and counted to ten. Her mother had always been threatened by the unspoken bond Hannah had shared with her father. "I'll be there soon, Mom. Just two more days, I promise."

"Your desire to stay there wouldn't have anything to do with the young man living in the house with you, would it? The one with the voice of a Renaissance poet?"

She exhaled slowly, choosing her words with care. "Jake is helping me as a favor to Dad. That's all there is to it. I can't put off dealing with Dad's house any longer. I'll be out there Sunday evening."

"I wish it were sooner." Her mother sighed. "Your father always did this to me."

"Did what?"

"One-upped me. No matter what I gave you for your birthday, his gift was invariably bigger and better. I don't mean to speak ill of the dead, but he could have been more considerate of my feelings when he planned this."

Hannah rolled her eyes. She'd been caught on this parental see saw before. "I hardly think that he planned his death."

"I wouldn't put anything past him."

"I love you, Mom."

"Love you too."

Hannah put her phone away. Another crisis narrowly averted. Why would her mother even consider buying a yoga studio in California? She had a perfectly fine studio in Maryland for Pete's sake. Mothers weren't the easiest to manage, especially one as led by her inner eye as her mother.

She found Jake sitting in the recliner. For a moment his needle sharp gaze brushed against her, then he relaxed. He seemed relieved about something. What?

Was his distress in relation to their agenda for today? It couldn't have been easy for him to see her father's handwriting on that letter. But, he didn't seem like the overly sentimental type. Perhaps he was anxious about finding the two remaining letters.

Or, he could be nervous about the search itself. She'd been gone for most of an hour. Maybe he'd started searching without her.

"Everything all right?" he asked.

"No problem yet, though with my mother anything is possible. She wants me to fly out there today, but I put her off. Patience isn't her strong suit."

"Is she buying a yoga studio?"

Hannah frowned and sat down on the utilitarian sofa across from the recliner. "I hope not. There's one for sale, and the movie director thinks it's a good deal, but that wasn't our original plan. Mom has a yoga studio in Maryland. She doesn't need one in California."

"You don't want her to buy the studio?"

"I don't have enough information to make a decision. Every other word out of Mom's mouth was Doug says this or Doug says that."

"Doug? Who's he?"

"A movie producer she met. It worries me that she's so enamored of him. She's only known him for a couple of days and yet she quotes him like he's proclaiming the gospel truth."

"She is a mature adult, capable of making her own decisions."

"But she thinks with her heart, not her pocketbook. I've balanced her checkbook for years because she insists that it's bad karma to quibble over money. How would she know if her bank statements were correct if she hasn't ever balanced her checkbook?"

"Sounds like you're more worried about your mother's money than you are about her."

That drew Hannah up short. Was she focusing on the wrong thing here? Should she be more concerned about her mother's happiness? "It may sound that way, but I want my mother to be happy. Mom said making a yoga video would make her happy, so I'm helping her make that happen."

"What if she decides Doug makes her happy?"

What an odd conversation to be having with Jake. Hannah had no doubt about what made her mother happy. Yoga did, dating didn't. To put it bluntly, her mother didn't date. "Doug is temporary. He won't be in the picture for long."

"What if you're wrong?"

Why was he being so pushy about this? Hannah shrugged. "I don't know. I haven't had to deal with Mom dating before. I'll do whatever makes her happy. I'd feel better if I knew more about this guy."

Jake was silent for a long minute. "What do you want to know about him? I might know someone that could help."

"Maybe I'll check him out once I've met the guy. Hire a private detective or something."

"At a minimum you'd need a background check and a credit report."

"Sounds good, but I'll bet it's expensive. I'm working with a tight budget. Quality assurance inspectors aren't at the top of the compensation scale."

"This guy I know, he owes me a favor. If you want to know about Doug, say the word."

Hannah blinked rapidly. "You'd do that for me?"

"Sure."

Nothing like having good data before making a decision. If Jake could get Doug checked out for free, she wasn't going to complain. "Let's do it. At least then I'll feel better about Mom being parted from her money."

Enough about her mother and her Doug. Time to get

back on track for the day. "Did you find them?"

Jake's gaze narrowed and he stilled. "Them who?"

From his frozen posture, Hannah was certain Jake was hiding something. And his face had been flushed when she'd come in from her walk. As if he'd been doing something he didn't want her to know about. Hmm. Jake was cut from the same fabric as her father. God save her from secretive men.

"The letters," she said. "Did you start searching for them?"

"I waited for you."

She watched him out of the corner of her eye. Something was off with his response, but she couldn't quite put her finger on it. "What have you been doing all morning?"

"You want a blow-by-blow detail of how I rinsed out the coffee cups, brushed my teeth, and got dressed?"

Hannah blushed. She deserved his snippy tone. "I'm sorry. I was projecting my personality onto you. If I'd been stuck here with nothing to do, I would have gone through every book in the house until I found another letter."

"There are a lot of books in this house."

"No kidding."

Jake reached for his cane and started to rise.

Hannah waved him down. "Don't get up. It's not good for your leg for you to be so mobile."

"I'm going to help you look for the letters."

"You can help from the chair. I'll bring the books over to you. As we go through each batch, we can stack them in the cartons."

Hannah leaned down and grabbed an armload of books from the lowest shelf of the nearest bookcase. When she stood, she noticed Jake's eyes gleamed appreciatively. Had he been staring at her butt when she bent over?

Why did her blood race at the idea? He was the type to flirt with any female who breathed.

The books accidentally slipped from her hand into his lap. The brunt of the weight fell on his good leg, but just for a moment, she saw a much different Jake. A very capable man, one who could intimidate with the merest glance.

"Sorry." Hannah scrambled to right the books in his lap. As she bent closer, she recognized his unique fragrance, a pleasing hint of musk which flowed around her like an exotic dessert, enticing, decadent, and forbidden.

Jake fought hard not to over react. He knew she was aware of the physical attraction between them. What he didn't know was if she intended to do anything about it.

She stacked the spines of the books in his lap precisely into a straight line and then sat down across the room thumbing through a stack of her own. Jake leafed through *Treasure Island* and *Black Beauty*. No letters.

After five years of working with D.C., Jake knew that the man didn't repeat himself. If there were letters hidden in this house, they weren't hidden in books. He would have offered his opinion on the matter if he'd been asked, but she hadn't sought his opinion. Hannah seemed determined to check every book, and so they did that.

He didn't mind because it put them working in close proximity. However, if she dropped another load of books in his lap so perilously close to the fly of his jeans, he wouldn't be responsible for his actions.

Jake nodded towards the sunny window. "What did you see out there?"

"Birds."

"That's all?"

Hannah smiled. "To be precise, I noticed birds and habitats. We have the backyard habitat here at the cottage, which reminds me I need to buy seeds for the feeder, the margin habitat where the lawn meets the forest, the forest, the meadow, and the wetlands there by the spring. This place is teeming with beautiful birds."

"You don't think of birds as rats with wings?"

Hannah put down an armload of books so that she could gesture with both hands. "Absolutely not. Birds have very complex behaviors. Males use vocalization to attract a mate, to claim territories, and to burn off excess energy stored overnight. Some ornithologists believe birdsong is the prelude to bird reproduction."

"You went out there this morning to watch birds get it on in the woods?" He would have gone with her if he'd known it was going to be an X-rated show. He eyed her speculatively. Did bird reproduction put her in an amorous mood?

She grinned. "Nothing like it, although it's over almost before you realize what happened. Birds pair up each spring to nest, with the larger birds mating for life. One thing that always amazes me is that even the birds with life-time mates fool around. Neither the male or female of a breeding pair is completely monogamous."

"So, birds are cheating adulterers?"

"Exactly. I wouldn't stand for it. If I had formed a lifelong bond with a mate, I would be crushed if he looked elsewhere for entertainment."

"You're not into casual sex?"

"That's not me." Hannah snapped a book shut and reached for another one.

"You're practically a dinosaur. Most folks today are very willing to hop in the sack with strangers."

She flashed him a tight smile. "I'm not most people."

No kidding. She was amazing and witty and self-sufficient. Was it any wonder he was hot for her?

She had backbone, that Montgomery stiff spine that didn't let anything get in the way of her goals. She had a vitality that energized him. And she had the most compelling eyes he'd ever seen.

Every room in this house had been painted the color of her gray green eyes, and it was driving him crazy seeing her against the backdrop that brought out the sparkling radiance in her lovely eyes.

Two hours later, they'd thumbed through every book in the house. "No letter," Jake said.

Hannah slumped on the sofa. "I should have expected

that. My father always did the unexpected. My fondest wish was that he would one day follow a schedule."

Jake laughed at the idea of anyone tying D.C. Montgomery to a schedule.

Hannah's gaze narrowed. "Did his unpredictability ever interfere with his work?"

Jake sobered instantly. Talking about work was off limits. "D.C. always took care of business, but he did it in his own way, in his own time."

"Amazing he could run a business that way. In my work for Potomac River Labs, I manage a master plan for all the research in our facility. Everyone operates on a strict schedule. If Potomac River managed their business the way my father did, it would be pure chaos."

"I don't think of chaos when I think of D.C."

"Tell me about him."

Jake took a deep breath and spoke from his heart. "D.C. Montgomery was the closest thing I ever had to a real father, and I'm ashamed to admit I let him down."

Chapter 7

Hannah's stomach lurched. Her equilibrium swung way off-kilter and she could have sworn the walls moved. She panted in shallow quick breaths as her fingers gripped the sofa armrest.

Her dad had been like a father to Jake?

Not. Fair. So not fair.

If her dad had spare time, he should have been doing dad stuff with her. Was it because she was a girl that he'd left her? The thought of him choosing to spend his time with Jake instead of her ripped at Hannah's insides like a steely claw, shredding her self-esteem.

She wanted to fold in on herself, to huddle in a tight little ball until the pain went away. This was why she had put this trip off for three months. Because she hadn't been a priority for her father for over twenty-two years. No matter how good she'd been, he had ignored her.

Every year, she'd asked Santa for the same thing. But Santa couldn't make her father come home either. Two nights before he walked out of her life, she'd had hysterics about the imaginary troll living under her bed. That night, she'd slept peacefully between her parents, but her childish outburst had a price. In the bottom of her heart, she knew the truth with sickening certainty.

She had driven her father away.

If she'd been a boy, a boy like Jake, he would have stayed. Boys didn't cry about imaginary trolls. Why couldn't she have been a boy?

Her hands fisted in the sofa cushion. "Didn't you already have a dad?"

His penetrating glare would have intimidated a

lesser woman. Hannah's chin jutted out, and she returned his fierce look.

"I never knew my father," Jake said. "My foster parents, Stuart and Gloria Brewer, are great people, but they didn't understand my need to color outside of the lines. D.C. took me on as a special project. It's because of him that I learned our trade so well."

Jake sounded so sincere, her anger lessened a bit. Her father wasn't her exclusive property. But still, given their occupation, Jake's claim seemed overstated. Her gaze narrowed. "How tough is the import and export business?"

"Tough enough. There's a lot of traveling, negotiating, and background analysis required before a deal is made."

Hannah gathered his words close to her heart. This was why she'd finally come here. To open this window of her father's life. She leaned forward. "Where was your store?"

"We worked out of Northern Virginia. Once a product request came in, we'd obtain the item in question for our clients. Then we'd ship the product directly to the requestor."

"Sounds complicated. How did you manage that without adhering to strict schedules?"

"There are schedules and there are schedules. We never had complaints on how we did business. Our clients always received one hundred percent satisfaction from our services."

She glanced around the utilitarian room. It was furnished with hand-me-downs. No big ticket items. No splashy accent pieces. She wanted to believe Jake, but what she saw didn't jive with his account. "Why aren't there any imports here? Why didn't my father collect souvenirs from the countries he visited?"

Jake shrugged. "I don't know."

After years of auditing records, she had developed a strong truth sense. And something here was off. She could practically smell it. What was Jake trying so hard not to tell her? "Why did you say you'd let my father down?"

He stared straight ahead. "If I'd paid closer attention to details, the way he taught me, everything would have been fine and he'd be alive today."

The storm blue walls of the living room pressed in on Hannah again. Questions boiled up and stuck on her tongue like flies on flypaper. Her breath came shallow and fast.

Jake's gaze softened, as if he were looking at a distant horizon. "D.C. died in my arms. I told him he was too mean to die, but he didn't listen to me. He made me promise I would come here and help you with the house. I promised him I wouldn't let him down a second time. I'm sorry, Hannah. I did what I could to save him but it wasn't enough."

Her father died in Jake's arms? She didn't believe him. The medical examiner had been very specific about the cause of her father's death. "My father had a fatal heart attack. For all we know, this wasn't his first one. My father believed he could beat anything his body threw at him."

Jake hung his head, scrubbed his eyes. "I feel horrible about D.C.'s death. If I could have that day back to do over, I'd rewrite history."

Hannah's raw emotions yo-yoed across the spectrum. How could she stay mad at Jake when he cared so much for her father? "I don't hold you personally responsible. I'm heartened that he didn't die alone. My father wasn't the easiest man to like, but he enjoyed being around people. It means a lot to me that you were there with him."

The truth of her words surprised her. She envied Jake for sharing her father's daily life, but he'd eased her father's passing. She owed him for that kindness.

Jake massaged his hurt thigh. "A part of me died with D.C. I'll never forget him, Hannah. I wouldn't be here if it wasn't for him."

She met his agonized gaze, shivering at the depth of his pain. "I don't understand."

"I can't talk about the details, but it means a great deal to me that you don't blame me for what happened."

Hannah gnawed on her bottom lip. She wanted Jake to tell her everything. How could she understand if he withheld information?

Judging by Jake's miserable expression, this topic was painful for him. She'd done enough probing for now. "It's hard for me to accept my father's mortality. I always think of him as larger than life, a superhero chasing down bad guys."

A muscle in Jake's cheek jumped. "D.C. always got the job done. Everyone in the industry respected his abilities."

Jake's compliment brought a soft glow to Hannah's face. She and Jake saw her father in the same light. Maybe they weren't so different after all.

As Hannah boxed the inspected books, she realized her initial impression of Jake was flawed. He wasn't entirely shallow and superficial. His grief and despair over her father's death proved he had a sensitive side.

And he'd been there for her father's last breath. *He'd been there for her father.* She'd been a continent away with no idea of her father's distress. Jake hadn't shied away from the distastefulness of death. He'd embraced it to ease her father's passing.

Jake wasn't so mysterious after all. Could this wandering playboy have a heart of gold? It was certainly something to consider.

****

The half-pound burger and fries Jake ordered at the gleaming white and chrome diner for lunch went a long way towards filling him up. Trouble was, he'd eaten so fast he had to sit and watch Hannah leisurely munch through her frilly salad.

Hannah's living arrangements seemed at odds with her independent nature. Why had she moved back home?

"You live with your mother?"

"I do." A becoming blush spread across Hannah's porcelain cheeks. "It's not because I have to. The arrangement works out better for me."

"You said something about an apartment before."

"My townhouse. I kept the townhouse as an investment when I moved back home."

"Sounds like you're already familiar with the property rental process."

Hannah swallowed a mouthful of curly lettuce. "I can tell you from experience that it's a royal pain to move the furniture. I stored my stuff in Mom's basement in case I ever saved up enough to buy another place."

"Why did you move out of your Mom's house in the first place?"

"Doesn't everyone want their own house when they grow up? I sure did, but the townhouse wasn't the right habitat for me. Too many people living so close together. And it seemed like I was over at Mom's house four evenings out of seven for yoga classes or dinner. The logical solution was to move back in with her."

"Didn't that negatively impact your social life?"

Hannah put down her fork and stared at him. "What is this, twenty questions? My social life didn't suffer from my move, thank you very much."

She hadn't given him the answer he wanted. Probably because he hadn't asked her the right question. Time to remedy that. "Let me rephrase that. Are you dating anyone right now?"

"I don't see that as any of your business."

It was very much his business. He wanted to get to know Hannah a whole lot better. If she had a boyfriend, the boyfriend wouldn't appreciate Jake moving in on Hannah.

"Why don't I ask the questions for awhile?" Hannah asked, picking up her fork and starting to eat again. "What kind of place do you live in?"

A man and a dark haired woman dressed in tailored

suits entered the diner. Not the sort who lived around here. When the couple sat two booths down from Jake, but both ignored his frank appraisal, his sensors went on alert. He leaned forward to answer Hannah's question, pitching his voice lower. "Are you talking about my mailing address?"

Hannah shrugged. "Sure, why not?"

"My foster parent's house."

"But you don't live there?"

"No."

"Where do you live?'

"I move around a lot."

Hannah leaned forward. "So, you're like a homeless person with no fixed address? You haul all of your belongings around with you everywhere you go?"

He winced. "Pretty much."

"How exhausting. The thought of dragging my entire wardrobe through airport security gives me the willies."

"I manage just fine." He had a self-storage unit near his foster parent's place in Philadelphia for his more unwieldy stuff. He got back to Philly a couple of times a year to drop off his accumulations.

The man and woman ordered, the woman changing how everything was prepared. The man met Jake's gaze and they shared a moment of understanding. He heard the man's "whatever you want, honey," and relaxed. These two were off the beaten track, but they weren't a threat.

"Tell me this," Hannah said. "With all that moving around, how do you find time for a social life?"

"There's always time for that." Jake grinned, pleased at this conversational direction.

"Are you dating anyone?"

White hot desire pulsed through him. He appreciated fine women, and Hannah was very fine. "My social calendar is wide open. Can I pencil you in?"

Her eyes flared then narrowed. "No. I don't appreciate you hitting on me because you're in a dry spot and I happen to be nearby. Let's stick to business matters and set the personal stuff aside."

****

Hannah wished she'd worn her dark glasses. It was bright enough in the offices of Holiday Realty to perform an intricate surgical operation. And she would've liked to have hidden behind dark glasses after lying to Jake. She had a feeling he'd seen right through her dismissal of dating him.

"Take these forms," Bertha Shifflet said. Bertha's big hair looked like it could house a dozen songbirds. "Fill them out and we'll talk about how soon you want to rent your property."

"As soon as possible," Hannah said, accepting the forms from Bertha. "The only hold-up is getting all the furniture out before I leave for California on Sunday."

"Don't worry about that, dearie. We'll rent it furnished. A remote place like that in the woods, folks might want to use it as a hunting base."

Hannah ground her teeth together. There would be no hunters living in her future wildlife sanctuary. "Absolutely not. No hunting on the property."

Bertha looked momentarily stricken. "All right. No hunters. Have you already decided on your rental fee?"

Hannah named a sum.

"No problem," Bertha said. "I'll advertise the cottage in the newspaper and on our website right away. At that price, you'll have it leased within the month. Did you bring me a picture of the property?"

She blinked. A picture. Darn. Why hadn't she thought of that?

"I have one," Jake said, pulling a color photo from his shirt pocket.

Hannah remembered to close her mouth. Jake was one surprise after another. She was the organized one. For him to assume her role showed just how unsettled she was. She certainly wasn't acting like herself around him. "Thanks."

"I need the listing fee and those forms filled out," Bertha said.

Hannah wrote the check and filled out the paperwork, but her mind wasn't on the rental agreement. It was on the man who'd invaded her dreams. He made her feel alive.

Dangerously so.

The ice queen would repel his advances. Which is what she'd done. But the sex kitten in her wasn't satisfied. The sex kitten wanted to party.

****

There was so much sunshine inside his truck, Jake barely felt the dull ache in his thigh. Every time he was with Hannah he felt like singing. After meeting with the rental agent in Thurmont, they'd picked up some groceries, found more cartons, and purchased bird seed. Hannah had insisted on a cornucopia of bird munchies.

"Why don't birds eat the same foods?" he asked, glancing back at the stacked bags of black oiled sunflower seeds, cracked corn, thistle, millet, and suet in the bed of his truck. From her appalled expression you'd have thought he'd blasphemed the holiest of sacred tenets.

Hannah gestured with her hand. "If birds ate the same diet then there would be a limited supply of food. Not nearly enough to sustain a varied population, and we would have fewer birds to study. Variety is every bit as important as diversity."

"Won't you mix those seeds together to fill the feeders? And won't an enterprising squirrel or chipmunk get most of the goodies?"

"They better not. This is nesting season. Birds need good nutrition at this time of year. I don't begrudge the squirrels and chipmunks their portion, but I don't want them to hog everything. As for mixing the seeds, heck no. I'll put the sunflower seeds in the hopper feeder, the cracked corn on the ground, the millet on the tall platform feeder, and the thistle in the tube feeder."

"You forgot one."

"The suet cakes go in the onion bag. I'll tie it to a tree branch."

"The suet—that's for the woodpecker that keeps banging on the side of the house? Why encourage him to come around?"

"Woodpeckers are great. They eat tree destroying insects. If one's been banging on the house, he's courting and letting the other males know he's claiming this area. What kind of woodpecker do we have?"

Jake shrugged as he made the first of a series of quick turns down back roads. He checked to make sure no one was following them. "It was black and white."

"Was there red on its neck or head?"

"I don't remember. The darn thing bangs on the house early in the morning. I wasn't interested in classifying it. I wanted to get back to sleep."

"If he comes again while I'm here, I'll let you know which kind we have. I saw both Downies and Hairys in the woods yesterday."

"There goes the neighborhood," Jake said. Hannah was very passionate about birds. He'd do well to keep that in mind. Otherwise, he'd get lots of her mini-lectures this weekend. "Are you this thorough about your work?"

"More so. I shift through data and double check results against written procedures. Why do you ask?"

"Curious. I wondered if you focus this intently on everything."

She nodded. "Quality assurance is a good fit for me."

She was intense. Passionate. Highly focused. Jake's blood heated thinking of how satisfying it would be to have all of that passion focused on him. He sure hoped she'd change her mind about keeping their relationship strictly business. He turned off the road onto the wooded lane that ended at the mountaintop cottage. "Is this how you spend your vacations?"

She shook her head. "This year is unusual. Family obligations are taking priority. I can only spend the weekend here packing up my father's cottage, so I hope we find those other two letters soon. Mom needs help with her yoga video, and that will keep me busy for the rest of my two weeks off. Otherwise, I'd be off on a birding trip, adding to my ABA life list. That's American Bird Association to you non-birders."

Another question nagged at Jake as he eased up the gravel lane. If Hannah was so capable, why had D.C. made him promise to help her get settled? What did the old man know that Jake didn't? D.C. believed in having redundant systems in his clandestine missions. Did he expect trouble here in this fairy tale cottage?

Trouble came in many shapes and forms. He wished he knew what kind of threat D.C. had been worried about. And he wished his leg was at one hundred percent so that he could handle any kind of threat.

D.C. knew about Jake's soft spot for women. Was D.C. counting on Jake's loyalty to keep him from seducing Hannah? That was a lot to ask, and Jake wasn't keen on that particular game plan anymore. He had a much different scheme in mind.

One in which he recuperated in Hannah's arms. Hannah's passion was just the tonic he needed to fully recover his strength.

Jake liked taking action and moving forward. Not possible with Hannah. She wasn't just any woman. She was D.C.'s daughter. Someone special.

A storybook princess even. Not the type to hop in the sack with a warty frog like Jake. It didn't take a tactical genius to reason out his dismal chances with her. And she'd already turned him down. He didn't like being shut out, but he'd respect her wishes.

When Jake lapsed into a brooding silence, Hannah wondered why. Had she talked his ears off about birds? Could be. She had a tendency to ramble on and on about birding.

Jake wasn't the type to tromp across hills and vales on the off chance of spotting a Bohemian Waxwing. But, she had. Not long ago, a call had come in from the Hot

Line phone tree, and Hannah had raced to an abandoned orchard to view a rarely seen bird in Maryland. In the huge flock of birds, there had been one Bohemian Waxwing. She remembered her heady exultation when she located the lone bird that was slightly bigger than the cedar waxwings, the one with a reddish tint to the undertail covert and yellow and white marks on its wings.

Though Jake didn't have a fascination for birds, he spent a lot of time studying people. She'd seen the way he checked the folks at the diner and the other locations they'd visited. And she'd observed firsthand how he studied her.

She had the distinct impression he could easily pick her out of a crowd, that he had her particular field marks memorized. In the avian world, his focused behavior would be considered courtship.

Courtship and mating. Couldn't she think of anything else? How would she get through this weekend if she mooned after the guy? Hannah groaned inwardly. Ever since he'd comforted her, she'd wondered what it would be like to kiss him. She longed to feel his arms around her again. The sex kitten in her purred happily at the thought.

Heat rose to Hannah's cheeks. It wasn't like her to obsess about courtship rituals.

Tense. She was definitely too tense. At last, something she knew how to fix. Yoga was the cure for tension. She managed a few deep breaths, posture visualizations, and positive affirmations, but relaxation eluded her.

Jake skirted the house and drove around to the rear. She'd noticed he'd parked there before as well. She broke the silence to ask, "Why do you park back here?"

"Expediency," he said, scanning the area. "It's closer to the back door."

There were just as many steps leading up to the back door as the front, but who was she to argue with his logic? It didn't matter to her where he parked.

"I'll carry the groceries in," she offered. Jake had embarrassed her by insisting on paying for the groceries, supplies, and their lunch. She wasn't helpless and she could jolly well unload the truck by herself. "You've done a lot on your hurt leg today."

"I'm okay." Jake hauled four of the plastic grocery bags out of the pickup bed and limped up the stairs with them.

Hannah followed with the remaining four bags of groceries, grumbling under her breath about stubborn males. Jake didn't take direction well. To get him to rest, she'd have to hog tie him to the recliner. The thought made her smile.

She refrigerated the cold items and headed for the back door. "I'll get the bird seed. Why don't you rest until dinner?"

Jake pushed off from the kitchen counter he'd been leaning against. "I can manage the bird food."

Hannah bristled at his terse reply. His limp was more pronounced now than it had been this morning. Why did he have to be so darn macho about unloading the truck?

Well, she could be stubborn too. She'd unload the truck before he got outside. Hannah speed walked to the truck. He hustled to keep up.

"I'm not sick, and I'm not weak," he said.

"You are hard headed and don't know when to stop," Hannah said, reaching for the sunflower seeds. When his hand brushed hers, a shocking current flashed up her arm and raced down her spine. Hannah jerked away from the incidental contact and accidentally elbowed him hard in the belly.

To her horror, Jake lost his balance and began to fall. "No!" she cried, lunging for him, but she was too late.

Like a slow motion scene in a movie, she was aware of everything happening one frame at a time. Jake's arms broke his fall moments before she landed on his chest. Air huffed out of her chest on impact.

Oh God. Oh God. Oh God.

Hannah's thoughts ran around in an endless circle. I've killed him. He survived world travel with my father, and I killed him over a few bags of bird seed. Oh God.

"Jake?" she whispered, raising her head. "Please be okay. I'm so sorry. I didn't mean to knock you down."

A muscle in his cheek twitched, but his eyes remained closed. Waves of heat steamed off his body inundating her senses with his savory aroma. Her mouth watered.

"Jake." She leaned closer to his angular jaw and his very kissable lips. What to do? What to do?

Her fingers sunk into his shoulders, and she gave him a not so gentle shake. One of his eyes arched open. "Is that any way to treat a man flat on his back?" he asked.

"Are you okay?" She gazed deeply into his dark brown eyes. For once, they did not seem cloaked in mystery. Instead, they brimmed with life. "Were you teasing me?"

"I was hoping for a little mouth-to-mouth resuscitation. What I got was a teeth jarring shake. Is that how you treat damaged birds, you shake the life back into them?"

"Of course not. I don't know what came over me." Hannah's gaze drifted down to his smoothly chiseled lips. Had he really wanted her to perform CPR on him? Now that she was touching him, she'd much rather throw out her good intentions and kiss him.

"Are you hurt?" she asked, dragging her gaze back up to his very warm, very inviting eyes. A girl could happily drown in their luminous depths.

"The only thing hurt here is my pride."

Hannah realized she was plastered to his chest. He was very warm and solid in places where their bodies intersected. She should quit fantasizing about kissing Jake and help him up off the grass.

But when she went to let go of his muscled shoulders, his hands clamped onto her wrists. "We've got to do something about this," he said.

Appalled, Hannah stilled. Did he know she'd been secretly obsessing about courtship rituals? Did he know she'd been savoring his unique masculine scent? "This?" she echoed weakly.

"This. You and me this."

"Oh. That this."

"I'm interested in you, Hannah."

Hannah chewed on her bottom lip and cocked her head to the side. "I'm aware of that."

His expression intensified. "I'd be interested in you even if I wasn't in a dry spell. Only, you said no. I respect that. But I'm hoping you've changed your mind. Kiss me?"

Was she breathing? It didn't feel like there was any air in her lungs. "I barely know you. This is insane."

"You and I have been striking sparks off each other since the moment we met. Kiss me."

Hannah stared again at his kissable lips. They were very close. What would it hurt to kiss him? She wanted to kiss him.

"What about your leg?" she asked.

"I guarantee you my leg isn't bothering me right now. I'm thinking about you, Hannah. About how you're going to taste, about how good you feel on top of me. About how great we're going to be together."

Hannah sucked air through her parted lips. Her nipples hardened at the velvet caress of his words. Oh Lord. She was seriously thinking about kissing him.

She must have given him some intangible sign because his gaze softened. His thumbs stroked the underside of her wrists. Goosebumps broke out on her flesh, a flame shot through her loins. She wanted to kiss him more than anything.

All of her nerves screamed encouragement. She wasn't one to sit on the fence. All the data pointed to one logical conclusion. This was her chance to find out if she was the ice queen or the sex kitten. She should kiss him. Right now.

Hannah leaned forward, trembling as her lips learned the shape and feel of him. With feathery kisses, she explored the intriguing contours of his mouth. Her pulse thundered in her ears. Her aroused breasts pressed into his muscular chest.

He tasted warm and delicious, like a steamy apple cobbler. She'd never been one to turn down dessert. Hannah went back in for another taste, this time touching the tip of her tongue to his lips. A hot surge of pleasure flooded through her and she sighed dreamily.

Jake's lips parted and he kissed her back. Boy, did he kiss her back, hot, deep, and demanding. He drank in her essence as if it was nectar. Instinctively, she nestled closer, her hunger for him overwhelming everything except her newfound feminine desire for completion.

She wanted him.

That was a shocker.

Most men thought she was frigid. She wasn't, but there was a difference between being frigid and being extremely selective. No man had ever felt this right. No man had ever made her want him with just one kiss.

Hannah shivered in feverish anticipation.

His hands stroked the length of her arms, then caressed her back. She gasped in pleasure at his tactile exploration, her spine arching into his touch. He trailed feathery kisses down her face, chin, and neck. Their gazes met. Undisguised sexual desire flared in his eyes.

He wanted her right back.

Would they make love out here in the yard?

The idea excited her, but a measure of common sense returned. Years of ingrained caution were difficult to erase even in the heat of passion. "Jake?" she murmured, her hands stroking the back of his head. His short hair was surprisingly soft to the touch.

"Yes. Oh God, yes," he mouthed against the laces of her shirt. His warm breath against her skin unearthed more buried passion. Her brain was bombarded by so many sensual messages that she almost succumbed to the tidal wave of desire.

Almost.

"Time out," Hannah said, her hands fisting in the soft grass. In a distance an ovenbird called teacher, teacher, teacher. Hannah didn't doubt for a moment that Jake could teach her lots of new things. Trouble was, Jake 101 wasn't on her elective list.

Jake planted one lingering kiss on her neck and lay back on the ground. His hands slid from her hips to rest heavily on her lower back. "Time out?"

His eyes were deep sparkling pools of chocolate that called her name. She wanted to lose herself in their depths. A lump formed in her throat. The urgency of her passion frightened her. She'd never before acted so wild and reckless. Time to put the brakes on before she crashed and burned. The fact that she didn't want to stop showed how far out of her comfort zone she had strayed.

Bad things happened to little girls who strayed from the straight and narrow path. Hannah shivered again.

"This isn't me," Hannah said, averting her gaze from Jake's soul searing eyes to his slightly crooked nose. All of her hormones chanted his name. She could barely think straight for all the racket. "I don't do things like this. I don't even know the woman who just kissed you like there was no tomorrow."

Jake's hands warmed her back. "I won't rush you, Hannah, but I won't lie to you about this. I want you."

"You do?" Hannah risked looking in his eyes again and got snagged on his very intense high beams. She couldn't look away if she tried.

Jake nodded. "And you want me right back. I see it in your eyes, I feel it in the way your body presses close to me. Right now, your head is filled with how I taste, how I smell, how I feel, and you want more." He stroked her back reassuringly. "We're going to be great together, sweetheart."

Hannah hummed inside. How could he tell from looking in her eyes? She couldn't deny that she wanted him, but she didn't act on every want she had. "I don't do one night stands, and I can't imagine that we will ever see each other again after this weekend."

"You're smart, but this isn't about smart. Desire is rarely logical. That's why it doesn't matter how long we've known each other. It's the connection that's important, and we connect, Hannah. Big time."

Hannah realized she was arching her back into the warm circles his hands were making on her back. If she didn't get off of him right away, she wouldn't be responsible for her actions. She pushed up from the ground.

His arms held then yielded. "Don't be scared of me, Hannah," Jake said in a whisper soft caress.

Hannah sat on the ground next to him, her fingers fisting in the short grass. The cooler air didn't begin to soothe the heat inside of her. "Don't you get it? It isn't you I'm scared of. It's me."

Chapter 8

Jake polished off the last of the manicotti with a satisfied sigh. At least one of his hungers was satisfied. His hunger for Hannah had grown beyond reasonable bounds. Good thing she'd had the sense to halt his seduction. Once she'd fallen into his arms, he'd thought of nothing else but making love to her.

Even now, the shape of her soft curves had him wishing their encounter hadn't begun and ended with that single kiss. But he had a responsibility to D.C. to fulfill and a hardened killer to track down. He needed to focus on those objectives. Besides, the last time he'd let down his guard around a woman, he'd paid dearly.

"Did you get enough to eat?" Hannah cocked her head at him, her wondrous eyes full of concern. Storm blue she'd called the matching paint shade on the walls. He privately thought the color should be called 'shimmering sunlight on a tropical sea.'

Jake nodded. "I did. Thanks. You're a good cook."

"My learning to cook was a necessity." Hannah sipped her water, a bittersweet expression on her face. "Both of my parents were so self-involved that supper was usually an afterthought."

Jake leaned back in his chair, his belly round and replete. "I guess your folks didn't stock the freezer with frozen dinners."

"Heck no. Mom insisted that everything we ate be fresh, but she'd forget to shop. Lots of nights our suppers were hunks of cheese and an apple."

"Sounds healthy."

"It's all right once in a while." Hannah reached for

his empty plate, stacked it on top of hers, and moved them off to the side. "I wanted variety in my diet so I learned how to cook. After a while, I did the grocery shopping too. Once my folks separated, my mom didn't bother with cooking again."

Hannah had personal experience with innovation and adaptation. He'd excelled at both in his previous line of employment. "I don't remember D.C. ever cooking."

"He traveled so much, he probably never had time to learn." Hannah leaned forward eagerly, perching her elbows on the table and supporting her chin on her fisted hands. "Speaking of traveling, I have a few questions. Do you know a Bearded Lady in Berlin?"

Her unexpected question brought to mind an old friend. The Bearded Lady, a male cross-dresser double agent who preferred lavender spandex to three piece suits, had been D.C.'s CIA contact in Germany. "Wilhelmina?"

Hannah gasped. "I didn't think the story was true. My father told me the oddest tales about the Bearded Lady. Is it true that she wore a gun holster on her thigh?"

"She believed in protecting herself. Willie kept a dagger in her high heeled boots that was sharp as anything you'd ever want to run across."

"Is she still alive?"

"Alive and dancing nightly at the Green Slipper."

"Amazing." Hannah shook her head. "What about the contortionist? What was his name?"

Jake stroked the roughened beard stubble on his cheek. Apparently D.C. had told Hannah odd bits and pieces about their travels, so he wasn't betraying his friend or his country by answering her questions. "Hashim? D.C. told you about Hashim?"

"Hashim. Yes, that was his name. My father said Hashim could curl up in the tightest of places, and once he hid inside a large urn in a restaurant for an entire day."

"Last I heard, Hashim was alive and well." The event

D.C. had mentioned to Hannah had been the high water mark of Hashim's career. Jake remembered the scorching heat and arid dryness of that day in the Middle East. After the evening meal, gunfire broke out in the eatery where Hashim had been eavesdropping on an arms broker. A stray bullet had penetrated Hashim's urn, blowing off his pinky finger. He'd been extracted immediately and received medical attention, but Hashim's clandestine career was over.

"Gosh," Hannah said. "I never believed these people were real. The way my father told the stories they seemed like exotic fairy tales. I thought he'd made Hashim and Wilhemina up."

Jake stared into his empty water glass. He knew exactly how she felt. He wished his horrors were fictional events. Would he ever be free of the mistakes of his past? "They were real all right."

"What did they have to do with the import business?"

Jake swallowed thickly. He knew the drill. Tell enough of the truth that his lie seemed truthful. When would he finally be free from the dead weight of all the lies?

"Sometimes, in foreign cultures, transactions aren't straight forward like they are here. Certain individuals have made a career out of expediting matters. D.C. and I frequently needed these people to help us close the deal."

"It sounds dangerous and exciting."

"Sometimes it was," Jake admitted, feeling lighter for his brush with truthfulness. She was watching him closely, in the same way she focused on one of her birds. Could she read his body language? Did she know he was hedging the truth?

"In fact, if I didn't know better," she continued with a shrewd gleam in her eye, "I'd guess that you two were in another line of work altogether and that the unusual people you came in contact with were your regular associates."

"That's quite an imagination you've got Hannah."

Her guess was too close to the truth for Jake's peace of mind. He fumbled for his cane and rose. "I'll do the dishes."

"You sure?" She followed him to the sink with the stacked plates.

"I'm sure. You cooked. I clean up. Oldest rule on the books."

"Hmm." She shot him a searching look and pulled the plates back out of his reach. "You're very adept at changing the subject. Didn't you enjoy working with my father?"

"I'll never regret the time I spent with D.C., but that part of my life is done. I've closed the book on it so to speak." Well, almost closed the book on it.

Her expression softened. "I understand. I know how painful the past can be."

Jake shot her an exasperated look. He didn't need her sympathy. He wasn't a weakling. "I don't want to talk about my work."

She broke into a breathtaking smile that set him back a couple of heartbeats. "See how easy that was? We're effectively communicating now. And you don't have to do the dishes. I'm not keeping score on who does what household chore. Rest your leg. I'll wash these."

She'd pushed him far enough. He wasn't the weak link on this team, and they were a team until he got her settled. He always pulled his weight on a team. He took the dishes from her. "Forget it. I'm washing the dishes."

She was a long time closing her mouth, but she didn't protest further. Jake removed the dish soap from under the sink. "By the way, I contacted my friend about running a background check on Doug Nichols."

"You did? When?"

"Before we left for town today. He's already looking into the matter for me." Jake had initiated the automated computer search first thing that morning.

The preliminary results suggested nothing out of the ordinary. No surprise there, but Jake wasn't finished yet.

He'd know the man's entire life story in a few more hours.

"He works weekends?" she asked.

A truthful grin hit Jake's face. "He works all the time."

"He must be a really good friend."

"Like I said. It's not a problem."

"Let me know if anything unusual turns up." Hannah turned to go then stopped and thought the better of it. "I don't remember you making any phone calls."

"You have a suspicious mind." As he sought a way to phrase his reply, Jake soaped up the sponge and scrubbed the plates. "My friend and I communicate via the Internet."

"You have a computer in your room?"

"A laptop. Is that a problem?"

"No. Of course not. It just took me by surprise, that's all."

She would truly be surprised if she knew the things his computer did. God willing, she'd never need to know.

Her eyes bored into his back, bombarding him with her silent questions. To her credit, she kept them to herself. He exhaled slowly, relieved that another hurdle had been crossed. Even so, he was profoundly aware that he'd just lied to her. Again.

"Do you know where the forms are that we got from the property management company?" she asked.

"On the coffee table. I reviewed them while you were cooking dinner," Jake said, rinsing off the last plate. D.C. hadn't invested in a dishwasher, which was another reason Jake had been eating frozen dinners. Fewer dishes to wash.

One thing was rapidly becoming apparent. Hannah had a lot of her father in her. She was very close to piecing together the truth of her father's life. He wanted to tell her the truth, but he couldn't.

Civilians were briefed on a need-to-know basis. Hannah didn't need to know. Not knowing would keep her safe. And the thought of anything bad happening to

Hannah was completely unacceptable.

****

A solitary dove cooed to Hannah's left as orange rays from the setting sun warmed the sky one last time. She shivered and rubbed her arms against the chill in the evening air.

She rocked on the porch, rental papers on her lap. She couldn't bring herself to look at them just yet. Living here would be nice. There would be no traffic, no congestion, and no work schedules. No income to speak of either.

But living here wouldn't bring her father back. He'd been a man of secrets, and that secrecy had driven her nuts. He'd taken his secrets with him to the grave, except for the other two letters he hid. Letters that she couldn't find.

Jake must have thought she was possessed when she paged through every book in the house this morning. She wanted to find the letters, wanted to understand her father, but she was chasing a ghost.

To make matters worse, Jake wasn't being honest with her. At dinner, she'd observed him closely. She'd seen that cold look come into his eyes, the same one her father had used when he was skirting the truth.

She wasn't blind.

Or stupid.

Jake was a liar.

Hannah couldn't tolerate liars.

In the waning light of dusk, the solitary dove mourned the passing of the day. Its plaintive cries of coo-ah, coo, coo, coos filled her heart with sadness. Nothing she did would bring her father back. It was time to realize that and move on.

It was absolutely too bad that this mountain property would make a perfect wildlife refuge. Or an even more perfect meditation center. She could easily envision people coming out here for relaxation.

But those large scale ideas took money. Big money.

She didn't have the means to live out the rest of her life following her heart's desire.

This place had to pay for itself or she had to sell it. She couldn't afford to indulge in any sentimentality. End of story.

"I brought your jacket out," Jake said. "It's cooling off as the sun goes down."

"Thanks." Hannah shrugged into the jacket as Jake sat in the rocker next to her. His thoughtfulness touched her, confusing her all over again. Every time she thought she had him pegged, he caught her off guard.

"Are you sure about your decision to rent this place?" he asked.

The storybook surroundings called to Hannah. But fairy tales weren't her reality. "Fraid so. It hurts to lease this lovely place, but I don't have much choice."

"Choices. It always comes down to choices, doesn't it?"

His philosophical insight troubled Hannah. "Who are you, Jake Sutherland?"

He visibly startled. "A man. Nothing more. Nothing less."

Being clever now, was he? "Easy to say, but few people know who they really are. Just coming up here has me reevaluating my life."

A chipmunk dashed across the lawn, its narrow white stripes visible in the deepening dusk. Hannah rocked slowly in the wicker rocker, wishing for answers to her questions.

"That's easy. You are definitely your father's daughter."

"Funny you should say that. I don't know who my father's daughter is. My mother's daughter I know real well, but she doesn't fit the mold up here. Have you ever felt like two people living in the same body?"

Jake's cane clattered noisily to the floor. He reached for it and slung it across the arms of his rocker. "Are we talking schizophrenia here?"

"Heck no. I'm talking about being the person that the situation warrants. It seems that my staying here, thinking about my father, has brought realms of submerged emotion and memories to mind. Does that ever happen to you? That you blend in so much until you don't know where the old you and the new you begin and end?"

"I know that feeling."

Hannah let out the breath she'd been holding. She didn't want Jake to think of her as crazy or schizophrenic. "It is very confusing."

"At least you don't have to choose between one identity and another," he said. "You know who you are, you've just been trying on a different aspect of your personality up here."

"Sounds like you've had some experience with this. Tell me, how do you get back to feeling like one person again?"

He took his time answering. His deliberateness irritated the heck out of her. Was he practicing his lines on himself before he spoke to her? Couldn't he answer spontaneously? That sure hadn't been the case with his kiss. Her ears were still steaming after rolling on the ground with him this afternoon.

Best not to think of that.

"You may not like my answer, but hear me out," he said. "In my experience, change is irreversible. Once you try something new, that experience sticks with you, even if you decide to go in the old direction."

He was right. She didn't like his answer. She didn't want to be her father's daughter. She just wanted to be herself. Her old self. Hannah chewed on her bottom lip as a faraway owl called out "who?" She didn't want to be a *who*. She wanted to be Hannah Montgomery.

Did her father know this would happen? Her mother had said it was sneaky of him to dangle the hidden letters in front of her, making her question the standards of her life.

She hated sneaky. She hated feeling torn between

her mother and her father. She hated that thinking about all of this was changing her.

Who was she?

Good question.

Jake nudged her with the gently edge of his cane. "Earth to Hannah. One minute we were having a conversation, communicating effectively as you'd say, and the next you were off somewhere in your head."

She was guilty of wool gathering. "You're right about a person changing. I was reflecting on recent events and my reaction to them."

"Sounds like you have regrets. Don't. It's a waste of time to relive the past. The future is where we're headed."

"But don't you ever want to go back and fix your mistakes?"

"It isn't possible."

"But, if it were, would you?"

His teeth flashed white and sharp in the darkness. "In a heartbeat."

Hannah liked that answer. Sitting here in the dark with Jake was comforting. It felt like they had moved beyond a superficial acquaintance. It felt like he cared about what she thought, about what happened to her. And that caring made her feel special. Cherished.

"How about you?" he asked. "If you could change something in your past, what would it be?"

"Easy. I had a fit about trolls under my bed when I was about seven years old. I'd like to fix the past so that night never happened. And you? What would you change?"

Jake wished there was only one incident in his past that haunted him. That wasn't the case. He'd screwed up majorly by trusting Ursula. Not something he could discuss with Hannah. There had been some minor professional screw ups. But his personal list of do-overs was extensive, stretching far back into his childhood.

He'd been through a slew of foster homes before he ended up with the Brewers. He hadn't made much effort to fit in because he'd been angry with his mother for abandoning him. He hadn't thought about his mother in years. "My mother," he said. "I'd do things differently with her."

"That's sweet."

"I wasn't easy to get along with when I was a kid."

"No kidding."

He ignored her sarcastic jab. "My Mom had it hard her whole life. I was unexpected. Having to deal with a kid she didn't want pushed her over the edge. If I could go back and change something, I'd be nicer to my mother, or maybe I'd wish I'd never been born. Maybe that would have given her a better chance at making a success of herself."

"I can't speak for all mothers, just mine who isn't quite typical, but she would never wish I hadn't been born. I can't imagine your mother wishing you'd never been born. Even if you complicated her life, she wanted you, or you wouldn't be here."

"Never thought of it quite that way. Thanks."

Hannah's familiar scent wove a subtle spell around him, making him long for things he couldn't have. Or could he?

She didn't trust him enough to sleep with him. Jake knew with bone deep certainty it was for the best if they didn't pursue an intimate relationship. But he wasn't done with trying to change her mind. He cleared his throat. "About this afternoon."

He heard her sharp intake of breath. Heard it and knew she'd been as affected by that sensual kiss as he'd been. Hope surged through him, a delta wing kite dancing on the wind.

"What about it?" she asked.

"Are we going to pretend that you didn't kiss me?"

"That would be lying and I hate lying," Hannah stated emphatically. "I kissed you. It's undeniable."

"I enjoyed kissing you back."

He was taking a risk by pressing her, but he couldn't

seem to get out of the way of the coming train wreck. "I'm a dog for bringing this up again, but I would like to get to know you better."

"I'd be a dog if I didn't say how much I've enjoyed your company," Hannah said. Her tone of voice reminded him of the mournful doves. "I dreaded coming up here, but your presence here made the unbearable bearable. You helped me feel like I wasn't alone in this, and I appreciate that."

"But?" he asked.

"But, this storybook place is not my reality. I have a life outside of this cozy mountain retreat."

"This could be your reality. Your father built this place for you."

"Do you think I don't know that?" Hannah's voice was no longer soft and cooing. Its shrillness grated on his ears.

"Then why are you walking away from it?"

Hannah stood and paced in front of him, rental papers in her hands. "You are a real pain in the butt, you know that. My father used to keep drilling away at me like this and I always hated it. I can't stay here. There are secrets here, embedded in the woodwork. I can feel them, and they eat at me."

"Secrets?"

"Secrets. My father lived apart from me for years. It's too late for me to make room for him in my heart. Its twenty-two years too late."

Jake pushed off the rocker and balanced on his good foot. He couldn't tell her she was right. He couldn't tell her a damn thing. "I'm sorry. I shouldn't have pushed you so hard."

"You know what I'm talking about, don't you?"

Her beautiful gray green eyes glittered at him. "I don't have any right to ask you to trust me, but I am. Asking you to trust me."

"How can I trust you? You're keeping secrets from me, too. Trust is a two way street."

"I trust you, Hannah. I respect the hell out of you. I

admire you for coming up here and trying to exorcise your father from your life."

"But you don't trust me enough to tell me your secrets?"

He squirmed in the darkness. "I can't."

"Then don't expect me to trust you. I won't settle for less than the truth. I don't care how many sparks fly between us. Passion isn't enough."

"You can't turn off that truth seeking part of you, can you?"

"What?"

"There's a part of you that analyzes everything, isn't there? A part that never turns off. I understand that, Hannah. Inside where it counts, I'm the same as you. I want everything to fall into place. I can't stand loose ends. But, don't make the mistake of thinking passion can be pigeonholed and organized like ordinary data points."

Hannah's spine stiffened. "Are you saying I can't be passionate? That I'm frigid?"

"Hell no. You are the most beautiful, exciting woman I've ever met. I'd like nothing better than to spend the next two weeks making love with you." Absently, he rubbed his fingertips in little circles on the handle of his cane. It was the same pattern he'd traced on her back earlier today. "You'd like it too."

"Two weeks?"

He'd started this and he would finish it. If Hannah wouldn't allow him to physically touch her, he'd touch her with his sensual words. "Have you ever spent two weeks in bed with a man? We'd feast on desire and let sweet passion be our guide. The magic you and I made would be incredible."

"Two weeks?"

"I'm not one for subtlety, Hannah. I've been on good behavior because of the favor I owe your father. But I'd much rather misbehave."

"Are you telling me that you're going to attack me tonight? That I need to barricade my bedroom door before

I go to sleep?"

He grimaced. Why did she misinterpret everything he said? He respected her boundaries. "Hannah. I want you. You said you needed to hear the truth. That's it. The basic truth. I'm a man, and I want you."

"Absolutely not. Not going to happen." Hannah veered away from him and stood next to the porch railing. "I won't indulge in an affair just so you can scratch your itch. I have higher standards than that."

A muscle in Jake's cheek twitched, and his eyes closed reflexively. Tells. Signs that could get a man killed in the field if he couldn't control them. But he wasn't in the field. He was arguing with an exasperating woman. And she couldn't see his tells in the dark.

Or know how much her lack of trust and barbed words hurt. "Just so there's no confusion. "The Great Romance" is over?"

Hannah nodded, the whites of her eyes shining in the darkness.

Her absolute and unwavering rejection of their potential knifed through him. D.C. had been wrong. Hannah didn't need his help. "I won't be here when you come back from California."

"That's probably for the best."

He heard the door slam as Hannah went inside. His heart sunk when he heard her confirming her Sunday plane reservations over the kitchen phone. *Way to go Sutherland. What were you thinking, pushing around a beautiful butterfly like Hannah? You're lucky she even lowered herself to kiss you.*

His heart ached. He hadn't thought he'd ever feel desire again, so his yearning for Hannah hadn't been a complete waste. It had shown him that he wasn't going to be angry forever, that he didn't distrust all women, just Ursula.

Revenge. He'd thought of little else as his leg had healed. He owed it to D.C. He owed it to himself to balance the scales of justice.

He wouldn't kill Ursula outright. Killing was too easy for the likes of her. He had something much worse in store for Ursula.

Chapter 9

Saturday dawned gray and damp. Dreary rain pelted Hannah's window, and she burrowed deeper under the covers. Not even the mouthwatering aroma of morning coffee got her moving. How would she get through this day?

Wouldn't it have been smarter to string Jake along until she'd at least finished packing up her father's stuff? Smarter maybe, but twice as hard.

The Great Romance was over. How depressing.

Did he think she was tedious, boring, and dull? Because that's what she'd concluded, and she didn't like her assessment one bit. After this weekend, she was going to get out more. Have some fun. She wasn't an ice queen.

That decided, Hannah rose, dressed, and ate breakfast. As she finished her banana, she heard Jake coming down the hall. She took a bracing breath. "Morning," she said in a neutral tone. She grimaced inwardly. Boring people talked in neutral tones.

"Morning. What's our agenda for today? Are we moving furniture?"

Hannah glanced up at him. He had on jeans, another black tee shirt, and an unbuttoned flannel shirt. Dark circles rimmed his eyes. Had Jake been unable to sleep too?

"I've decided to rent this place furnished." Hannah didn't like him looking down at her with his shuttered gaze. She rose to be on equal footing with him. "I figure it won't take long to go through his personal effects."

Jake's flat expression didn't change. Had being here with her sucked the life out of him? Hannah chewed on her bottom lip. She wanted to bring Jake back from that cold place where he was dwelling.

She crossed the kitchen to throw away her banana peel and wash out her cereal bowl. "I didn't ask this before, but is there anything of his that you want? Furniture, books, clothes?"

Jake leaned in the doorway, his arms barred across his chest. "No thanks. Hard to travel light with a recliner in your suitcase."

"Oh." She knew that he traveled light. "Are you sure? What about a book? They're all timeless classics."

"He wanted you to have them."

"I already have them. At Mom's."

Jake stared at her. Hannah stared back. Okay. It was weird that her father had replicated her library at home. But, was it significant? They had already paged through every book.

Hannah skittered out the doorway to look at the stacked cartons of books. If the books had been arranged in any coded order, she'd messed that up yesterday when she unshelved them to search for hidden letters.

The vacant shelves taunted her. The books belonged here. If she was leaving the furnishings for a renter, the shelves shouldn't be empty. "I'll leave the books here."

"A renter might not take care of them. There's probably room in your mother's basement to store them."

"No." In her heart Hannah knew the books belonged here. "I want them to stay in the cottage. I'll reshelf them before I leave tomorrow."

Jake shrugged. "Suit yourself."

Hannah couldn't articulate why she felt so strongly about the books. She hoped she did better at sorting through her father's clothing. "I planned to gather his clothing in black plastic trash bags and donate them to a charity this afternoon."

"Sounds like a plan."

After she pushed past him and snagged the box of trash bags, Jake followed at his own pace. He'd seen the hurt and bewilderment in her eyes, but he couldn't snap out of his dark mood after spending most of the night surfing the Internet.

He'd heard her rustling around during the night, so he knew she hadn't slept much more than he had. When the rain had started around three a.m., he put the finishing touches on his lure for Ursula. He'd been studying her for months, and he knew she wouldn't be able to resist this particular gambit.

He hated waiting, but his waiting was nearly done. His plan was simple. Ruin Ursula financially and discredit her. If the rebels she ran with didn't kill her, Jake would. Then he'd be free to live his own life.

Meanwhile, he had to help Hannah. He entered her bedroom. The bed was made, of course. Not one wrinkle to be seen on that pristine surface. Unlike his own rumpled bed.

"Should we take the clothes off the hangers?" Hannah stopped near the closet.

"Whatever you want." Her clipped voice had him scanning the room for danger. Nothing out of place in here. Still, he remained watchful.

Hannah opened the closet, and then she sagged backwards. Moisture pooled in her eyes. Jake limped over to her, wanting to gather her in his arms. But, she'd made it painfully clear that she didn't want him touching her. "What is it?" he asked.

"Can't you smell it?" Hannah stepped back and hugged her arms to her middle. She stared wide-eyed at the closet of D.C.'s clothes.

Jake stuck his head in the closet and sniffed cautiously. He brushed his hands across D.C.'s shirts and pants. No toxic vapors in this closet. "Sorry, I don't smell anything."

"It's him. My father. The closet smells like he did. Every time I open that door his after shave wafts out and smacks me right between the eyes."

Jake took another sniff. She was right. The clothes

smelled like D.C. "I'll empty his closet for you."

Relief flared in Hannah's eyes. But before Jake could congratulate himself for solving her problem, she surprised him. "No. I have to face this head on."

He recognized her plucky Montgomery pride. He'd let her do the task, but they'd do it his way. "Why don't I hand you his things one at a time?"

"All right. I want to check his pockets anyway, in case he stashed a letter in his clothes."

Jake reached in the closet and pulled out a blue oxford shirt. He limped over to the bed and handed it to her.

Hannah took the shirt off the hanger, checked the shirt pocket, and folded it up. Then she placed the hanger in one garbage bag and the shirt in another. "Next," she said, her voice flat.

Every time he carried an item to her, her feminine presence teased his nose. D.C.'s lingering after shave didn't bother him, but Hannah's fragrance sure did. Being near her and not touching her was torture.

Jake quickly emptied the closet and started on the dressers. He immediately found Hannah's underwear and wished he hadn't. He didn't mind that the items were white and practical. He minded that they were Hannah's. That they had touched her exquisite, luscious body.

"I'll empty the bathroom cabinets while you finish up in here," he said to get away from her. In the bathroom, he splashed cold water on his face. Pretending the big romance was over wasn't a cake walk. Because it wasn't over for him, not by any stretch of the imagination.

He quickly found he'd made a mistake in retreating to the bathroom. It was no longer a masculine bastion. It smelled like Hannah. Fresh. Woodsy. Natural. Sunshiney. Jake groaned. Come on, Sunday.

****

After her father's personal effects were loaded in her car, Hannah allowed herself a deep breath. She'd discouraged Jake's insistence on using his vehicle by saying her trunk would be drier than the bed of his pickup. He'd not been gracious in defeat.

He limped out to her car, holding out his hand for her keys. "I'll drive."

"I'll drive."

His face darkened. "I know where we're going."

She opened the driver's door of her white Volvo sedan and slid inside. "Good. You can be my navigator."

He stumped over and sat in the passenger seat, resting his cane beside his seat. Her car seemed much smaller with him in it. She edged down the graveled drive, windshield wipers on intermittent speed now that the rain had nearly stopped. She followed his directions and soon had the car unloaded.

When the charity workers asked if she wanted a receipt, she said no. She didn't want another reminder of her father's life. She was moving on. There'd been no letters in his clothes. She'd search the rest of the house this afternoon and evening, but first she'd gas up for her trip to the airport.

She pulled into the station and fueled her car. Jake hovered nearby. He'd stepped out of the car when she did and done that predatory thing with his eyes. From the way he acted, she half-expected King Kong to jump out of the gas pump and try to carry her off.

She'd feel much better if he wasn't hovering. She rooted through her pocket for a few loose bills. "Would you mind getting me a bottle of water?"

With another scan around the property, he agreed, brushing aside her money.

Hannah sagged against her car. Sunday afternoon couldn't come soon enough for her. Jake's edginess was contagious. If it wasn't for those letters, she'd leave and go home right now. But she wanted to find those letters because she needed closure on her father's life. And for better or worse, Jake was her best chance for closure.

"Hannah?"

The familiar voice snapped Hannah out of her

reverie. She glanced up at the dapper, balding man approaching her from the red convertible. "Dr. Esteban? What are you doing up here?"

"Your assistant said you were staying near this town. I came up yesterday hoping to run into you. I've got to talk to you."

She flashed him a cold, professional smile. "I'm on vacation."

"You told Amanda to delay my audit, to do Coolidge's study first."

Her fingers gripped the plastic coated pistol handle of the gas line. Esteban was standing too close. The cloves of his breath mint mingled with the gasoline fumes. "I did."

"I can't afford the delay. You've got to put my study first."

The gas pump clicked off. Hannah removed the nozzle and holstered the line. "I don't have to do anything. The quality assurance unit is an independent aspect of the laboratory."

Esteban grabbed her arm. "Don't get in my way, girl."

Hannah yanked her arm out of his grasp. "You've crossed the line. I will report your behavior to Dr. Price."

He grabbed for her again, but she danced away in time. He followed her. "You're going to ruin me! Price won't let me publish until the audit is done. And Reed is preparing to submit his study."

Price was the big boss of the lab. Reed didn't work for them, but in the past, he'd published findings contrary to Esteban's. "I can't help you."

"Yes, you can."

One minute Esteban was looming over her, the next he was sprawled against the side of her Volvo.

"Who are you?" Jake snarled. Esteban shrank from him.

Hannah bit her lip at the menace in Jake's voice. "He's Jerry Esteban from Potomac River Labs."

"Call off your guard dog, Hannah," Esteban pleaded. "I can make this worth your while."

Hannah's eyes rounded. Esteban was trying to bribe her?

Jake grabbed Esteban's shirt. The two men were evenly matched in height and weight, but Esteban wasn't moving a muscle to defend himself.

"Call the cops," Jake said.

Hannah didn't want to call the cops. This was a professional matter, something that could be worked out by effective communication. "He didn't do anything, Jake. We were just talking."

Jake glared at Esteban. "He grabbed your arm. That's assault. And he tried to bribe you. For all we know, he tried to run your car off the road the other day. That's three strikes. This guy will be lucky if he ever sees daylight again."

Esteban's face paled. "Hannah, please, I beg you. My reputation is at stake. If Reed publishes first, I'll be out in the street."

Hannah heard the truth in his words. "Let him go, Jake."

Jake stepped back, but he stood between Hannah and Esteban.

"Hannah," Esteban pleaded. "Help me out here."

Hannah peered around Jake's shoulder. "I am helping you out. I'm allowing you a second chance. I can't control when anyone publishes, and I sure can't salvage your professional reputation. You're in charge of your destiny."

He hung his head. "My destiny sucks.'

"You have no one but yourself to blame. Dr. Price set up Potomac Labs to produce high quality research. You've had every opportunity to excel. The data audit won't change that."

"I'm doomed."

"Get out of here," Jake snarled. "You threaten her again, and I'll bury you."

Esteban scurried back to his car and fled.

Hannah stared at Jake. "You wouldn't really hurt

him, would you?"

Jake limped over to pick up his cane and her water bottle. He grinned for the first time that day. "Me? I'm injured, remember?"

Hannah wasn't so sure.

****

When Hannah mentioned she wanted sweet potatoes for dinner, Jake used to opportunity to slip away alone. Grafton met him at the nearly empty fast food place in town.

"I thought you had a tail on Esteban," Jake stated baldly over a late afternoon snack.

Grafton sipped his coffee. "He checked out okay. There was no reason to tail him."

"He threatened Hannah. Grabbed her and threatened her. The man isn't stable."

Grafton sighed. "I'll run him through the system again, but he's not a threat to national security."

Translated, Esteban was low priority. The fried chicken Jake was eating turned to sawdust in his mouth. He shoved the plate aside. "What about D.C.'s case? Where do you stand on that?"

Grafton pointed at the discarded food. "You not going to eat that?"

"No." Jake had better food waiting for him at home. Hannah's food. "What about D.C.'s killer?"

Grafton plowed into the chicken. "This is tasty. " He glanced around the empty room. "Two of the men we believed were involved were found dead last week."

"Last week? Why wasn't I informed?"

"You no longer work for the agency, Jake. I'm only telling you now as a matter of friendship."

"Who were they?"

"Ruger and LaFleur."

Jake knew of them. Small time operators on the European scene. What business did they have in the Middle East? Probably the same business as the woman who betrayed him. "What about Ursula? Have you found her?"

Grafton shook his head. "Sorry. She's gone to ground. Patience. We'll flush her out."

Jake pressed his palm on the Formica table top and leaned forward. "Patience? I've been patient. It's been three months since D.C. was killed."

"These things take time."

"If one of us had been taken out, D.C. would've found our killers by now."

"True, but neither of us is the great D.C. We'll find them, lad."

Jake gritted his teeth together. The Giraffe wasn't the sharpest knife in the drawer, but he got results in due time.

"What about you?" Grafton asked around a mouthful of chicken. "Have you remembered anything else since that day?"

He'd relived that day about a thousand times. They'd been meeting a contact and all hell had broken loose. It had been a setup from the word go.

"I've got nothing," Jake said simply.

"Nothing will keep you alive," Grafton said. "Stay out of this. The CIA will take care of the matter. We've got the resources and the connections."

And Jake had nothing. That's what Grafton was implying.

Jake held his silence. He trusted Grafton, but it was increasingly clear to him that there was a leak in the information highway. That leak had cost D.C. his life. Jake would plug that leak or die trying.

****

From the porch, Hannah watched Jake's truck until it disappeared into the woods. Thank God she'd thought of those sweet potatoes so she could have a moment alone. She immediately called her coworker. "Esteban came up here and tried to bribe me."

"Get out!" Amanda said. "Did you flatten him?"

Hannah hugged the phone to her ear. "When he tried

to grab me, I moved out of his reach."

"That wouldn't stop Esteban."

"Actually it didn't. But my friend Jake straightened him out."

"Jake flattened Esteban?"

"Jake got his attention. He won't be bothering me anymore, but I felt like I should warn you about Esteban."

"Does this mean I shouldn't go out with hottie Arturio tonight?"

"You should be careful, whatever you do. I'm calling Dr. Price right now and mentioning the incident."

"What about the audit schedule?"

"Unless Dr. Price asks you to change it, leave it alone. Esteban will self-destruct."

After a few minutes of small talk, Hannah hung up and called the lab's director. He was alarmed and promised to take up the matter with Esteban personally.

Sunbeams danced around her. Though it was tempting to loiter outside for the rest of the afternoon, Hannah wanted to look through the house, alone. She walked through the living room, cataloging the hiding places for letters. They could be inside the sofa cushions, taped to the bottom of the recliner. In the kitchen, there were lots of mostly empty cupboards. She should definitely search those.

She glanced down the hall to her bedroom and bath. They'd searched those rooms today as they collected her father's personal items. She blushed remembering Jake gazing at her undies. She wished they were silky and lacy, but she'd never seen the point of silk and lace. Until now.

There were other rooms in this house. Jake's bedroom and bath. She hadn't seen those.

She strode briskly down the hall. Jake's bathroom held a toothbrush, a bar of soap, and a few towels. Nothing else. Where was his stuff?

She headed across the hall and opened his door. Clothes littered the floor. His twin-sized bed was unmade.

His toiletries lined the bureau. A lumpy canvas bag filled one corner of the room. His laptop sat folded on the narrow desk.

Assuming the letters weren't in his belongings, they might be in the bureau, under the bed, or in the closet. She quickly checked all three. To her amazement, none of Jake's clothes were in the closet or the bureau drawers. The lumpy canvas bag held his clean clothes.

She gazed longingly at his computer. She'd love to open that and snoop around, but that wasn't right. The computer was Jake's. It hadn't been her father's.

She rocked back on her heels. Then she saw Jake glowering at her from the doorway. "What are you doing in my room?"

She stood, her chin going up. Why hadn't she heard his truck come up the drive or him coming into the house? "Looking for the letters."

"They're not in here. I don't even believe there are any more letters. I looked through this house pretty good when I first arrived. If the letters were here, I would've found them. And if I had them, I'd give them to you. There's no need to snoop through my things."

Heat steamed off her face. "I should've asked your permission."

Jake limped over and sat heavily on his bed. "You don't have to ask permission. This is your house."

His magnanimous attitude bugged her. The ice queen wouldn't be affected by his manly presence, but the sex kitten—she noticed how fine he looked. "Big talk coming from a man who had his hand on my underwear this morning."

His eyes gleamed. "Would you like to put your hands on my underwear, Hannah?"

What had she done? The big romance was supposed to be over. Hannah edged towards the door. "I think I'll start dinner."

Jake's masculine chuckle followed her down the hall.

Chapter 10

Hannah was exhausted. Walking through the Los Angeles airport late at night added another surreal touch to a surreal day. She adjusted the shoulder strap of her father's Zeiss binoculars so that they wouldn't bang against her overnight bag.

It had been a long, long day. She'd spent the morning tromping through the woods, exploring the lay of the land. She'd spent the early afternoon searching for the two hidden letters, but her heart hadn't been in it. Nothing had felt right since they'd declared the big romance over. It shouldn't matter. She dealt with facts, not feelings. Feelings changed. Feelings weren't reliable. Facts, on the other hand, were indisputable.

She veered around the young mother and the stopped stroller in the busy carpeted walkway. All around her people were rushing ahead, and she didn't feel like rushing. Every step she took seemed headed in the wrong direction.

As for her father's letters, they were too well hidden to find. She had poked and puttered and looked high and low. Mostly when Jake was holed up in his room doing God knows what with his computer. If her father wanted her to find the letters, he shouldn't have been so secretive.

Why couldn't he have been a normal father? One who wasn't afraid to tell his daughter that he loved her while he was alive. Why did he wait to tell her in a letter that she couldn't respond to?

The whole situation was disheartening. She couldn't live in the fairy tale house. She couldn't earn a second chance with her father. She hadn't learned why he'd acted as he did, why he held himself apart from her. And Jake was as secretive as her father.

Jake had stood tall on the porch and watched her drive away, reminding her of a soldier on sentry duty. Watching, waiting. But Jake wouldn't wait long. He had plans to move on. Hannah clenched her teeth so hard pain shot up the side of her face.

It was past eleven p.m. California time, and she'd been up way too long. A nap on the plane would have sufficed, but every time she closed her eyes, she thought of Jake. Funny how in such a short time he'd become so deeply embedded in her critical thought processes.

Hannah passed the security check station and saw her mother. Libby Montgomery wore a fire engine red sheath dress with matching jacket and red strappy sandals. Her pale blonde hair had been cut in wispy layers to frame her oval face. Something was different about her eyes, they seemed bluer and more vibrant than Hannah had ever seen them.

Hannah's mother swept her into an exuberant hug. "I'm so happy to see you. Did you have a good flight? What do you think about my new outfit? And my new hair cut?"

Everything seemed too bright out here. Hannah wished it was daytime so that she could hide behind her sunglasses. "Good to see you too, Mom. Nice outfit. Great hair."

"Come on. I have a limo waiting for us."

Hannah's cost conscious heels dug in against the tide of humanity pushing them towards the exit. "A limo? Isn't that expensive?"

"Who's counting? I figured you'd be out here soon enough to watch over my millions."

"You won't have any money left if you aren't careful with it." Hannah veered towards baggage claim. "I have another suitcase."

"I'll ask the driver to get it for us."

"It's my suitcase. I'll get it."

As soon as the words left her mouth, Hannah was

appalled. She sounded like she was back at the cottage arguing with Jake over who would do the dishes. Did it matter who got her suitcase? If she went with her mother, they could sit in the quiet of the limo and someone else would worry about her suitcase.

"On second thought, you're right," Hannah said. "Ask the driver to get my other bag."

Libby beamed. "I knew you'd take right to California. I love it out here. Doug says I'm a Californian at heart."

A flare of alarm flashed through Hannah. Had Doug already insinuated himself in her mother's daily life? "Is Doug in the limo?"

The noise outside the airport made Hannah want to shrink inside. Car horns blared, people shouted in Spanish and English, and everywhere she looked, folks had cell phones glued to their ears. The thick smell of diesel exhaust weighed down her lungs. She needed to get to bed. Soon.

"No dear. You'll meet Doug in a few hours. After we ate dinner this evening, he left for an evening appointment. He's joining us later for a nightcap. I can't wait to introduce you two."

A nightcap. Translation: late night drinks with seduction on his mind. How far under this man's spell was her mother? "I'd rather meet him tomorrow, Mom. I'm beat. I want to fall in bed and sleep for days."

"As you wish. But you're going to love the suite I booked for us. We have lots of elbow room and a cozy kitchen as well."

Hannah's stomach knotted. "A suite? Isn't that terribly expensive?"

Libby's excitement visibly slipped a notch. "A hotel room didn't feel right. My aura was troubled in the smaller space, but I love the suite. Lots of privacy."

"Privacy comes with a hefty price tag, Mom."

"Don't start on me, Hannah girl. This is how I want to spend my money."

Hannah flashed back to the pointed question Jake

had asked her. Was she interested in her mother or the money? Why couldn't she relax and enjoy herself?

She'd start by squaring things with her Mom. "I'm sure the suite will be perfect."

Libby grinned. "I was hoping you'd see it that way. I've lined up appointments for us all day tomorrow, starting at nine."

Hannah yawned and sank further into the plush limo seat. "What sort of appointments?"

"To see the most perfect yoga studio in the world, of course, but we're also going shopping. You need different clothes for California. Those dark colors you favor won't do. We're updating your look."

Hannah turned to gaze out the window. Cars whizzed past. Didn't Californians ever sleep? "What if I don't want to be updated?"

"Don't be ridiculous. You're way overdue for a change. New clothes and a new hair style are absolute musts. Besides, you're looking a little off, if you don't mind my saying so. Is anything wrong?"

Everything was wrong. "Other than staying in Dad's house with a strange man for the last five days? Anything besides that you mean?"

"You don't have to sound so snippy about it."

Hannah pinned her mother with a sharp gaze and then looked away. "You could have come with me, Mom."

"You needed to do this by yourself. I made my peace with your father years ago. You clung to the belief that we would be a family again."

Hannah mentally reeled from the one-two punch of her mother's words. How long had her mother known about Hannah's secret wish? Why hadn't they ever had this conversation before? Hannah turned back to her mother. "Did you love him, Mom?"

"Of course I did. I wouldn't have married him if I didn't love him."

"Why was he so secretive?"

Libby shrugged. "Why do I love to be surrounded by

people? Because that's my nature. I can't change who I am anymore than your father could change who he was."

The driver returned with Hannah's bag and then they were underway. Moving away from the airport only added to Hannah's dismay. Loose ends. That's what her life had become. A series of loose ends.

Hannah stared at her knees. "Once Dad went away, I hardly got to see him. I pretended I didn't care, but his absence hurt. Now he's left his house to me, and I don't know what to do with it."

"D.C. always had reasons for the things he did." Libby sighed sadly. "Not that I agreed with his reasons, but there was no changing his mind once it was made up. He lived for his work."

Hannah couldn't think of any explanation for her father's house. "So much about his life doesn't make sense. It irritates me that I can't organize his life into a logical matrix. If he didn't want a family, why did he get married? Why did he have a kid?"

"I can't answer those questions, dear. Our marriage was an attraction of opposites, and there were many times when marriage was a struggle for us."

Hannah cocked her head. "I never knew that."

"You were so little then, so serious already. Lord knows I did what I could to introduce you to fun, but you always tended towards books and your birds."

"You taught me yoga."

Libby shot Hannah a mysterious smile. "At least I didn't fail totally. What else is bothering you? Is this about the young man?"

"Jake? You think I'm snippy because of Jake?"

"Your young man is the only new element of interest in the picture."

Hannah leaned back in her seat, barring her arms across her chest. "Jake is not my young man. He's every bit as secretive as Dad was and twice as arrogant. He won't rest his injured leg, and he told me point blank that he wanted to sleep with me."

"Ah."

"I don't want to discuss my sex life with my mother." Tears welled in Hannah's eyes. "I don't feel like myself anymore. Why can't everything go back to the way it was four months ago? I knew how to be that Hannah Montgomery."

Libby drew her close. Hannah drank in the comfort her mother offered. All the other stuff fell away, and she was her mother's daughter once again.

"Don't cry, baby girl," her mother said, patting Hannah's back. "We're making a fresh start here in California. Maybe both of us will get laid out here."

Hannah rolled her eyes at her mother's absurd comment. She lifted her head from her mother's chest. "Mom! I don't want to hear about your sex life."

Her mother continued as if Hannah hadn't spoken. "I loved your father, Hannah. I never stopped loving him. But he didn't love me enough to live with me. Now he's gone, and I'm finally free to make different choices. I feel lighter than I have in years. Coming out here and making this video is going to turn my life around. You'll feel the same way once you've had a good night's sleep."

Hannah was too tired to argue. Her knotted shoulders felt as if they'd never been stretched, her head weighed a hundred pounds.

When the limo driver discharged them at the hotel entryway, the doorman greeted them personally. "Ms. Montgomery. This must be your lovely daughter Hannah."

Hannah nodded tersely. She wanted to return the man's welcoming smile, but she was all smiled out. If she didn't get to bed soon, she would fall asleep standing up.

Following a brief elevator ride, Hannah was shown into their spacious and airy suite. She barely glimpsed the gleaming ceramic tile floor and fancy furnishings. All of her attention was on her bed. Slipping off her shoes, Hannah sunk down onto the plush mattress. With a big yawn, she pulled the spread over her and called it a night.

Her last thoughts were of the forested property and the maddening man she'd left behind. The corners of her mouth tugged up in a fleeting smile.

****

Jake stared blankly at the pale ceiling in his shadowy bedroom. He'd come in here to rest after Hannah left, and he hadn't stirred as the hours ticked off the day.

The sun had set, and his mood had dimmed with the waning light. He was hollow inside. Empty, like a spent shell casing.

He should move on.

He had a killer to track down, and one last debt to pay his late partner, the debt of justice. D.C. had been a man of sterling character, a man who had made a difference.

Would the same ever be said about Jake?

It hurt knowing that Hannah had rejected him without giving him a chance. Her stellar Montgomery standards wouldn't accommodate the scrappy boy who had clawed his way up from the wrong side of the tracks. She'd known he wasn't good enough.

The house echoed without her. Memories of her just-right curves taunted him, filling him with the impossible need to touch her again.

The right thing to do was to pack up and leave. That was the right thing, but it was the one thing he could not do. Now that he was free to leave, staying here was exactly what he wanted to do. Leaving felt wrong.

Like unfinished business.

As a hunter, he'd often relied on his natural instincts. Through the years, they'd stood him in good stead, and on more than one occasion, they'd saved his life. He wasn't about to start ignoring his instincts now.

Watching Hannah drive out of his life had been tough. She left without looking back, and he couldn't explain the crushing lethargy he felt. He'd been fine before she came, he should be fine now. Only he didn't feel fine. He felt like someone had punched him in the stomach and turned out the lights.

Technically the rental agency could start showing this property today, but despite the realtor's claim, Jake didn't think there would be much demand for this isolated place. He was counting on that lack of demand to ensure his privacy while he summoned his energy.

He hadn't noticed his confinement so much before Hannah came. Now it definitely felt like something was missing in his life. Correction, someone was missing.

Hannah.

He envied her close connection to her mother. He hadn't been so lucky. He hadn't known nurturing or support until he'd landed on the Brewer's doorstep in his teens. His foster parents had given him room to make mistakes, room to grow and try new things.

It was thanks to their constancy that he'd received an education and hadn't ended up in prison which was where he'd been heading. Looking back, he was sorry that he'd given them such a hard time. They were decent people. And in spite of everything, they cared about him.

Maybe he should call them, touch base, and see how they were doing. They thought he was still overseas, working with his partner at their import business. He had never liked lying to them about his job, but that had come with the territory.

He hadn't informed them of his injury or his changed job status because he didn't want to burden them with his problems. But right now, he could use a little caring and compassion.

In a completely spontaneous move, he picked up the phone and dialed their number. "Gloria? It's Jake."

"Jake! It's wonderful to hear your voice," Gloria said, with infectious enthusiasm. "Are you on your way home?"

Guilt gnawed at Jake. Should he tell her he'd been in the U.S. for months? He winced. He hated lying to her. "Sorry. I'm still tied up with work. I had a free moment and thought I'd call."

"Isn't that nice? I've been fine. Stu's had a time of it

recently. The hard part was not knowing what was wrong. We've gotten real familiar with the Emergency Room staff."

Jake gripped the phone tighter as cold seeped into his bones. He didn't have much of a family, but the Brewers were all he had. If something happened to them, he'd have no one.

He should have called sooner. He should have swallowed his pride and returned home right after he was discharged from the CIA. "The hospital? Where is Stuart now? Is he okay?"

"Now, now. I didn't mean to alarm you. It's not like you can do anything from overseas. He didn't want to worry you, so we didn't call that emergency number you gave us. Turned out his problem was a kidney stone. He passed a large one, and then he went through a medical procedure to make sure that didn't happen again."

"So, he's all right?"

"Heck, yeah. He's around here somewhere. Let me get him for you."

Jake heard her put the phone down and call Stuart's name. He imagined her walking through their tiny suburban house, taking pride in its immaculate condition. Some warmth seeped back into his chilled body.

"Jake, that you, boy?"

At the sound of that grizzled old voice, something inside of Jake broke. He had needed a connection with someone, needed to feel that he mattered. He mattered to the Brewers. "It's me, old man. I heard you haven't been feeling well."

"Don't believe everything you hear. You know how Gloria likes to go on about pain and suffering. I'm hale and hearty, and no one is going to tell me otherwise. If I have anything to say about it, I'll still be here sixty years from now."

Jake exhaled slowly. "You take care of yourself and Gloria. I want to see you two when I get done here."

Gloria's voice chimed in again. "I'm on the other line

so don't talk about me any more."

"You need to find another job," Stuart continued as if Gloria hadn't spoken. "One that you're not married to."

"I've been thinking along those lines myself." That much was true. It was past time for a career change. "Thinking I might do some freelance consulting work."

"Freelance? Does that mean you'll still travel as much as you do now?"

Jake was making this up as he went along. He had no idea what his future held. It was a big black box as far as he was concerned. On the other hand, he didn't want to let Stuart and Gloria down. "I'm thinking to get a place, have a home base, that sort of thing."

"That's wonderful. Does this mean that a young woman has finally caught your eye?"

Jake closed his eyes against the gloom of his dark room and a vibrant picture formed in his mind of Hannah. She'd caught his eye all right. Caught his eye and held it like super glue. His gut twisted at the knowledge that she didn't want him. "There's no young woman in the picture."

His words came out more forcefully than he'd planned. To his trained ear he sounded defensive. Would Stuart and Gloria notice?

"Quit riding the boy, Stuart," Gloria said. "He'll know when the right girl comes along. How have you been, Jake? We haven't heard from you in months."

It occurred to Jake that he'd been lying to these nice people for years, ever since he'd become a CIA operative. The necessary lies weighed heavily on his conscience. "I'm fine. I had a problem with my leg a couple of months ago but it's better now."

"Problem? What kind of problem?" Gloria asked.

Now he'd done it. He hadn't meant to get Gloria upset. This was what came from telling half truths. Half-assed explanations.

This was why he hadn't called them before. He sighed deeply and came up with the correct spin for this story. "Don't be alarmed. It wasn't that big of a deal." He'd skirted death, but his partner hadn't.

"Why didn't you call us?" Gloria demanded.

"I didn't want to worry you," Jake said in a calming voice.

"We're your family. We want to be bothered with your news, good or bad. You should have called."

"Now Gloria, don't give the boy a hard time," Stuart said. "He said it wasn't a big deal. No need to send your blood pressure sky rocketing through the roof."

"Definitely not," Jake said. "I also wanted you to know that I'd be done here in a few weeks. If it's convenient, I could swing by Philly and see you guys."

"Do you have a firm date yet for when you're coming home?"

"Not yet. I'll let you know as soon as I can break free."

"We'd love to have a welcome home party for you," Gloria said. "Just give me a few days notice to pull something together."

Stuart cleared his throat. "Jake, you come home real soon. It's awful quiet around here. We miss you."

"I miss you too." It startled him how much he meant those words. He'd never missed being away from home before.

A few minutes later, he was alone in the dark again. But he didn't feel quite so lonely. Someone cared for him. Someone thought he was worth having around.

Too bad it wasn't Hannah.

****

Hannah jumped into her mother's busy schedule. She wanted to please her mother, wanted to approve of the choices her mother had made in this strange land. It wasn't easy.

Doug Nichols was her first challenge. His limo driver drove them to the yoga studio. Doug reminded her of the plastic fashion doll that all the popular girls had played with. Everything about Doug seemed perfect and somehow fake, like an entertainment version of the real thing.

Doug's favorite topic was how wonderful Libby Montgomery was. "You have such a marvelous artistic talent, Lib," he'd said with regard to her drawings. A few minutes later he'd commented on Lib's great sense of style, then on her invigorating vitality. It was enough to make Hannah gag.

And who gave him the right to call her mother Lib?

That sounded entirely too familiar and too personal for a business relationship between a video producer and his client-to-be. She didn't like the way his arm draped possessively over her mother's shoulders, the way he accepted her mother's wacky ideas as if they had been handed down on stone tablets.

Hannah hated him on sight, but she wasn't about to mention that to her mother.

Even with his plastic perfection, Doug Nichols was easily ten years younger than her mother. Women Hannah's age were dating men Doug's age. Hannah silently questioned the wisdom of this May/December relationship.

Worse, the location he'd lined up for the video seemed perfect. It was exactly what Hannah and her mother had envisioned for the yoga studio. Clean austere lines in a serene setting. "This is very nice," Hannah said as she toured the vacant building.

"Isn't this just the best place? I can feel the peacefulness within these walls. I just know buying this place is the right thing to do."

"How much?" Hannah asked.

Her mother named an astronomical price.

The studio was expensive, exorbitantly so. Out of her mother's price range if she seriously wanted to make the video. She'd be bankrupt and deeply leveraged before she even started filming. But Hannah didn't want to burst her mother's bubble.

"Isn't the soft natural light perfect?" Libby asked. "Shouldn't we go right over to the realtor's office and buy this place?"

"Let's think about this for a day or so," Hannah suggested. "No need to jump right into a large purchase like this. Have you priced the other options?"

"She's not usually so grumpy," Libby whispered to Doug.

"I'm not grumpy. I am looking after your bottom line. Don't you want to make your video?" Her teeth clenched as she stared at her mother.

"Of course, dear. That's the whole point of coming out here," Libby said.

If kids were this difficult, Hannah was never having any. "What about the other studios?"

Doug cleared his throat. "I looked at the list Lib brought out with her and those properties are second rate. This is the perfect place for filming the video."

Hannah didn't care for Doug's patronizing attitude. "I'd like to see the other studios. What is it that you love about this place?"

"The lighting is right, the studio is right, the location is right, and Lib loves it," Doug said with a wink at Libby.

"I do like this place," Libby added. "The energy flow is very positive in this room. It's very harmonious."

"So you haven't seen any other studios?"

"This place is perfect. Why cloud our minds with extraneous details?"

Hannah grimaced. Her mother didn't understand that her inheritance was finite. "I'd like to see the other studios and run cost comparisons."

"What if someone buys this studio out from under us?" Libby asked.

"We'll manage." Hannah couldn't believe this was the only suitable studio. And if it was so perfect, why couldn't they lease it from the current owner? Anything would be better than buying a property clear across the country.

Hannah massaged her throbbing temples. She'd be more clear-headed if this darn headache would leave her alone.

Jet lag, most likely. Time would fix that. And yet as the hours of the day ticked past, through her massage, her manicure, and her hair highlights, her head didn't clear. By late afternoon, she knew she needed a break. Shopping for a new wardrobe would have to wait. Her mother fussed over the change in plans, until Doug agreed to take her sightseeing while Hannah rested.

Hannah lay on the hotel bed and listened to the blessed silence. She used a deep breathing technique to get more oxygen in her system. The trouble was, as soon as she freed her mind, thoughts of Jake stole into her head.

She'd only known him for five days, but he'd made a big impression. He was the sexiest man she'd ever met, and he made her think she wasn't the ice queen. She missed him.

She could have bent her rules for him. They were two consenting adults who were attracted to each other. If only his secretive nature hadn't put her off, she wouldn't be in California with the worst headache of her life.

When would she have the opportunity again to date a man like Jake? Never. She'd probably never run across anyone like him again. His type didn't bother with quality assurance.

The Jakes of this world saw what they liked and took it. They didn't worry about precision and accuracy. They went with the flow. They were spontaneous. They were fun.

Now she was in California, and he was in Maryland. Or was he?

He'd said he would be gone when she returned.

How depressing.

Her one chance at a hot liaison, and she'd blown it with her conservative thinking. The whole concept of emotional vulnerability was too risky for comfort.

But, she couldn't stop thinking about that erotic kiss. Sure, she'd started it, but he'd finished it, leaving her breathless for more. No way would she delete that from her memory banks. It would remain the gold standard for kisses.

If only she wasn't such a coward. If only she had forgotten her rules and stepped forward, she'd be in his arms right now. He'd offered to spend two weeks in bed with her.

Hannah had no doubt that two weeks in bed with Jake would exceed anything she'd ever envisioned in her wildest fantasies. She couldn't imagine what sort of woman she'd be after such an experience. Wild. Wanton. Carefree.

The room phone rang. Hannah reached over and picked it up on the second ring. "Hello."

"Hannah, it's Jake."

The rough growl of Jake's voice had Hannah's complete attention. Hannah snugged the phone up next to her head on the downy soft pillow. She imagined him wearing those low cut jeans and nothing else. She sighed dreamily. "Jake. How did you find me?"

"I believe I mentioned a friend that could find anyone. Your cell phone is turned off."

He sounded good. Strong even. Almost like he was in the next room. "So it is."

He'd probably called because he missed her so much. Cool, because she missed him more. "What's up?"

"I have something for you."

Hannah's mind skittered happily ahead to several distinct gifts that men traditionally gave women they were pursuing. What would he have chosen for her? Candy? Perfume? Jewelry? Her expectations soared skyward. "What? What is it?"

"I promised you information on Doug Nichols. The preliminary results indicate he doesn't have any skeletons in his closet. He is exactly who he claims to be."

"Oh. Too bad." Hannah sighed, doubly disappointed. Doug was a legitimate businessman. Jake hadn't missed her at all. Two bits of depressing news.

Still, it was great to hear his voice. She tightened her

grip on the phone.

"You don't like him?" Jake asked.

"He dishes out buttery compliments to my mother every time he opens his mouth. It's annoying." Hannah's comment sounded sour to her ears. "Let me clarify that. Doug seems too good to be true, and I've found that anything too good to be true usually is."

"You are naturally cautious."

"I wish you'd found some dirt on the man. That would make my life easier."

Jake was silent a moment. "The background search isn't complete. There's still a chance he's a bad guy. I'll let you know when the search is complete."

"Thanks."

"Everything okay out there?" Jake asked after another long pause.

"Sure, why wouldn't it be?"

"You sound different, that's all."

She missed him so much it hurt, and it was only Monday afternoon. Hearing his voice was wonderful, but it wasn't enough. She couldn't touch him from California, couldn't see the way his powerful muscles flexed, couldn't sniff out the yummy Jake-laden air that made her mouth water. Her hand fisted in her bed covers. "The flight took a lot out of me."

"Flying zaps me too."

"That must have put a crimp in your import business."

"No kidding."

Was he teasing her? She couldn't tell. "How's your leg?"

"It's fine."

"Fine-fine or fine it hurts?"

"You have a suspicious mind."

"It goes with my detail-oriented personality."

"My leg's okay."

What she wanted to talk about was how much she missed him. How good it was to hear his voice. "Well, it's been good talking to you," she said when it seemed that too much time had elapsed since he last spoke.

He was silent.

"Jake?"

"Hmm?"

"I'm glad you called." Oh God. Did she really say that? What happened to being calm and cool and in control?

"Me too. You take care now, okay?"

"Sure. You too."

There was no click on the line. "You didn't hang up."

"That's true."

Was he flirting with her? Why wasn't there a manual for phone calls? Hannah fiddled with her hair. "Hanging up isn't a competitive sport."

"So you hang up first."

"I will. Bye."

Hannah was still smiling as she hung up the phone. Her headache was gone, but now she had a new problem. Jake would be calling again. Her blood already raced in anticipation. Not a good sign.

Chapter 11

After dinner that evening, her mother insisted Hannah accompany them to a nightclub. "It'll be good for you to get out and meet people your age," Libby had said.

Clubbing wasn't Hannah's idea of fun, but she wanted to make her mother happy. The music was loud, the drinks were watery, and the place was swimming with people. She wasn't overweight by any means, but the aesthetically thin people with blonde highlights made her feel as broad as a barge.

Hannah felt like the lone Bohemian waxwing in a flock of cedar waxwings. A little lost, a little befuddled, but grateful for the relative safety of the flock.

She met Tad, Jerry, Clint, and Kyle and was soundly disappointed in all four. Their attention seemed fragmented, as if she were a stand-in until someone better came along. Their conversations seemed contrived and boring. Their eyes didn't eat her up.

She had never purposefully endured such misery, and she couldn't wait for the ordeal to end. It wasn't until she listed the collective faults of the men that she understood what she had done. One man was too tall, another too short, another too blonde, another one too happy.

None of these men were Jake. None measured up to his rakishly dangerous good looks. None tried to order her around. None looked at her like she made the sun come up every morning.

"You're not having any fun," Libby said when she briefly sat out a dance.

Hannah traced her finger around the rim of her half

empty cocktail. "I'm feeling out of place. I'd be more at ease if there were birds here to watch."

"You and your moldy old birds. Forget about your birds for the evening. Relax and enjoy yourself. Isn't this place great?"

Doug twirled her mother away, and Hannah was left to contemplate the flashing lights and overly warm, crowded room by herself. Relaxation wasn't the issue. This was about as relaxed as she ever got. Her real problem could be summed up in two words.

Jake Sutherland.

She had run from the passion he'd offered, but she couldn't deny her deep seated longings for him. It wasn't like her to be so cowardly. Usually if she wanted something, she figured out how to achieve her goal and implemented her plan.

Trouble was she didn't know how to have Jake and protect herself at the same time. She didn't indulge in casual affairs.

Not that sleeping with Jake would be casual. It would be as elemental as fire and water, as precarious as shifting sand. She liked having her feet planted solidly on the ground. All of her logic and commonsense told her to avoid the certain danger of Jake.

But, playing it safe was making her miserable. Was she a perennial wallflower in the dance of life?

Ever since she'd met Jake, her thoughts hadn't been her own. It astounded her that she could be fascinated by a man so full of secrets. If she gave into this fierce longing she had to be with him, was she destined to follow in her mother's lonely footsteps?

At the end of the dance set, Hannah stood and signaled her mother over. "I'm going back to the hotel, Mom."

"Aren't you having a good time?"

"I'm beat. It's been a long day."

"Wait a minute. I'll go with you."

"I don't want to ruin your evening."

"You're not ruining anything. Doug can do without me for one night. Let me tell him what our plans are."

After a moment's private conversation, Doug walked Libby and Hannah out to the curb and hailed them a cab. Hannah looked away as Doug took Libby in his arms and murmured, "Later, doll."

Hannah slid across the back seat of the cab and heaved a sigh of relief. In the crowd of glittering high heels, she'd been a well-worn slipper. Serviceable. Dull. And entirely too aware of how out of place she was.

Seeing people paired off in couples hadn't helped her sense of isolation either. Instead, she'd been reminded of her oddness. She had no one to pair off with, and at the rate she was going, there wouldn't be anyone in her near future either. Her shoulders sagged.

Even her mother had someone, although Hannah wished Doug wasn't in the picture. It was difficult enough to keep her mother focused on business matters without any distractions. Doug's involvement was a huge negative in Hannah's mind.

"I'm worried about you, dear," Libby said, once they were underway. "I've never seen you so unhappy. What, or should I say, who is the problem?"

Hannah studied the three lanes of cars stopped next to them for a traffic light. In the past, she'd shared her troubles with her mother. This problem was different, so much more personal.

But, she didn't have a close girlfriend to confide in, and it wasn't like she could figure out what to do on her own anyhow. Hannah chewed on her lip. It was possible that an objective opinion would be very beneficial.

What did she have to lose? Her mother had already been through this at least once. She drew in a breath. "There's this man—"

Libby clapped her hands in delight. "I can't tell you how long I've waited to hear those words. Tell me everything about this man in your life."

The cab accelerated around a corner, and Hannah

braced against the arm rest. "I feel conflicted about entering into a relationship with him. It seems to me that if it isn't a good idea then I should be able to talk myself out of it. That's not happening, even though I have serious reservations."

"Go on," Libby said, touching Hannah's arm. "I want to hear the juicy details."

Hannah's stomach lurched. It was harder to talk about her need for Jake than she'd thought it would be. "There aren't any juicy details. Fear kept me from getting involved with him."

Her mother studied her for a long moment. "Does he pass the last thing, first thing test?"

"What's that?"

"Do you think of him at night before you drop off to sleep?"

Hannah nodded in affirmation.

"Is he the first thing on your mind when you wake up?"

"Sure, but physical attraction doesn't mean it's a good idea to sleep with him. The factors that make this particular relationship a bad idea haven't changed."

"My dear analytical and very practical Hannah. When it comes to love, no one has all the answers. You just have to trust that everything will turn out all right."

"Love? Who said anything about love?"

"I did. I am intimately acquainted with this subject. As soon as I met your father, I couldn't think clearly."

"Muddled thinking means love?" Hannah groaned. "I'm doomed. This person has a lot of Dad's bad habits."

"Don't let fear hold you back. Love doesn't come along too often."

"Are you in love with Doug?"

"Doug is entertaining and fun. What we have is companionship and shared interests. That's not love. Or at least it's not the immediate and desperate love I had for your father. Doug is easy-going; D.C. was always difficult."

"The thing is, after growing up with a distant father like Dad, I want someone who will be there with me through thick and thin. I don't want to make a big mistake."

"There are no guarantees in life, dear. You could find the absolutely perfect person tonight, and he could be killed in a freak accident tomorrow. Love is what's important."

Hannah shoved her fingers through her bangs, pushing her hair back towards the crown of her head. "Love. Is that what this nauseatingly vulnerable roller coaster feeling is?"

"That bad, huh?"

Hannah nodded. She blinked back the tears that filled her eyes. She was not going to cry. "What am I going to do?"

Libby pulled Hannah into her arms and stroked her back. "There's only one thing to do. Go back and see if you can make it work."

Hannah's blood quickened at the thought of seeing Jake again. She couldn't begin to imagine the rest of it. But how she wanted to.

"Are you going to keep me in suspense forever?" Libby asked. "Who are you in love with?"

Libby's ethereal perfume surrounded Hannah, and it felt safe to tell her the rest of it now. "His name is Jake Sutherland. He's the man living in Dad's house."

Libby stiffened and leaned back. "Your father's friend?"

"His former business partner," Hannah corrected.

"Hmm. He has to be trustworthy or D.C. wouldn't have had anything to do with him. You say he's like D.C.?"

"He thinks the world of Dad, acts like him too."

"I can see where that would be confusing."

Hannah warmed to her topic. "Jake tries to boss me around. And he's stubborn as a mule. I wouldn't be doing myself any favors if I got involved with him."

"He's hot, right?"

"Hotter than a July firecracker." Thinking about how Jake filled out a pair of jeans and a T-shirt shirt brought a fond smile to Hannah's face. "He asked me to spend the rest of my vacation in his bed. I'm certain he was serious."

Libby chuckled knowingly. "I'm sure he was. Don't be afraid of your passionate nature, sweetheart. You'll do just fine."

"Mom, that's not the point. I barely know Jake. It was outrageous for him to say he wanted to spend two weeks in bed with me. I shouldn't reward him for being so forward."

"I have a feeling you are more like me than you want to admit. The chemistry between your father and me was immediate. It was never convenient, but it was always there. This Jake may not be everything you desire in a man, but he must come pretty darn close. I say, go back there. Get naked. Have fun."

To circumvent a well-worn lecture on the therapeutic value of sex, Hannah hastily interjected, "But Mom, what about his secrets? I can't stand that he's lying to me."

The cab halted in the hotel's driveway. The color drained from Libby's face. "Lying isn't good. I changed my mind. Don't go back to him. Treat him like he's got the plague."

Her mother's sudden change of opinion shocked Hannah, depressing her further. Jake, what have you done to me, she silently cried.

****

Tuesday evening, Hannah sent her mother off to dinner with Doug and indulged in room service. After spending the day touring yoga studios and joining in two yoga classes, Hannah needed some time to herself. She didn't want to smile and discuss her mother's yoga video plans with another soul. She didn't want to hear Doug compliment her mother one more time. She didn't want to be nice to anyone else. She turned off her cell phone.

She polished off the last of her fruit salad and leaned

back in her chair. By all accounts she should be exhausted. She'd been exhausted when she said goodbye to her mother and Doug.

But eating dinner alone had recharged her flagging energy levels. Not that she felt like running a marathon, but she didn't feel like taking a nap either. She felt oddly restless.

It was clear that her mother wanted the first studio or nothing. The studios they had visited today seemed adequate to Hannah, but they hadn't suited her mother. Libby had found serious fault with them.

In two days, Hannah had gone from being very positive about this video project to thinking it would never come together. Her mother's ideas didn't mesh with the reality of her financial constraints. The cold hard reality was that they couldn't afford to make any mistakes in the production of the video, not with such a limited supply of cash.

Hannah didn't want to disappoint her mother, but she didn't know how to make this right. The only words that wanted to come out of her mouth were no, no, and no. How could she turn this around so that she could say yes?

She had no idea.

Living in a hotel, no matter how luxurious, wasn't Hannah's style. She missed open air, natural habitats, and walks in the woods. She'd never be a city girl. California didn't do a whole lot for her either.

She'd never been homesick before, but mid-Maryland pulled at her mind, calling her back to its gently rolling hills. She wanted to go home.

Home. In the past, home had been exactly two places. Her mother's house and her townhouse. But now, when Hannah thought of home, her thoughts didn't turn to where she lived. Instead, she dreamed of a cozy fairy tale cottage in the woods and Jake.

The trouble with being still and resting was that her thoughts ricocheted back to him every time she had a free moment. She needed to do something to take her mind off of Jake. Stretching, she stood and walked the dinner cart to the hall corridor.

A bath would be nice. Soaking in hot water with a good book sounded delightful. She would definitely feel better after a long soak.

The room phone rang as she was running her bath. She turned off the water. It could be Jake. Her blood raced as she made her way to the phone. "Hello?"

"Hello right back."

It was Jake. Hannah's heart pounded as she perched on the edge of her bed. "Is everything all right?"

"Why do you ask?"

"This is going to sound silly, but I can't seem to settle down. I feel out of sorts and it's getting to be too long since my flight to call this disorienting feeling jet lag."

"Understandable, given the pressure you're under. How's the yoga video coming along?"

Hannah sighed and dropped her tensed shoulders. "Nothing is decided. Mom won't settle for anything less than the most expensive studio. She won't compromise. It's maddening."

"Why don't you take a break and go watch some birds?"

"I might just do that."

Jake exhaled slowly. "I called because I found something on Nichols. It may not be relevant, but I promised I'd let you know if I discovered anything. He doesn't have a driver's license."

Hannah's interest perked up. "That's odd. Who doesn't have a driver's license in this day and age?"

"My thoughts exactly, so I asked for information on him for the last twenty years."

"And?"

"Impatient, are you?"

"Don't toy with me. If something is wrong with Doug Nichols, I need to protect my mother. As it is, I'm not certain Mom has enough money to do this project the way she wants. I don't need her hooking up with a bloodsucking loser."

"I don't say he was a loser. There was an auto accident almost twenty years ago. Nichols' brother Vern died in the accident. Vern was driving. In the obituary, donations are directed to the American Epilepsy Foundation."

"What does this have to do with Doug?"

"I can't confirm this, but, given the family history, it seems likely that Doug may have epilepsy."

"And that keeps him from getting a driver's license?"

"Not officially. It may be his choice not to drive."

"I've never seen him having a seizure."

"With the medicines available these days, you wouldn't. That's why I said this information may not be relevant."

Hannah's shoulders sagged. "That's it? That's all the dirt you could dig up on this guy?"

"I could keep looking if you like. I didn't have his entire life investigated. Maybe Nichols had to repeat second grade."

Hannah winced. "No. That's not necessary. I was hoping for something like embezzlement, or old gambling debts, or poor financial stewardship. Something that might convince my mother to step back from this association."

"Is it the professional or the personal side of their relationship that's bugging you?"

Hannah didn't like the way his question sliced into her. She was big enough to accept that her mother was dating, wasn't she? "I just don't like him."

"This is the first man your mother's dated since your parents divorced, right?"

"So?"

"So, it may take some getting used to the idea. You haven't had to share your mother in a long time. Does it bother you that she's seeing so much of Nichols?"

Hannah flopped back on the bed. "Of course it bothers me. I hardly know anything about him."

"Do you want a copy of his background faxed to the hotel so that you can review it at your leisure?"

Alarm shot through Hannah. Her mother would have a cow if she knew Hannah had a dossier on her lover. "No. Don't fax anything. Everyone knows Doug here at the hotel."

"All right. If you change your mind, let me know."

"Thanks for looking into this for me."

"No problem."

"I guess this is goodbye," Hannah said, curling on her side.

"If you want it to be goodbye."

Hannah sighed. Night had fallen while she talked to Jake. She didn't want to say goodbye, but she didn't want to give him false hope either. "It's for the best."

"If you say so."

"We've been through this. Nothing has changed."

Jake remained silent. She couldn't even hear him breathing. Was he still on the line?

She didn't want to do this, but she could hardly claim she was having second thoughts. When he didn't say anything else, she could only assume he agreed with her. "Bye, Jake, and thanks again for your help."

Before she lost her nerve, she hung up. She wasn't going to get trapped into listening for him to hang up. He'd probably sit there with the phone to his ear like he did last night.

A great weariness descended on her. Taking a long bath was out of the question. She was too tired to even take her clothes off. Her eyes filled with tears, but she was too exhausted to will them away. Clutching a pillow to the hollow place in her middle, she cried herself to sleep.

****

Doug had a pressing business appointment the next day at lunchtime, so Hannah unexpectedly had her mother to herself. She'd been mulling over Jake's finding all morning and she had decided to tell her mother what she'd learned. Her mother would be upset, but she would thank Hannah later. Besides, if it had been the other way around and her mother knew something potentially damaging about Jake, she'd want to know.

This bustling café was about as private a spot as they were likely to have today. Hannah sipped at her flavored water and then leaned forward. "Mom, there's something I need to talk to you about."

Libby glanced over the top of her menu. "What's that dear?"

"I found out something about Doug. Have you noticed that he doesn't drive?"

"How could I miss that? He has a fulltime driver."

"Do you know why?"

"I assumed it was because he could afford it. What's this about Hannah?"

"I'm worried about how much time you're spending with Doug. I had him checked out, and—"

"You what?" Libby interrupted, snapping her menu shut.

Hannah leaned closer to her mother. "I had him investigated. We are talking about turning over most of your inheritance to him. I wanted to make sure he was who he said he was. It was a precaution."

"Good grief. Doug Nichols is a fine man with a vibrant aura. I can't believe you'd go digging around in his life. This is an outrage."

Hannah shifted uneasily in her seat. "Lower your voice, Mom. You're attracting attention."

"Do you think I care? You've been spying on Doug, for heaven's sake. You invaded his privacy."

Hannah grimaced. How could she have forgotten her mother's dramatic streak? Breaking this news in a public place was not one of her brighter ideas. "I had good intentions. I did it to protect you."

"Do you think my money is that important to me? If it were to go away tomorrow, I wouldn't care. The yoga video will be fun to make, but if I don't get to make it, the world won't end. Can't you see that I'm finally free?"

"Free? From what?"

"From everything." Libby's eyes glittered. "Doug makes me happy. Why can't you accept that?"

Hannah waved the waitress away. They weren't ready to order. "You're my mother. Of course I want you to be happy." Something Jake said vaulted to the front of her thoughts. "But I haven't had to share you in a very long time. Your personal relationship with Doug is an adjustment for me, too."

Libby drew in a series of double breaths and held them. Hannah knew from countless yoga classes that her mother was trying to increase the oxygen level in her bloodstream. She could use some clear thinking right about now too.

"I hadn't considered my situation from your point of view," Libby said as she exhaled slowly.

Hannah covered her mother's hand with her own. "I want you to be happy. I'm not selfish enough to think that I have you to myself for the rest of my life."

"Just as I expect you to find someone you want to share your life with."

"But, if I really liked someone, seemed absolutely absorbed by someone, and it had happened all of a sudden, wouldn't you be concerned? Wouldn't you want to check him out?"

"I see your point. I want to meet your young man. I don't think I need to have him investigated though. I rely on my own judgment. His aura will tell me more than any background report."

"Let's keep Jake's aura out of the conversation for now. You'll be happy to know that Doug is exactly what he says he is, a successful movie producer. There are no skeletons or disasters in his recent financial records."

"But?"

"But there was a car accident a long time ago. Doug's brother Vern was driving. It is believed that the accident was a result of an epileptic seizure."

"Poor Doug. He must have been terribly crushed when his only brother died."

Her mother wasn't connecting the right dots. Hannah decided to help her along. "There's a fairly good chance Doug has epilepsy, Mom. Has he ever said anything about it to you?"

"He doesn't talk about his personal life. I thought that was a bonus. Nothing more dreadful than a man who won't shut up about the past. His forward looking attitude suits me fine."

"I don't know if the information means anything, but I felt I should tell you."

Libby's gaze sharpened. "Who else knows? Who did this investigating?"

"My friend Jake. He said he knew someone who did this sort of thing. I'm sure they were extremely discreet in their inquiries. It won't be in tomorrow's paper, if that's what you're worried about."

Libby's complexion paled. "I should hope not."

"You know how I hate secrets. I couldn't stand knowing something about him that I thought you needed to know."

"Don't you like Doug?"

Hannah weighed her words with care. "It doesn't matter if I like him or not. You like him, and he seems crazy about you. What's important is that he treats you right."

Libby sniffed into a napkin. "I'd like that to be between Doug and myself. I don't want folks poking around in my life. How would you feel if the tables were turned?"

"I'd think you were looking out for me."

"That's where our opinions differ."

"So how do we make this work?"

"Easy. You worry about your love life. I'll worry about mine."

"Deal."

Hannah opened her menu. There was only one item

she wanted to try. But Jake on the half shell wasn't on the appetizer list. Pity.

Chapter 12

"Hello, this is Bertha Shifflet from the rental agency. This is a courtesy call to let you know that I'll be bringing a prospective client by the property in an hour."

Jake stared at the answering machine in surprise. Well, damn. A possible renter.

Go figure.

He had no intention of being here while someone toured Hannah's cottage. Jake hurriedly shoved his dirty clothes and laptop computer in his duffel bag. Then he collected the trash and the perishable food items from the refrigerator and tossed them in his truck along with his belongings. His frozen dinners he iced down in a small cooler he kept in the bed of his truck.

On the kitchen counter, three over-ripe bananas hung on a tubular stand. Hannah hadn't finished them off before she left. He couldn't bring himself to throw them out. Hannah loved bananas, and in his mind as long as he kept them, there was an outside chance she'd come back. He carefully carried the stand out to the cab of his truck and deposited it in the passenger seat. He made one last walk through of the cottage, checking to make sure he hadn't overlooked any personal items.

In Hannah's bedside drawer he found the fairy tale book. That stopped him cold. Why hadn't she taken the book with her? Seeing the small book in the drawer made him think she didn't want any part of her father's inheritance.

Not the house.

Not her father.

Not her father's former business partner. His cheeks

stung with failure.

But, he'd fulfilled his promise to D.C. He'd watched over the house until Hannah arrived to claim it. He'd helped her donate D.C.'s clothes to a charity. He'd accompanied her to the rental agency.

His job here was done. It occurred to him as he drove down the mountain that there was no need to return to the cottage because his belongings were already in the truck. Only, he didn't have a fix on Ursula, and he didn't see any point in running blind. Best to stay holed up until she took his bait.

Jake parked at a diner across the street from the rental agency. With a heavy heart, he watched Bertha Shifflet drive off with a big-haired blonde wearing unfashionably large dark sunglasses. D.C. wouldn't like how this was turning out, but Jake had done his best.

Inside the diner he ordered a burger and fries. He picked at his lunch until the rental agent and client returned thirty minutes later. Out of habit, he observed Bertha and her client parting ways. Nothing seemed out of the ordinary. Just a routine meeting between a rental agent and her client. Nothing to worry about.

So, why was he suddenly so antsy?

Why did he want to rush back to the cottage and sweep it for listening devices?

Jake drove back to the cottage and methodically unloaded his truck. His nose wrinkled at the lingering smell of Bertha's cheap perfume in the kitchen. He didn't like outsiders in his personal space, but there was little he could do about that. Hannah was determined to make this place pay for itself, and she needed a renter for that.

He stowed his gear in his bedroom, connected his laptop, and checked to see where the women had been. The piece of string he'd placed on the top of the refrigerator door was askew, so they'd looked inside. The bedside drawer in the master bedroom had been opened. He knew because the drawer was no longer pulled out exactly one matchstick width.

Bertha and her client had opened doors and drawers. Big deal. A renter should look at those things. He shouldn't be paranoid about their activities. This wasn't his place. It was Hannah's, and this was what she wanted.

He wished Hannah were here right now. Wished she were in his arms. Wished that she hadn't seen right through him.

Though he'd waited here alone for three months, his memories of this place would forever be tied to Hannah. He would never forget the sensual kiss she'd given him. That kiss had implied promises of delights to come, promises that had been withdrawn when clear thinking returned.

He ought to be used to broken promises by now.

****

Jake stood on the back porch and stared at the frenetic chipmunk chowing down on sunflower seeds at dusk. Hannah had said she didn't begrudge the chipmunks their share of the food, but she hadn't told him how much he should allow them to eat. If this guy didn't slow down soon, Jake was going to have to sign him up for Weight Watchers.

In the four days since Hannah's departure, he'd devoted himself to finding Ursula. His diligence had finally paid off. This afternoon his computer search had unearthed a credit card issued to Joan Gruber of Germany, Joan Gruber being a collation of the names Joan Andress and Ursula Gruber. In the last few days, she'd spent a day each in Philadelphia, Chicago, and Atlanta.

Her choice of destinations hit close to home. His homes. He'd lived in those cities at one time or another. Last night she'd flown into the Baltimore Washington International Airport. At BWI, she'd rented a compact car and disappeared.

D.C.'s killer wasn't even trying to cover her tracks.

She was close.

Too close for his comfort.

He'd planned to be the hunter, not the hunted. What would flush her out of hiding? It had to be something urgent.

Did she have terrorist contacts in this area?

Yesterday he'd been working on another train of thought. What if Ursula's stumbling onto their Middle East mission hadn't been accidental? What if it had been planned? Jake had gone through her background files and known associates and he'd pieced together a chilling picture.

Her chance meeting and friendship with Jake might have been part of a long range strategy. Their sexual relationship might have been a coldly calculated matter, not a random union of two physically attracted individuals.

She'd probably faked her orgasms.

Birds chided the foraging chipmunk with loud repeated calls. If Hannah was here she would tell him what kinds of birds were making the ruckus. She'd know when the chipmunk had had enough too. From the birds' point of view, the chipmunk was a loose end.

Loose ends were always trouble.

A chilling thought slid down his spine as the shadows of day lengthened around him. Ursula's sleeper cell had apparently been activated by D.C.'s push to clean up loose ends before his retirement. What intel did the agency have on the sleeper cell? Jake needed to know.

Had something changed in the international picture during the last three months? What if someone on Ursula's side had also been wounded during the shootout and later had died? D.C. had fired off several rounds of ammunition as he'd run to pull Jake to safety.

It was a possibility Jake couldn't ignore.

He called the Giraffe. "Grafton? Got a minute?"

"Always have a minute for a former colleague," Graham Grafton said in a booming, cheerful voice. "How's the leg, Sutherland?"

Jake didn't bother to suppress his annoyance. "My leg's fine. What's the status on the case?"

Grafton sighed heavily. "I'm afraid our leads have gone cold."

Jake didn't like that answer. When leads went cold, agents were redirected. "How many agents are working on finding D.C.'s killer?"

"Hey, don't shoot the messenger. We had half a dozen agents for the first two weeks. Folks got pulled off one by one to work more urgent cases. You know the drill."

He knew it all right. He'd lived it for eight years. "So, you're it?"

"I'm it for now, and I've got three other active cases at the moment. Since we're still short a team, everyone has more work to do."

If D.C. had been alive, he would have closed those open cases by now. D.C. had been that good. The fact that the current investigation had gone three months and stalled was not a good sign. "Did you find out anything more about Ruger and LaFleur? What about the woman?"

"I told you all I knew on Ruger and LaFleur. The woman hasn't resurfaced."

Jake knew that wasn't true. "What about a second shooter?"

"Our investigation supported a second shooter, but the trajectory of the bullet that killed D.C. came from the area where the person of interest was."

Jake had had enough of agency double speak. "Christ, Grafton. It's been three months and that's all you've got? Who was she working for? Why did she shoot D.C.?"

"I don't have anything else for you. Like I said, the leads went cold."

D.C. was probably rolling in his grave. Even sitting in a remote mountaintop cottage Jake had more active leads than Grafton. "The other shooter. What do we know about him?"

"Both shooters are still at large. We have no ID on

the second shooter."

"Any chance the second shooter got injured or died?"

"We monitored area hospitals for over two weeks. There were no unaccounted for gunshot wounds."

Jake swore under his breath. "Then you'd better locate the first shooter. I won't rest until D.C.'s killer pays for her crime."

"I'll catch her," Grafton said. "She can't hide forever."

"Bring D.C.'s killer to justice. That's what I want."

"You've got a one track mind. Why don't you come down to the office, Sutherland? We could grab a beer, shoot the breeze, and talk about the good old days."

"This is not a social call," Jake said. "How hard can it be to find one woman?"

Jake pocketed his phone with disgust. Grafton would never find Ursula at this rate. Good thing Jake had been conducting his own independent investigation.

Why was Ursula looking for him? Was he a loose end she needed to tie up? That didn't make a whole lot of sense. She'd had plenty of chances to kill him during their affair. Not to mention, he'd been an easy mark during D.C.'s last moments on earth. If she was so coldly calculating, she wouldn't have shown mercy when he was vulnerable.

Had something changed in the big picture? D.C. wouldn't have had any trouble figuring this out. He would have put the scene together, worked backwards, and tracked down the responsible individuals long before now. Only D.C. couldn't work this case. He was dead.

"Go on. Git." Jake shook his cane at the endlessly foraging chipmunk, but the fat pest didn't pay him any attention. Hell, he was so good at this spook stuff that he was invisible to wildlife.

The only person he'd wanted to really see him was Hannah, and that had blown up in his face. He'd been as honest as possible with her, and she'd still walked away from him. It didn't matter that he knew it was a bad idea to get involved with her. It didn't matter that sleeping with Hannah would complicate his revenge plans enormously.

He wanted her, and his need for her was getting worse by the minute. The hollowness in his gut was large enough for a flash flood to roar through.

Get a grip, man. She's living it up out there in sunny California. She's probably in with the juice bar crowd. Some producer will cast her in commercials for natural products and she'll be on magazine covers.

He'd be a distant memory, if that. Darkness swirled around him. He should go in, get some supper, but he wasn't hungry. When she'd headed out, she'd taken part of him with her.

How could he go on the offensive against Ursula, put his life on the line, when he didn't feel whole? Not even the gunshot wound to the thigh had slowed him down this much. With his leg, he'd known that it was only a matter of time before he healed. Now it seemed he would be lethargic forever.

Jake shook the cobwebs from his head.

He'd done his job. He'd stayed here and helped Hannah get the house squared away. The major loose end concerning the cottage was those two missing letters. It bothered him that he couldn't find them, but maybe his partner hadn't written any more letters before his untimely death.

Who knew?

He'd been partners with D.C. for a long time, but he had never completely understood how the man's mind worked. D.C. had seen patterns where everyone else saw chaos, and he had been infallible. Too bad he hadn't passed on his superior discernment skills on to his junior partner.

Had D.C. stayed away from his beloved family to keep them safe?

If so, that was being extremely paranoid, and it definitely wasn't how Jake wanted to live his life. If he ever settled down, and that was a very huge if, he'd want a woman who made a house into a home, a woman who filled his soul with joy and laughter.

A woman like Hannah.

He growled out loud, and the chipmunk finally got the message. It scampered off into the shadowy forest.

Jake went inside, bypassing the frozen dinners in the freezer and heading to his laptop in his bedroom. He sat down gingerly, easing weight off his injured leg and went to work.

When the pressure plate alarm went off, Jake visibly started at the shrill double rings. The glow from the computer screen didn't fill the dark room. He'd been sitting at the computer for hours, looking for backdoors and links where there were none.

Hearing the alarm sent a sharp spike of adrenaline in his bloodstream. What time was it anyway? Late. After eleven p.m.

He had a visitor?

He wasn't expecting anyone.

Anxiety arrowed through him. It was too soon to confront Ursula. He wasn't ready. Not that he had any choice. If his visitor was Ursula, he was about to come face to face with a cold blooded killer. Swift action was needed.

Shutting down his computer, he rummaged through his duffel bag for his gun and limped quickly to the front window, shutting off household lights as he went. In minutes, a pair of headlights appeared. High beams.

Jake swallowed hard. No one would be coming up here accidentally this time of night. This was no meter reader, no lost newspaper delivery person. Chances were that this was trouble with a capital T.

This sudden intrusion had his blood pounding in his ears and his leg tightening up. His reflexes weren't lightning fast. Fear gripped him as it never had before.

If his skin had been flayed open, he couldn't have felt any more vulnerable. He hadn't slept in days. He hadn't eaten either. Why had he let the external perimeter defenses of the cottage lull him into a sense of false security? If it was Ursula coming up the drive, chances were that Hannah's fairy tale cottage would soon be riddled with stray bullets. He didn't want that to happen, but he wasn't going to voluntarily take a bullet either.

The car stopped at the end of the drive, but the motor continued to idle, as if the person inside were confused or lost. Jake cursed his injured leg. If he were fully mobile, he would slip out the back and circle around behind the vehicle.

As it was, he was pinned as surely as a bug in a science fair display. Granted he was armed and he had the home field advantage, but given his physical limitations, he doubted that would be enough to overcome a skilled adversary.

He crouched between the front window and the door. The car lights and the engine remained on. Very open and above board. Not the work of a trained professional.

A covert agent would have parked their vehicle away from the location and proceeded on foot. They would not have announced their presence so blatantly.

He let out a long breath. If this wasn't his execution squad, who was it? Exactly three people knew he was staying here. D.C.'s lawyer. Bertha Shifflet, the rental agent. And Hannah. Hannah was in California and the others were unlikely to intrude without calling first.

Who was out there? Who would drive up an unfamiliar gravel lane so late at night?

Local kids looking for a place to neck? With the lights out, the house appeared vacant, and his truck was parked around back. A chance visitor wouldn't know the house was occupied.

This was Hannah's house. Whoever was sitting out there in the car had no business being here. Pressing his back into the wall, he extended his heightened senses to the perimeter of the yard.

The coldness of the gun seeped into his hand. With his ears tuned to the night, he listened intently. There was something familiar about the sound of the car engine. A Volvo, for sure. Hope flared brilliantly from the smallest glimmer to a blazing bonfire.

Was it possible?

Was Hannah out there?

The slightest twitch rippled through Jake's impassive cheek. If Hannah was outside, what the heck was he doing in here? Jake shoved the gun in the back of his jeans and strode purposefully out the front door and toward the car.

Under the thin sliver of a crescent moon, he dared to believe that Hannah was here. The color of the vehicle glowed ghostly white, bringing a smile to his lips. Hannah's Volvo.

But his heart sunk at the sight of her hunched over the steering wheel. Was she ill? He rapped his bare knuckles on the smooth glass of her window, leaning in close to better see her.

At the sudden noise, Hannah jerked upright with a scream.

Her shrill cry of terror had adrenaline sluicing through his veins. Instinctively, he used his body to shield her, whipping his gun from his waistband. Time suspended as he scanned the wooded area for deadly threats.

Though his eyes darted from shadow to shadow, there was no perceivable external threat. The shadows in the yard were just that, shadows.

No armed assassins.

No marauding bears.

His nerves pinged. He called upon his CIA training to slow his rapid breathing. Why didn't she hop out of that car and into his arms where she belonged?

As if she could read his thoughts, Hannah shut the car off and opened her door. "You scared the hell out of me, Jake Sutherland. Why are the lights off in the house?"

Jake wanted to fuss at her for scaring the daylights

out of him with her scream. He wanted to sweep her in his arms and twirl her in dizzy circles. Instead, he drank in the sight of her like a thirsty traveler who had stumbled into an oasis.

The dome light of the car illuminated her pale face and the dark circles under her eyes. California must not have agreed with her.

"That's a gun in your hand!" Hannah exclaimed. "Are you going to shoot me?"

Jake clicked on the safety and stuffed the gun in his waistband. "I live alone in the woods. A man's got a right to defend what's his."

Those words filled him with renewed purpose. In that moment, he realized he would defend Hannah's house and her life without question. Hannah was his, she just didn't know it yet. A smile welled up from deep within.

"I can't believe you even own a gun," she said.

"The world's a dangerous place." Her delicate wildflower scent blanketed him, drugging his senses, weakening his resolve to leave her untouched. But why should he take the high road? She'd come back looking tired and unhappy. Whether she admitted it or not, she needed him.

And he damned well needed her.

What would she do if he leaned in and kissed her? He studied her face in a slow appreciative sweep. He settled for placing his hands on either side of the car roof behind her. "You're back."

"I am." Hannah's hand fluttered over her heart. "But you just took ten years off of my life. What are you doing skulking around in the dark? And why aren't any lights on in the house?"

"When I realized a car was approaching, I turned them off."

She gazed towards the forested lane. "How did you know a car was coming?"

Jake couldn't resist the pull of her. He edged closer, reveling in the sensual heat toasting the air between them. "A buried pressure sensor triggers an alarm in the house when someone comes up the drive."

Hannah frowned. "An alarm. Why didn't you tell me about it before?"

He leaned in just enough to nuzzle her neck. She shivered in response, and his senses shifted into overdrive. His fingers tingled with the anticipation of gliding over her silky skin. "You didn't ask."

"I don't recall seeing an alarm system." Her words were husky with awareness.

Encouraged, he traced the creamy skin of her jaw line. "Remind me to show it to you sometime."

Her rosy lips drew him, but he resisted their siren-like call. It was imperative that they reach an understanding before they went any further down this road. "I missed you."

Her eyes glowed with feminine secrets. She leaned into his hand. "I missed you."

"Why did you come back, Hannah?" He had to know if she would acknowledge the intangible connection they shared.

"I could say my mother didn't need me, but she does. I couldn't bear to think you'd be gone when I returned in two weeks. The truth is, I came back for you, Jake."

Jake's heart swelled.

She'd come back for him.

And he'd had the good fortune to be waiting for her.

Wanting her, needing her more, he sighed out her name as he swept her into his arms and kissed her. Passion roared through his veins, spurring him to action. His hands explored her luscious terrain. He wanted to take her now, against the car. But he hesitated, wanting her in his bed, rumpled sheets framing her naked body.

When Hannah kissed him with equal fervor, instinct overrode his attempt at caution. "Inside." If not for his injured leg, he'd have carried her there. Instead, his fingers interlaced with hers, and he strode directly to the bedroom. As they stood before the bed, her eyes locked on his and a tremor ran through her arm. "Nervous?" he asked.

She studied him, her tenseness at odds with the desire in her Montgomery blue eyes. "A little."

"Don't be." Jake rubbed the back of her hand with the pad of his thumb. He wanted her, and he believed she wanted him. He prayed for both of their sakes that he could soothe her anxiety. "I'm the same man in here that I was out there. And you're the same woman who flew across the country to make love to me. We both want this, unless you've changed your mind?"

Hannah gave a little laugh. "No, I haven't changed my mind. But I need a minute in the bathroom to freshen up."

Relieved by her answer, Jake reclined on his side on the bed, his head propped up on his hand. Something hard pressed into his back, and he belatedly remembered his gun was stuffed in his waistband. Best to put that away in the bedside drawer. And while he was at it, he withdrew the just-in-case condoms from his wallet and tucked them under his pillow.

Though he wanted to make love to Hannah more than anything, a small voice in his head warned him against the folly of putting himself at the mercy of a woman, something he swore he'd never do after Ursula's betrayal. Hannah wasn't Ursula. Not by a long shot. She was D.C.'s daughter. She wouldn't betray him.

Hannah paused on the threshold. Light from the hallway shone down on her shoulders, haloing her lightened hair. The body hugging clothes were new too. He whistled under his breath. He hoped his tongue wasn't lolling wolfishly.

"So."

From her pensive tone, Jake realized her nerves had gotten the better of her. He ramped back his desire and sat up, patting the quilt. "Come here. I'll rub your back."

"That sounds divine." Hannah crossed the room, toed off her shoes, and climbed up in the vee of his legs. "I've been cooped up in the middle seat of an airplane between two strangers for hours. I was afraid to go to sleep for fear of drooling on one of them."

Jake chuckled as he rubbed her back, starting at her shoulder blades and working his way down her back in opposing circles. She felt so good, so right. "You're a drooler?"

"Not that I know of, but that was the worst possible thing I could imagine happening." She arched against his hands. "Ooh, that feels great."

His fingers smoothed over the womanly swell of her hips as he kissed the base of her neck. His body telegraphed his need to make love to Hannah, but he kept the pace slow, not wanting to scare her off by going too fast.

"Oh, Jake," she mouthed as he blazed a trail of kisses along the slender column of her neck. She turned to him, kissing him hungrily.

Heat seared him at her eagerness. He skimmed his hands up her torso and caressed the outline of her breasts. "You're driving me wild, Hannah."

On a half-moan, half-shudder, she tugged at his shirt. "I've thought of nothing else since you kissed me."

At her admission, his caution shattered. Like smart missiles, his hands closed over her pert breasts. He marveled at the feel of them, their weight, how perfectly round and wonderful they felt in his hands.

"You're beautiful," he whispered, dipping his head to taste.

She yanked at his belt. "I can't wait another minute."

He stayed her shaking hands. "Let me do that."

"Move faster," she urged.

Fast suited him just fine. Like a man possessed, Jake tossed his shirt over his head and tugged his jeans over his hips. As they crumpled to the floor, he glanced her way. The light from the hall spilled over her shoulder, her naked shoulder.

He swallowed thickly, stunned by her magnificence,

humbled by her trust. He deeply regretted missing watching her clothes come off. Then another thought plowed into him, shaking him to the core.

It was happening again. He was so wrapped up in Hannah that he was missing the big picture. A few missed signs here and there could cost a fellow his life. He'd been down this lusty road before, and it had ended badly.

How could he be objective about the future when all of his focus was on the here and now?

Chapter 13

All her life, caution had practically been Hannah's middle name, but tonight she'd flung caution to the wind. She wanted to take the risk, to dare all.

Tonight she was going to make love for the first time ever.

With Jake. A man she'd known for barely a week. Being separated from him had left her empty. So she'd remedied that by flying back from California to claim him.

Tonight when she'd driven up to the darkened house, fear had taken hold of her.

She'd believed she was too late.

And then Jake had materialized, a specter in the night.

Scary stuff. Quality assurance auditors observed life after the fact. They didn't live in the moment.

That's why she had to move fast. To make sure the moment didn't pass her by. She wanted him as a woman wants a man, beside her, touching her, completing her.

Hannah stilled. Jake still wore his boxers. She'd shed every stitch of her clothes. Here she was, naked and vulnerable. She pointed at his boxers. "You forgot something."

Jake gave her a knowing smile, sat up, and reached for her. "I forgot nothing. A man's got a right to some modesty when he's getting jumped by a hot woman."

Warmth coursed through her. Jake thought she was hot. She stroked the dark, exciting hairs arrowing down his chest. "What nice muscles you have, Jake."

His fingers slid through her hair, then caressed the side of her face. Hannah made a small muffled sound at the pleasurable sensation. Though his touch felt wonderful, she wanted more. Heat pooled deep inside her core as erotic images of him touching her filled her head.

"You are so beautiful, Hannah." Jake's reverent tones sent another blast of warmth down her spine. She didn't want to talk. She wanted him more than anything.

Tingles of mind-reeling sensation shot into her body wherever he touched her. The combination of electrical heat and friction on her skin was akin to throwing a lighted match into a box of heart pine kindling. Hungry flames bathed the precious tinder of her emotions, igniting her every feminine instinct.

His questing fingers circled her firm breast. A little moan tumbled from Hannah's mouth as his thumb brushed over her pebbled nipple. "Your hands are magic," she whispered. If he didn't make love to her immediately, she would die. She caught his shoulders and tugged him to her. "Now. Let's do it right now."

His eyes glittered. "Let's take our time."

"I can't wait. Don't you want me?"

Jake produced a foil packet, ripped it open with his teeth, and slicked it on. "I want to show you how much I want you."

Excitement filled her at his words, but when he rolled her on top of him, her courage faltered. What if her inexperience turned him off? Would he resent having to show her the ropes?

Jake seemed to sense her hesitation. His hands rested warm and heavy on her ribs. "Is everything okay?"

It wasn't. Her heart raced. Her body ached with feelings she didn't understand. "I can't think clearly."

"We just took care of the thinking part. From here on in, thinking is not required." He surged into her, his forward momentum dispatching the slight resistance he encountered. Jake quivered deep inside her, then he went still. "Hannah?"

The concern in his voice touched her deeply. He was worried he'd hurt her. But she wasn't hurt. Far from it.

She had never felt so gloriously full before, never known it could be like this between a man and a woman. The wonders of the universe were almost within her grasp. Joy swept through her and liberated her rusty voice.

She pressed herself against him. "Don't stop."

His hands closed over her hips. "We need to go slow. This is your first time. Our first time."

"Don't need time," she said between the hot kisses she planted on his face. "If you don't start moving again, I'm taking charge."

He moved all right. Until her mind hazed. Until the room faded and there was nothing but him.

Until she saw stars.

Then she spiraled over a soaring cliff, gliding like a majestic hawk on a veering midday thermal. Weightless, boneless. Drifting feather light above an out of focus landscape. She slowly floated back to reality.

Blood thundered through her veins. Deep within her, a smile bubbled up and she let it out, laying her head on Jake's chest. Living in the moment was definitely the way to go.

****

Jake stroked Hannah's naked back. Satisfaction coursed through his veins. He'd known it would be good with Hannah, but he hadn't known how good. On a scale of one to ten, the experience had rated a twenty.

Damn they were good together.

He could definitely get used to being with Hannah. The floral essence of her silky hair soothed him. Every time he smelled her hair, he'd remember this evening and the wonder of holding pure sunshine.

Tension rippled through him. Did Hannah feel the same way? His worry grew. She'd been a virgin. He'd never been a woman's first before. What if he'd disappointed her? An educated woman like her had probably had certain expectations. How was he to know if he'd met them?

Hell.

He should have taken things slower. A woman's first should be special.

A faint vibration rumbled across his chest, interrupting his musings. Was she purring?

His body tightened in response. Not good.

He drew on his energy reserves to roll over and deposit her next to him on the mattress. She clung to him like a gentle summer rain. He groaned as the nubs of her breasts pressed sharply into his abdomen.

"What?" she asked, her voice thick with sensual lethargy.

"Lay next to me. Are you cold?"

She laughed hoarsely, snuggling into his side. "Not a chance."

"Was it—all right for you? Can I get you anything?"

She laughed against his ribs, the husky vibration winding his body tighter. "It was better than all right. I may never walk again." She feathered her fingers down his side, over his hips, as if she was memorizing the shape of him. "You were wonderful."

Jake drew in a sharp breath at her not so innocent caress. "Careful. You're playing with fire."

"I think I'm addicted to fire. When can we make love again?"

Weren't virgins supposed to be shy and retiring? Shouldn't he be gracious and exercise restraint? "Uh, later. Later is good."

Her hand flared across his abdomen, her fingers inching closer to the taunt area that ached for her touch. He caught her hand before it found trouble. He inhaled deeply, letting the delectable feminine bouquet of Hannah roll over his tongue like fine wine.

"You need some time to recuperate?" Her eyes twinkled with mischief. "How long? Seconds? Minutes? Hours?"

Drawing her hand to his lips, he kissed the underside of her wrist. "This isn't a NASCAR event. There's no penalty for extended down time. And you'll be sore. The last thing I'd ever want is to hurt you."

"I'm fine. Really. And you don't understand. I've read book after book on this subject. I've got lots of ideas I want to try out."

She wiggled suggestively.

His brain was filled with wanting her, and she seemed to be having the same thoughts. He was hammer hard, way past the jump-in-a-cold-shower place. He'd never wanted a woman so much in his entire life.

Jake hesitated. Four months ago he'd wanted Ursula too. He'd been thinking Ursula was the woman he wanted to share his life with, then she'd killed D.C. and shot him in the leg.

Clearly, he didn't have the best sense of self-preservation once sex became part of the equation. It would be best if he slowed this down a bit.

With regret, he uttered words he didn't want to say. "We should probably wait."

Surprise flickered across her face, then hurt. "You don't want me?"

Damn. Obviously she had no idea how much he wanted her. He guided her hand to his arousal. "I want you so much I'm about to burst from it. You do something to me, Hannah girl. I could spend the entire night making love with you."

In response, she straddled his chest. "So, what's the problem, tough guy? I want more, and so do you. I don't see a disconnect here."

Her glorious breasts bounced in front of his eyes, and Jake gave up the fight. A man could only take so much tender torture. He reached for her and tried out some ideas of his own. This time it wasn't fast and furious between them. This time he drew out her pleasure until her ardent response elevated him to previously unknown heights, until she gazed at him with those lovely luminous eyes, until she whispered his name in breathless abandon.

His release was hard and fast, leaving him

breathless. Jake cradled her in his arms, wishing that this wondrous moment wasn't just a snapshot in time. But his experience had proven that this sense of togetherness was an illusion. With time, the glow would fade, and they would drift apart. In a sense, this was the beginning of the end.

His affairs never lasted.

He knew better than to wish otherwise.

Foolishly, the thought of losing Hannah left him empty and aching. He shoved those feelings aside. As a boy from the wrong side of the tracks, he'd seen plenty of worn out and broken down people. He was one of them. There were no picket fences in his future.

Summoning his defenses around him, he let the bitterness of the past numb his heart. And he focused on his number one priority, avenging D.C.'s death.

****

Morning came and went. Just before noon, Hannah stumbled out of bed and into the shower, glorying in her womanliness. Jake was everything she'd hoped for in a lover. Tender. Passionate. Ardent. She couldn't hold in her satisfied smile.

Now that they'd shared so much between them, she was certain the issue of trust had been resolved. Making love with Jake had given her new insight into her feelings. She loved him without reservation. No question about it.

She trusted him with her heart.

Surely he felt the same way about her.

Clean, dry, and refreshed, she headed for the kitchen to rustle up a late breakfast. Jake sat at the kitchen table enjoying a cup of coffee. Hannah blushed furiously at the sight of his bare chest and low slung jeans. She'd spent a lot of time touching his body, kissing that skin.

She averted her eyes hastily and searched for something else to look at. The sickly sweet smell of overripe banana immediately caught her attention. She grimaced as she walked towards the tubular banana stand. "You should have thrown these bananas out days ago."

Jake lounged back in his kitchen chair and shrugged. There was a smug warmth to his eyes that she now recognized as male satisfaction. "I kept them for you."

"They're too ripe to eat and I'm not planning on making banana bread. No point in keeping them." The soft mushy fruit molded to her fingers. Grimacing, she slid the brown bananas off the stand with the intent of depositing them in the trash can.

Instead, the stand toppled and skittered across the countertop. The retaining knob separated from the stand and bounced to the floor. Hannah discarded the mushy bananas, then she leaned over to pick the knob up. When she did, a white piece of paper coiled snugly in the tube of the banana stand caught her eye.

She hadn't forgotten about the hidden letters from her father. Could this be one of them? Her heart pounded in her throat. "Jake, there's something in here. Do you think it's a message from my father?"

Jake came forward, rotating the banana stand in his hand until he could grip the edge of the paper. He removed the paper scrap and handed it to Hannah.

"My hands are shaking too much to do this," Hannah said as she accepted the tiny roll of paper. "What could my father have to say that required so much secrecy?"

Jake kept his own counsel and steered her over to a chair at the kitchen table. Hannah's mind raced with wild suppositions, ideas that she'd formulated over the years as she fantasized about the reasons why her father was habitually absent.

He'd been to the moon in a super classified spacecraft, or he'd been off negotiating world peace in an underground bunker, or he'd discovered the cure for cancer in a top secret research laboratory. Whatever his secret was, it had to be ground breaking, vitally important news.

Nothing else made any sense.

Hannah unrolled the slip of paper with precise movements. Her euphoria over this being the best morning of her life took a backseat to the gnawing uncertainty eating away at her insides.

Apprehension stiffened her trembling fingers. Her empty stomach twisted and turned until she wanted to double over to protect herself from harm.

Lord.

Why couldn't she have this time alone with Jake without worrying about anything else?

Her father had always had lousy timing. Death hadn't changed that one bit. His intrusive presence in the room seemed almost tangible.

"Did you know this was in here?" she asked.

The warmth winked out of Jake's eyes. "No."

Alarmed, she leaned forward, elbows on the table. She didn't want the man she loved to disappear behind a cold, impenetrable mask. She wanted to spend the day with the generous, passionate man who had made love to her through the night. "I didn't cross the country to play hide and seek with my father. I came back for you."

Jake's lips thinned. "Remember that."

His eyes were guarded now, as if he were ready for an attack. Not a good sign. "Anything you want to tell me, Jake?"

"Your father's last letter upset you. I'm preparing for more of the same."

His flat tone confused her. "You think I shouldn't read it?"

"I think you will read it, no matter what I say. I'm concerned about the content of the message. D.C. wasn't the most sensitive guy in the world."

"No kidding." Hannah's grip tightened on the small roll of paper. She wouldn't let Jake take it away from her. Not that she thought he would, but just in case.

This was as good a time as any to see if the trust thing was a two way street. She would answer any question he asked of her, but would he reciprocate? "I know you've been keeping something from me. Something big. Is it about my father?"

Jake barred his arms across his chest. "I can neither confirm or deny in response to your question."

Hannah let go of one end of the letter, and it recoiled into a tightly wound miniature scroll again. "Dammit, Jake. That's just the kind of maddening double talk my father used to give me when I wanted a straight answer out of him. After what we shared last night, don't you trust me?

His eyes glittered. "I trust you. I don't trust a letter from a dead man."

Hannah's fingers curled into tight fists. "Don't lie to me. If you trusted me, you would tell me what's wrong. Instead, you're shutting me out."

"I'm keeping you safe. I'd do anything for you, Hannah. I shouldn't have to tell you that."

"Anything but tell me the truth."

"Truth is relative. There are no absolutes in life."

Hannah's jaw dropped. A wave of outrage rolled through her, followed by a swift undertow of nausea. If she wasn't already sitting down, she probably would have lost her footing in the dizzying aftermath. "You don't trust me? I crossed the country to be with you, and you're shutting me out. I demand the truth."

Jake's eyes glittered with icy steel. His voice, the same voice that had caressed her with husky endearments, sliced deeply into her heart. "A woman once tried to control me with sex. Never again will I let myself be so stupid. I care for you, Hannah. I want to be with you. That's the limit of what I can give you."

Heat steamed off her face. She should have known better. This man didn't believe in families or love or affection. He believed in sex, which she had willingly provided to him.

She held his gaze for a long moment before she looked away from his coldly penetrating stare. There was so much she wanted from this man, so much she wanted to give to him, that it soured her stomach to realize he didn't share the same goals. "It's not enough. I want more from you."

When he didn't respond, she told herself it didn't matter. He didn't matter. She wouldn't let him.

Defiantly, she picked up the letter from her father and unrolled it. She silently scanned the text, squinting to make out the very small handwriting.

My dearest Hannah. I hope you're sitting down to read this. Please know that I loved you and your mother every minute of my life. You were in my thoughts and prayers, day and night. I stayed away to keep you safe from my work with the CIA. I'm a spy, baby girl. I've circled the globe keeping it safe from terrorists and other threats. I'm not supposed to tell, but I figure my bosses can hardly punish me if I'm dead. I know how you hate secrets. That's why I'm breaking my silence now so that you will know, once and for all. My absences were never because I didn't want to be there with you. You've got a good head on your shoulders. You'll understand that our country needed me. Your mother already knows, but even the truth didn't keep her from divorcing me. Love, Dad

Hannah read the letter through a second time. The silence in the kitchen was awful. She looked up from the letter to find Jake regarding her intently. Her father was a spy.

That meant his partner was a spy.

She'd spent the night making love to a professional liar.

An awful black hole swirled in her middle, pulling at the truths she knew, threatening to destabilize her entire universe. Her father had lied to her. Her mother had concealed the truth from her. Her lover couldn't confirm or deny anything.

Did everyone think Hannah wasn't responsible enough to be trusted with the truth? Did they believe she needed to be coddled? That she couldn't handle the real world?

The irony of the situation struck her. She'd spent her whole life searching for truth and the people she'd trusted the most, her mother and father and even her lover, had conspired to keep the truth from her. Had her whole life been a sham?

Her heart thudded wildly. The room spun slowly on its axis, and Hannah physically reeled from the disorienting sensation. She gasped in gulps of air and blinked without seeing. She'd never felt more alone in her life.

A touch to her shoulder nearly made her jump out of her skin. "Hannah?"

She met Jake's troubled gaze, but his deceit colored her vision. He'd lied about his career, about the time he'd spent with her father. What else had he lied about? Her stomach turned at the possibility that he'd lied about wanting her. "You're a liar," she said.

"What did the letter say, Hannah?"

"Read it for yourself." She threw the coiled paper at him and hurried out onto the front porch. The noon day sun was high overhead, but she didn't feel warmed by the bright light or the cheery chip notes coming from the nearby forest.

Hannah shivered.

She might never feel warm again.

Her entire life was built on a house of lies.

Had her father come home exhausted from his job because he had been dodging bullets in some tiny corner of the world?

How much of what he'd told her over the years were lies? He'd seemed to be so full of integrity. So righteous about doing the right thing in a given situation.

How could she possibly sort out truth from fiction in such a smoldering mess of lies? Her father had loved telling stories. Had his entertaining adventures been a figment of his overactive imagination?

He'd said he loved her. How was she supposed to believe him? Was she supposed to rejoice that he'd had such a successful career?

His career had cost him his wife and daughter.

God. That hurt.

She'd come in second in her father's attentions. But, she was his only child. Shouldn't she have received top billing?

What did her father know of love anyway? It seemed that he used the word to salve his guilty conscience for being away so much. His idea of love had been contacting her once or twice a year. That was an undisputable truth, she knew because she'd lived it.

She felt so empty inside, she wanted to die.

"Now you know what your father did for a living."

Hannah whirled to face Jake.

Her secretive spy lover.

She'd known it was a mistake to get involved with him, but she'd done it anyway. Now she had to face the consequences of her rash impulses. She leaned against the porch rail and froze him with a frigid look. "You lied to me."

"I'd do anything to keep you safe, Hannah."

Jake had worked with her father. He'd learned his craft from the master of all liars. Why should she believe a word he said? "Ha. You lied to me to keep me from knowing your secrets. That's the real truth."

Jake leaned back against the side of the house. The eight feet between them yawned as wide and deep as the Atlantic Ocean. "The CIA has rules about disclosure. Knowledge is distributed on a need-to-know basis inside the agency. It's never shared outside the agency."

"Well, I'm sick and tired of lies," Hannah said, rubbing the goose bumps on her arms. She might never be warm again. "My parents lied to me. Not just one little lie, but years of lies. Do you know how upsetting that is?"

"I don't know your mother, but your father loved you. You were all he talked about. How proud he was of you, how well you did in school and in your career."

Hannah didn't want to believe Jake's words. He was

a liar, too. But a small flicker of warmth licked at the blanket of cold inside of her. "I don't believe you."

"Your father shouldn't have told you he was an agent, but now that you know, you have to keep it to yourself."

Hannah gestured upward with her arms. "Great. Now I'm part of the conspiracy of liars?"

Jake's expression darkened. "Lady, you are pushing every one of my buttons this morning. If I didn't know you'd just received a major shock, I'd take issue with your cavalier attitude."

"Go ahead. Take issue with my attitude. At least it's real. Not made up." Hannah's voice sounded thin and squeaky, but she couldn't do anything about it. "What are you going to do if I tell someone? Kill me?"

Jake uncoiled from the side of the house like a lethal predator. His limp didn't slow him down one bit. His hands clamped down on her shoulders, perilously close to her neck. She didn't know if he was going to shake her or choke the life out of her.

His nearness filled her with longing. She had given him everything she had to offer, everything she had been holding in reserve for the man she loved. It hurt to remember how joyous and uninhibited their lovemaking had been.

Hannah found it difficult to swallow, but her chin jutted a little higher. Though her insides were raw and she barely knew what to believe, she wouldn't crumble. Her Montgomery pride would see her through this gigantic disaster.

She sensed she had pushed him close to some imaginary line, a line he never crossed. She'd recently crossed a similar line, and now she was filled with regret at making that choice.

He'd lied to her.

She couldn't forget that.

Ever.

In anger, she lashed out with words. "What now? Are you going to snap my neck? Is that a technique you learned from the top secret super spy manual?"

Jake's fingers tightened on her neck, and then he drew near, kissing her fiercely. She didn't want to respond to him, didn't want to remember the soaring passion they had shared, but his searing kiss wouldn't allow her to forget.

The raw need in him called to her. In this, at least, he was being truthful with her. This passion they shared was real, not a lie. She responded to him honestly, breathlessly, until she panted for more. He broke off the kiss abruptly and crushed her against his chest.

In spite of her pain and anger, she realized he was hurting too. On this elemental level, she yearned to comfort him, to take away his pain as a life long mate might do. He brought out a nurturing side of her that she'd never suspected she had. She stroked his back to soothe his distress.

What was she going to do?

She was in love with a man who didn't trust her.

Even though she was spitting mad at him, his kiss had taken her mind off her anger for long enough to sense his anguish. It felt weird to worry about him when her peace of mind dangled by a fraying thread.

Was his pain an empathic reaction to her distress?

The thought that he might care so much filled her with an uneasy tenderness. So much was changing that she barely knew which end was up.

She clung to Jake. He was the only solid object in her world.

His arms tightened around her, and she closed her eyes against the sudden moisture that threatened to overwhelm her. His heart beat steadily against the ear she had pressed to his chest. She inhaled deeply, feeling safe in his arms, wishing her troubles would magically disappear. They wouldn't, of course. Trouble never went away of its own accord.

"Jake?"

"There's no going back, Hannah. You and I have

something here. I know you're angry about the lies, and you have every right to be. All I'm asking is that you give me time to work some things out."

Fresh alarm flooded her system, and with it came a mind-numbing fear of the unknown. Did he have a wife and four kids tucked away in Baltimore? She lifted her head to look him square in the eye. "Things? What kinds of things?"

His gaze burned her with icy intensity. "Like taking care of the person that murdered D.C. and ruined my leg."

Comprehension rushed in like a monstrous ocean wave crashing on a tranquil shore. Her brain reeled from the sudden onslaught. Her father's death wasn't accidental?

Nausea swamped her senses, weakened her knees. She reeled under the staggering blow that came with raw unadulterated truth.

She backed away from Jake, one hand covering her mouth, one hand holding her queasy stomach. Her brain couldn't process his horrific statement. She inhaled a quick shaky breath. Then another.

Murder.

She just couldn't get past that word.

Someone had purposefully ended her father's life? She had to know more. Her need for truth clawed at her until she summoned the breath to voice the questions that screamed through her head. "Murdered? My father was murdered?"

Chapter 14

Jake rubbed the back of his neck.

Damn.

What the hell was wrong with him?

He hadn't meant to blurt that out.

Birds chirped in the trees, but on the cottage porch there was icy silence. His shoulders bowed from the avalanche of lies from the past sliding forward to bury him. He sagged against the porch rail.

He was so tired of lies. They kept him on edge, taunting him with the altered reality of the truth he had to profess, the altered truth he had to live.

But Hannah, she was pure and beautiful. The lies would ruin her too. He couldn't stand by and do nothing. If Hannah wanted truth, he'd give it to her.

"CIA field jobs are dangerous," Jake began. "D.C. didn't like living apart from his family, but that was the choice he made for your protection."

She gripped the back of a rocking chair. "But murder? What about his heart attack?"

"The death certificate said his heart stopped beating, and it did. It failed to mention that he'd been shot through the heart." Saying those words out loud eased more weight off his bowed shoulders.

Hannah's trembling hand went to her mouth. "I hardly know what to say."

He hated that her face was so pale. "D.C. died in my arms. That's why I have to make this right."

"Is that why you have a gun?"

"I have a gun because the world is not a nice place. There's plenty of evil out there. I don't believe in taking chances with my safety."

"You're going to shoot the person who killed my father?" Hannah's voice rose as she spoke.

Jake closed his eyes momentarily to escape her needle sharp gaze. "There are many ways to exact justice. Death would be too easy for this person. I have in mind something much more painful."

Her eyes narrowed in suspicion. "You said you were retired."

"I am retired. The CIA has no use in the field for guys who can't blend in. My limp marks me in more ways than one."

"Should you even be considering this? Shouldn't the CIA handle the investigation?"

The sunlight dimmed as a cloud passed overhead. His skin cooled, but the effect was negligible compared to the ice storm in his gut. "I'm not useless. Honor demands I make this right."

"Don't put words in my mouth. I didn't say you were useless."

"So, you understand why I have to do this?"

Hannah paced the length of the porch and back, stopping close enough for him to grab her. "I *understand* nothing. You're going after a person who's a killer? Why can't you walk away and be thankful you're still alive?"

"I can't."

"You won't. Big difference."

He wanted her to accept him for what he was. That was probably unrealistic now that she knew the truth. Jake softened his voice. "It doesn't have to affect us, Hannah. When the time is right I'll take a trip, and when I come back it will be over."

"This was the trip you mentioned to me earlier? Tracking down my father's killer? That's what you've been planning all along?"

He held her fiery gaze. "I'm going to take care of this. I know what I'm doing."

"Yeah, right. Last time you went up against this

person ended so well."

"Mistakes were made. I won't make a mistake this time. That's a promise."

"My entire life is a minefield of broken promises," Hannah said wearily as she turned from him again.

To his right a bird sang as if nothing was wrong in the world. The bird must not be experiencing the strong tremors which were shaking the underpinnings of Jake's existence. He wanted Hannah, but he also wanted justice for D.C.

Hannah didn't share his desire for justice. She wanted him to walk away from the goal that had sustained him these last three months. That wasn't going to happen. He kept the promises he made.

What did Hannah think of him?

His hands clenched into tight fists. It mattered what she thought of him. A woman like Hannah, soft and beautiful, what would she want with a washed up, banged up guy like himself? There were probably hundreds of men out there that were more suited to her refined tastes.

One basic fact gave him hope. She'd chosen him. She'd made love to him, not some other guy. He couldn't lose sight of that crucial detail. Her response to his desperate kiss moments ago proved that she wasn't repulsed by him. That kind of bone deep wanting didn't go away on a whim.

At least it didn't for him. He wasn't ready to walk away from her. Not by a long shot. He wanted to spend many nights with this woman. One night of passion hadn't been enough to staunch a lifetime of searching and loneliness.

But she might walk away from him. That thought sent him back into the shaky footing of mental quicksand. Shadows from his past had cast their tainted light on his present, and it scared him that he couldn't control the outcome of this situation.

Hannah played the game of life by strict rules. She might be inclined to ignore her physical needs because of her hard and fast principles. His gut knotted painfully.

Why did D.C. do this to him? They'd been partners. Close partners, and that fellowship had meant the world to Jake. D.C. had been his mentor, his surrogate father even. After a lifetime of lies, why had D.C. chosen to go out in a blaze of truth?

If not for that note, he and Hannah would already be back in bed.

A man didn't get what he wanted by letting things slip through his fingers. He closed the distance between them, taking her hand in his, willing her to remember the passion they'd shared. "This changes nothing between us, Hannah."

Hannah drew in a shaky breath. She longed to sink into the reassuring heat radiating from his touch. She longed to forget the shocking words of her father's letter, but she couldn't turn her mind off.

"Maybe not for you, but I can't sort out my thoughts and feelings so quickly." Hannah struggled through the stark facts and dark emotions clogging up her head. "My emotions are raw when it comes to my father, and this new information caught me off guard. I can't take this news in stride. This is very personal for me. I have to sort out the lies my parents told me and figure out who I am."

His whisper soft caress on the back of her hand sent chills down her spine. "I know who you are. A very desirable woman, Hannah. I want us to be together, to share passion in each other's arms."

She shivered at the warmth and intimacy infused in his voice. Incredibly, she wanted to jump in his arms and let the world take care of itself. Not very realistic. Definitely not responsible, and definitely not her. "I can't focus right now. I feel so mixed up."

"What are you saying?"

"I care for you, Jake. I wouldn't have slept with you if I didn't." She sighed. "I came up here to get to know my father better, and now I discover I never knew him at all. I can't get my bearings. The compass I've used to orient myself for my entire life is defective."

She hoped he would give her some space, but he didn't step back. Not that he was crowding her, but he wasn't giving her any wiggle room either. Heat poured across the slight distance between their bodies. What would she do if he pressed her to make a decision about their future right now?

His plan to avenge her father's murder sounded extremely dangerous. The thought of Jake getting hurt or killed rocked her to her core. "I don't want you going after a killer."

He stiffened. "Exacting justice is important to me."

"And your life isn't important?"

"I pay my debts."

"Your debt is to my father?"

He nodded tersely.

"I'm his heir, and I'm canceling the debt. Don't do it."

"It's not so straightforward. There are loose ends."

Hannah paused at that. Loose ends. She hated them. They unraveled when you least expected them to.

Jake wasn't a loose end. He was someone she very much wanted in her life. For more than a one night stand, maybe even forever. She loved him.

What chance of a future did they have if he got himself killed? She had to make him see that his noble plan was ill-conceived. "If you care anything for me, don't do this."

Silence echoed across the porch. Even the birds of the forest quieted. "Don't put conditions on me," Jake said, his voice low and dangerous. "I won't be manipulated by a woman."

She had to stand firm, even though his wounded tone ate at her. "Call it what you will. I don't have much to bargain with. I won't sleep with you if you go after this killer."

"Fine."

He didn't sound fine. In fact, he sounded like someone who had been pushed into a corner he didn't want to be in. A strategic retreat was in order. "Look. We both need a time out here. I'm going for a walk in the woods. You do whatever it is you do to recharge, and we'll continue this conversation later."

A mask fell over Jake's face. His eyes turned cold, calculating. She imagined him processing their conversation and arriving at the exact conclusion she had. Or at least that's what she told herself when he didn't reach for her again.

Hannah made what she thought was a very fine exit, stopping by her car to calmly collect her cell phone, her Zeiss field glasses, and her *Sibley's Field Guide to Birds*. After pocketing her phone, she strung the binoculars across her chest bandolier fashion and crammed her guide inside the back waistband of her pants.

He could have stopped her with a word, but he didn't. His pointed silence unnerved her. The distance between her car and the porch was nearly thirty feet, only it felt like a mere inch or two separated them. Why didn't he say anything?

She didn't breathe easily until she reached the relative shelter of the forest. In the dark understory, she marched pointedly away from Jake and the story book cottage her father had built for her. Over the course of the last twenty-four hours she had experienced extreme emotions, and she didn't know how to deal with the fallout.

How resilient was she? It wasn't a question she'd thought much about. In the past, she'd assumed she could handle anything life threw at her. Now she wasn't so sure.

Emotions weren't straightforward. Data could be dealt with in a linear fashion. Emotions, as she was finding out, tended to be circular and confusing.

She loved Jake. She loved the house her father had built for her. She hated her father's lies. She hated Jake's lies. She loved spending the night in Jake's arms. She hated finding out the truth of her father's life through posthumous letters. Was it any wonder she couldn't think straight?

Why did fate have to rear its ugly head? She could have gone her whole life without knowing her parents were liars or that the man she loved was set on killing someone.

Why couldn't she have fallen in love with a librarian or a pharmacist? Why did she have to fall in love with a glorified hit man?

She should have gone with her first impression of Jacob Sutherland. He was a dangerous predator. The biggest, baddest wolf out there.

The forest fell silent as she crunched over twigs and swatted branches out of her way. She didn't blame the wildlife for fearing her. She was in a dangerous, edgy mood.

She felt like screaming. Or at least giving someone hell. And she knew just the person that deserved to hear a piece of her mind.

Good thing she had her cell phone. She whipped it out and punched in a number she knew by heart.

****

Jake didn't want Hannah to walk away from him, but he was afraid of spooking her. He tended to be heavy handed when it came to obtaining what he wanted. He wanted Hannah with a relentless certainty.

No telling what she might accuse him of if he didn't give her the time and space she needed this afternoon.

She was only getting a brief reprieve. They would settle this issue today. He wanted her in his bed and in his life.

He rubbed his chin and the coarse stubble of his fledgling beard grated across his palm like abrasive sandpaper. No wonder Hannah had run off. He needed a shave and a shower. Maybe then he'd stop thinking about a certain storm blue eyed nymph that had him tied in knots.

As the water sluiced over his body, his jittery

thoughts settled. There was no reason he couldn't have Hannah and seek justice for D.C. He would spend the next week with Hannah, then he'd take care of that other business when she went back to work.

Simple as that. Why didn't Hannah see that those two spheres of his life didn't have to touch? He had no trouble keeping them separate. She shouldn't question his judgment.

She wouldn't have known about his quest to bring Ursula to justice if it hadn't been for D.C.'s latest letter.

If he had thrown those bananas away as soon as they got brown, she wouldn't have found the trouble-making letter. But he hadn't. He couldn't bear to throw away anything she'd touched. And as long as those bananas sat there on the stand, there had been a chance she might come back. And she had returned—for him.

Jake dressed hastily, his thoughts centered on Hannah. She had come back, but the mushy brown bananas had been his downfall. Things would have been much more straightforward between him and Hannah without that second letter.

Darn D.C. for trying to square things with his daughter. Jake sat down at the desk in his room and fired up his computer. A quick check of the grounds surveillance cameras revealed Hannah was on the way to the meadow. A walk of that length gave him plenty of time to check on Ursula's latest whereabouts.

He quickly found what he was looking for. Ursula had used her credit card to stay at a hotel near the Baltimore Airport. Rooms were cheaper there than at downtown hotels. She'd registered under her old alias, Joan Andress, and stayed for two nights, then she'd checked out.

What are you up to, Ursula? Jake searched for a paper and pen to write down the name of the hotel. When he opened the desk drawer, he found writing materials, and something else.

His sunglasses.

Not just any sunglasses.

The sunglasses he'd left in Ursula's bedroom the last time they'd been together. He'd left from her place to attend that fatal meeting with D.C. His sunglasses had no business being in this drawer, in this house, or even on this continent.

His blood went glacial.

Ursula had been here. In this house.

And by leaving the sunglasses, she'd let him know the game was on.

Was she watching the cottage right now? Had she discovered and disabled the remote external sensors when she was here in the house?

Hannah.

Hannah was out there by herself.

Hannah wasn't safe.

Jake tried her on her cell phone, only he got shunted directly to her voice mail. He hung up, worry eating at his stomach. He checked the perimeter cameras and couldn't locate her.

He ran his fingers through his hair. What was he going to do? He had to get Hannah away from the cottage.

Where would she be safe?

A place far from here. Ursula had no gripe with Hannah. Her beef was with him.

He threw Hannah's clothes and toiletries back in her suitcase and loaded them in his truck. As soon as he found Hannah, he was bundling her off to LA again. She'd be safe there. Or at least, safer than here.

Grabbing his gun and his cane, he left the safety of the cottage and melted into the woods to find her. The forest seemed unusually quiet. His heart raced.

He wasn't a man given to bouts of prayer, but he prayed for Hannah's safety.

He had to find her in time.

Chapter 15

"What's got you so riled up this morning?" Libby asked.

Hannah gritted her teeth and marched through the dense forest. This conversation wouldn't go well if her mother trivialized Hannah's unsettled emotions. "I found another letter. Dad told me the truth about his job. His *real* job. Both of you lied to me about his spy career."

"Oh, that. Well, I was never happy about the secrecy that surrounded D.C., but I got over that. What I hated was the hours. He'd be gone for weeks at a time, then he'd come home so tired he could barely hold his head up. I'd nurse him back to health, and he'd take off again."

"Why didn't you ever tell me?"

"Because he made me swear on my mother's grave not to tell anyone."

"I can't believe you kept this from me. I'm stunned that neither one of you trusted me enough to tell me the truth. I'm repeating myself but I can't help it. I can't believe you lied to me all these years. How many other lies have you told me, Mom? How do I sort out the truth from fiction?"

"Oh sweetheart, I'm sorry you're so upset. We never meant to hurt you. Your father insisted that it was safer for you to not know about his career when you were a kid. Then there never seemed to be a good time to tell you. D.C. was always talking about the need-to-know basis, and that stuck with me in regard to his career."

Hannah sighed in exasperation. "You trust me to do your taxes, you trust me with access to your inheritance, but you don't trust me enough to level with me about

Dad's true occupation? That doesn't make any sense."

"When you put it that way, it sounds bad. But, that's not how it was. Your father was a difficult man. He was so adamant about keeping you safe that I followed his lead. You can't fault me for keeping you safe."

"Mom. I'm twenty-nine years old. How old do I have to be before you tell me the truth? How many lies have you fed me over the years?"

"Why do you think I turned to yoga? I wasn't always the picture of peace and serenity that I am today. Living with your father's secrets had me walking on pins and needles."

"The lies, Mom. What else did you lie to me about?"

"You make it sound like a giant conspiracy. The only thing I ever lied to you about was your father's career."

"Would you have ever told me if he hadn't?"

"No. It was his place to tell you, not mine."

"I'm crushed at your lack of trust."

"You'll understand someday. You'll have someone that you care about more than life itself, and you will do anything in your power to keep them safe."

Old hurts boiled up out of Hannah's past. One incident in particular came to mind. "Did you know he wasn't going to make the sunflower pageant in first grade?"

"Yes, I did."

"You could have saved me a lot of heartache if you'd told me ahead of time."

"I couldn't, dear. And besides, there was always a chance he'd be back in time. I knew how much you wanted him to be there, and if I could have made it happen, I'd have made him show up."

Hannah gripped her phone tightly. Bright light shone through the thinning canopy of green leaves just ahead. "I'm having trouble assimilating all of this."

"You'll be fine, dear. I raised you to be a strong woman. You have never crumbled at the sight of adversity before. Speaking of adversaries, how did the big reunion go?"

"That part went well." Hannah's cheeks burned with embarrassment. "Amazingly well, but Dad's letter changes everything. I can't trust Jake either. As Dad's former partner, he's a part of the conspiracy of lies."

"Did you sleep with him?"

"Mom! What happened to our agreement to keep our noses out of each other's love lives?" Hannah glanced over her shoulder as if she were worried someone nearby might overhear her conversation. There was no one in the immediate vicinity, but who knew what spy gadgets were embedded in these woods.

"I know you're grown up and all, but it's important to me that you made a good choice."

"How can I know if I made a good choice when my whole life is based on lies?"

"I only want the best for you, dear. Sex can release massive amounts of tension."

"All right. You win. The sex was great. Are you happy?"

"Take a deep breath, Hannah. Let the air fill your lungs and seep into the places where you are tense. Be aware of your breathing, and you will find the truths that you seek."

Hannah groaned out loud. "I don't need yoga instruction, Mom. Deep breathing isn't going to fix this mess."

"It certainly won't if you don't try it." Libby sighed into the phone. "Do you love him?"

Bright sunlight blinded Hannah as she stepped out from the deep shade of the forest and into the tranquil meadow. Maybe she was better off with yoga platitudes. She wasn't ready to speak of her feelings for Jake. Especially not to her Mom.

How could she love Jake when he was all wrong for her? The only criterion that she absolutely never gave an inch on was lying. In the past, she'd cut guys off on the first date if she suspected they lied to her. Jake had boldfaced lied to her. Not once, but repeatedly.

And he had plans to track down a killer. Plans that made her blood run cold. If anything happened to him, she'd die. She blinked copiously to clear the moisture pooling in her eyes.

"It's all right, baby," Libby said. "I know what it's like to love a man that keeps secrets. It's not easy, but love is the most wonderful thing in the world."

Hannah headed towards the low slung bench by the flowing spring. The bright sunshine warmed her shoulders. "How can I trust Jake when I know he lies to me?"

"Your heart will tell you what to do."

"It isn't so easy. Jake claims he has unfinished business that relates to Dad. He plans to take care of this business soon, and I'm afraid for him, Mom. He already got hurt once, and Dad died from this unfinished business."

Her mother sighed. "I always knew that job wasn't good for D.C. You can only flirt with death so many times without risking your own life."

"I don't approve of violence. Have you forgotten that?"

"I haven't forgotten anything, dear. I'm not that old or senile. Hiding my fear for your father's safety has made me daffy over the years. I've searched for serenity in a world filled with bad people and harbored guilt that I couldn't do more to keep my loved one safe."

"How did you survive this gnawing uncertainty, Mom?"

"The same way you're going to. By putting one foot in front of the other. You can't make your young man chose a certain path. All you can do is outline the choices before him."

"I wish I had stayed out in California with you. If I had, I wouldn't have found Dad's second letter, and I most certainly wouldn't have slept with a man that might be a cold blooded killer."

"There's no point in second guessing yourself. You made the best choice you could at the time."

Hannah sat on the rustic bench, her shoulders rigid with tension. "I could have avoided this misery if I had listened to my inner eye the first time I laid eyes on Jake Sutherland."

"What did you see?"

"A dangerous predator."

Libby chuckled. "You're a strong woman, sweetheart. A weak man wouldn't stand a chance with you."

"I'm not sleeping with him again."

"That doesn't sound like the truth to me. I can practically hear the sparks flying over the phone. Do you need me to head back east and referee?"

Hannah winced at the thought. There was enough drama already between her and Jake without adding a third party to the mix. Besides, she had to focus on the root of the problem. Talking Jake out of tracking down a cold blooded killer was essential. "I'll manage."

"You can always fly back to Los Angeles. I'd love to have your company, and Doug knows tons of bachelors out here if your young man doesn't work out."

Definitely time to get off the phone if her mother was playing matchmaker. She didn't want to run into another man's arms. It was Jake's arms she wanted. "I want to work this out on my own, Mom. Thanks anyway. But, about Doug. Did you have a chance to talk to him about his brother? Did you ask Doug why he doesn't drive?"

"Doug changed the subject as soon as I mentioned his brother's name. Then he asked me how I knew about his brother. He thought that information had been pretty well buried."

Hannah thought about that a minute. Jake was a former CIA agent and probably still had agency contacts. That would explain how he'd gotten the information so quickly. "Not so buried that the CIA didn't know. How did you explain that one to him?"

"I said that you'd had him checked out."

Hannah winced. Good thing she wasn't going to see Doug anytime soon. "I bet he took that well."

"The thing is, I really enjoy Doug's company. And if the CIA couldn't dig up anything worse than a reckless brother, then I think that speaks fairly well of Doug's integrity."

"Good point. What did he say about not driving?"

"He said he'd talk to me about it later."

"Why later?"

"I don't know. When did you get such a suspicious mind?"

"Right about the time I got a spy for a father."

"That's a low blow."

"Welcome to my world." Another question popped into Hannah's head and out of her mouth. "Do you miss Dad, Mom?"

"Sweetheart, I missed D.C. for years. In the beginning, I cried every night he didn't come home. I begged him to change careers, but he never did. It hurt me to see him come home so exhausted. I couldn't live that life anymore. That's when we got divorced."

"What about love? Did you love him?"

"Still do, but the difference is that now I don't feel weighed down by that love. It can be a burden to love someone."

"I already understand that much. Why didn't you stop loving Daddy? Wouldn't that have been easier?"

"Your father knew, because I told him, that he could walk back into my life any time he wished. My only condition was that he quit his job."

"That's why you never dated after the divorce?"

"Yes. I never stopped loving D.C."

Hannah thought of the nearly twenty years her mother had lived apart from her husband. A long lonely time. Would her love for Jake run that deep? "I can see where it was a burden to love Dad. Why didn't he quit his job?"

"There was always one more mission he had to finish.

He said he was going to get out, but he never did. I clung to the hope that he'd come back to me. To us. He's gone now, and for the first time, I'm free to make different choices."

"I'd say you were past due, Mom. I never thought I'd be saying this, but I'm glad you found someone to keep you company."

"Doug is a sweetie. I'm sure his problems are minor issues. He's such a nice man."

"I'm going to withhold judgment on that last part until I know the facts."

"Are you feeling better, dear?"

"Yeah. Thanks for listening, Mom."

"Anytime. Let me know how things turn out with Jake."

"I will. Love you, Mom."

"Love you, too."

Hannah ended the call and turned her phone off. She didn't need any additional distractions while she figured out how to deal with Jake. Being in love was a lot like having the flu. Her muscles ached, her skin felt clammy, and she was lightheaded.

Glancing up at the cloudless blue sky, she saw a hawk high in the sky, so high that he was a black dot in a sea of endless blue. It must feel wonderful to soar at such heights. To leave your problems behind and glide effortlessly on invisible air currents.

Hawks didn't have to worry about secretive men. Or their dangerous plans to catch murderers.

Hannah's gaze returned to the earth. More little blue flowers had cropped up since she was here last. A titmouse darted past carrying moss, then a bluebird with a beak full of grass flew by. They were nesting, just as she and Jake were nesting in the cottage. She inhaled the pulse of the tranquil meadow until it centered her.

Her mother had been right. She had to make her own choices. She couldn't expect Jake to change his plans because of her. He didn't think of their relationship as long term. He'd been very up front about that.

It was her feelings of love for Jake that messed everything up. She had expectations, expectations that went beyond the bounds of their current relationship.

All at once, the clearing went silent, the only sound that of the wind whispering mournfully through nearby tree boughs. Alarmed, Hannah turned this way and that, searching for the cause of the silence. The image of an angry bear came to mind, and it frightened her.

Moments later, Jake burst through the clearing. His limp was very pronounced. He'd followed her? "Why isn't your phone on?" he demanded.

His accusatory tone added to her growing unease. Hannah stood up as he approached. "I heard the signal of another call coming in, but I was talking to my mother in California so I didn't flip over to pick up the call. Has something happened?"

He roughly clasped her arm. "Come on. I'm putting you on a plane to California this afternoon."

Hannah's mouth gaped open at his absurd statement. "What? You want me to spend the rest of my vacation with my mother?"

"Yes."

She planted her feet squarely on the ground. Blindly following orders wasn't her style. "What brought this on?"

"You want to take things slowly, and you had planned to spend your vacation helping your mother. I think it's best to follow your original plan."

His words washed over her like the bracingly cold spring water flowing next to the bench. She understood what he'd said, but what he'd left unsaid ate at her confidence. Jake didn't want her around. He wasn't willing to work things out.

She'd taken the biggest chance of her life with him and he was calling it quits over their first argument? Clarification was needed. "What about you and me?"

His fingers tightened on her arm. He started limping towards the edge of the woods. "Once you get back from

California, we'll reevaluate."

Hannah tried to shake off his heavy handed grip and couldn't. She dug her heels into the soft meadow grass. "I deserve better than being hustled out of town like yesterday's news. Why are you acting like you can't get rid of me soon enough?"

Jake let go of her. He turned slowly and fixed her with unblinking eyes. "I thought it over and you were right. We need some time apart."

The flatness in his gaze chilled her through and through. There was no mistaking his intention. None at all. He didn't want her around. She was being dumped.

Nausea swept through her, pulling her stomach up into her throat. One hand moved protectively to her hollow middle. If she didn't hold on, the pain from his unexpected about face would rip her in two. Her head reeled from lack of oxygen.

That she could fix.

She inhaled shakily, once, twice. The lightheadedness didn't go away, but Montgomery pride demanded that she pull herself together. Sheer determination solidified the rubbery bones in her legs, stiffened her spine.

When Jake reached for her again, she shied away from him. "Don't touch me. I know the way."

She hurried through the forest, blinking tears back in her eyes. She wouldn't reward him with so much as a sniffle. Never would she let him know how much his rejection hurt her.

Her hopes and dreams shattered in one fell swoop. Her vision clouded over and the bright light went out of her future. She knew she was making lots of noise as she strode through the forest, but she couldn't hear a sound. It was as if she'd been struck deaf and dumb and all she had for solace were her tormented thoughts.

Why had she been so stupid to open herself to this kind of pain? We need some time apart, Jake had said. Those words echoed endlessly through the void inside of her. He didn't care that he'd broken her heart. He didn't care that last night had been the most wonderful experience of her life.

She loved him and he'd used her feelings to get her to sleep with him. Earlier today he'd pretended that their lovemaking meant something to him, but he didn't keep up the pretense for long. He'd used her.

She couldn't get out off this mountain soon enough.

Why didn't she leave her keys in her car? If she had, then she could leave without ever going back into that house. Dizziness threatened but she breathed her way through it.

Okay. She had to go in the house. Her purse was in her bedroom. She'd grab it and then leave.

"Hannah," Jake called.

Apparently he wanted to humiliate her further. She wouldn't stop and accommodate him. She'd accommodated him plenty last night.

If she didn't get out of here in the next minute she was going to be violently ill.

She ignored him and raced into the house, but it was as if she'd never even been there. Her belongings were gone. Vanished. Sucked into a giant black hole that had whirled through the house in her absence.

A glance at her watch showed she'd been gone for less than two hours. Two hours. What a difference those two hours had made.

In two hours she'd gone from thinking she cared too much for Jake to finding out he didn't care for her at all. He'd used her and now he was done with her. He'd already erased her presence in the house. Once she left, she'd be erased from his life.

She was so mad she could spit.

Hannah picked up an empty glass from the kitchen counter and hurled it across the room. The spine tingling sound of breaking glass appealed to her dangerous mood. She'd break every glass in the house. She'd show him what she thought of being cast aside.

Through the kitchen window, she saw Jake climb in his truck. Outrage roared in her veins as she threw another glass against the wall. How dare he leave now. She was leaving. Not him.

Anger fueled her rapid steps. She stopped in front of his truck. If he was leaving, he'd have to run her down because she wasn't moving until she got some answers. "Where's my stuff?"

Jake nodded towards the bed of his truck. "Get in."

She couldn't see his eyes through his close-fitting wrap around sunglasses. She couldn't read the granite-like set of his facial features either. It was as if he'd erected a concrete wall between them. Hannah rubbed the goose bumps on her arms. "Forget it. Where's my stuff?"

"Your stuff is in my truck. I'll drive you to the airport. I'll make sure your car gets to your mother's place while you're gone." He revved the motor. "Let's go."

He had her purse with her car keys. Her stuff was in his truck. She didn't have many choices here. Hannah threw her hands up in the air. Jake Sutherland was a lunatic. He was completely unreasonable. If he wanted to drive her to the airport, fine. Who was she to argue with a crazy man?

Biting her lip, she buckled herself into his passenger seat and shoved on her dark glasses. During the two hour ride to Baltimore, she maintained her frigid silence. Jake didn't utter a word. He didn't turn on the radio.

By the time they arrived at the Baltimore Washington International airport, Hannah wanted to scream her frustration, but what was the point? Her exhortations would fall on deaf ears. Jake had already decided he didn't want her around. There was no way he'd want to hear she had been stupid enough to fall in love with him.

Jake pulled up at the Departing Flights terminal and offered her a folded piece of paper.

She recoiled. "What's that?"

He dropped the paper in her lap. "Your electronic

ticket. Your flight is departing in three hours."

Hannah scanned the page. He'd bought her a first class ticket to Los Angeles. "I can't take this."

"You can and will use that ticket," he said, removing her from his truck. He deposited both of her bags at the skycap station.

Hannah's head felt as hollow as her middle. Why couldn't she think of a single clever comeback? Scarlet O'Hara had never let Rhett Butler get the best of her. Scarlet always gave as good as she got.

It hurt too much to think.

She stared blankly at the first class ticket. Was that what one night of hot sex with Jake was worth? A first class airline ticket to California?

She couldn't move. This was the last time she'd ever see the man she loved. Any minute now, he'd start up his truck and roar out of her life. It wasn't right that his leaving should upset her, but it did.

Jake fixed her with a penetrating stare. "Be careful."

"This way, miss," the skycap said.

Hannah didn't look back. Numbly, she followed the man with her bags. She didn't want to go to California, but here she was at the airport. Jake had all but shoehorned her into the plane. Obviously, Maryland wasn't big enough for the both of them.

At the check-in counter, Hannah went through the motions, producing her ID and answering the requisite questions. The clerk stapled the luggage tags on her ticket envelope and dismissed her with a cardboard smile.

Around her, people bustled to their destinations. In a daze, Hannah joined the queue, passed through security, then found an empty seat near her gate.

All she could think of was that she hadn't folded like a rag doll even though that's exactly what she wanted to do. She hadn't broken down in abject misery. Not one tear had rolled down her flaming cheeks.

Hannah fixed her gaze on the busy tarmac and wished she could rerun the last five hours of her life.

Only, time didn't rewind like a recording. Time marched relentlessly forward, dragging everyone along in its magnetic tractor beam.

How was it possible to be so mad at Jake that she could barely speak and yet at the same time, love him so desperately? That didn't make any sense. The only thing that seemed real was the deep ache in her heart. It wasn't going away anytime soon.

One fat tear, then another slipped over the rim of her eyelids. She didn't have to be strong any longer, but she was too much of a Montgomery to fall apart in front of strangers. She needed privacy for this meltdown.

Sloppy raindrop-sized tears rolled down her cheeks. Hannah quickly gathered her belongings and retreated to a dark restroom cubicle. She had the presence of mind to lock the stall door, and then she sank to her knees. The deluge of tears fogged her mind to all but a few facts.

Jake didn't care about her.

He didn't love her.

Raw emotion arced through her like powerful lightning strikes. Hannah hung onto her knees and let the storm of pain overtake her.

Why did love hurt so much?

Chapter 16

It took everything Jake had to drive away from the airport. He reminded himself that this was for the best. This way Hannah would be safe.

That's what he kept telling himself, but the deep seated aching in his bones didn't let up. He cared about Hannah, cared more than he was supposed to care. And because of his caring, he'd lost her respect.

He'd seen the abject pain in her eyes, and because of his all consuming need to keep her safe, he hadn't corrected her false impression. He'd allowed her to think the worst of him because that would keep her out of Ursula's reach.

Ursula's trip to the States wasn't incidental. She'd been methodically checking his old haunts and now she'd found his current location. How had she found him? His former addresses had been buried so deep in agency files that it would have taken an expert to find him, and even then it should have taken months to get this close.

Which meant the problem was bigger than one woman. If Ursula had insider information, a mole in the CIA was feeding her information. A chilling realization.

CIA field agents were self-sufficient loners like Jake, good at blending in, good at being invisible. If an agent was giving away secrets, how long had that been going on? A rogue agent could do a lot of damage. He could also provide up-front intel on current missions.

Is that what happened on D.C.'s last mission? If Ursula had inside help all along, then there was a chance Jake hadn't screwed up.

His heart stilled as that thought sunk in. If he hadn't

messed up, then D.C.'s murder had been coldly calculated. He'd never looked at it that way before, but it felt right. Continuing with that line of reasoning, the Middle East mission had been doomed from the beginning.

But why? Who wanted D.C. and Jake out of the way?

His thoughts came faster. D.C. had been the target all along. If they'd wanted Jake, he would be dead by now. But he'd gotten by with a warning shot to his leg.

Why?

What was this all about?

Murders were committed for power, money, or personal reasons. D.C. had turned down multiple promotions to come in out of the field, so he wasn't in a position of power in the agency. D.C. had contacts everywhere, though, and he'd known everyone. Had that knowledge ultimately gotten him killed?

When it came to personal reasons, Jake drew a blank. D.C. had lived a monk-like existence, preferring libraries and solitude when they had down time.

There had been money involved in D.C.'s death, but the beneficiaries were his ex-wife and his daughter, neither of which wanted him dead. That only left the work angle.

What if D.C. had found the mole? What would he have done with that information?

D.C. always, without fail, followed the money. If he had discovered an agent had money coming in from the wrong sources, what might he have done?

Summoned the authorities?

Tried to make things right?

Thrown in with the double agent? Not D.C. He'd never betray his country. D.C. would've corrected the problem. Just as Jake was doing.

So, how did D.C. come by this fatal information?

He and Jake had been a team. D.C. had the brains and intuition, Jake the computer expertise and the leg work.

Chances were good that Jake had turned up some

info which had gotten D.C.'s attention. What? Jake mentally reviewed information requests D.C. had given him over the few months prior to his death. Nothing even mildly suspicious came to mind.

Jake banged his palm against the steering wheel. There had to be something. He'd sit down with his computer as soon as he got home and retrace their steps. Something was there. It had to be.

When he found it, he would take swift action. D.C.'s death would be avenged. And he'd get Hannah back.

A cold fire burned in his belly. Every nerve ending in his body vibrated with outrage. The enemy had made a deadly mistake. By coming onto Jake's turf, they would play by Jake's rules.

Advantage—Jake.

****

Her eyes had run dry by the time she heard the rapid patter of little feet run into the bathroom. The footsteps got progressively louder, then quieter. Hannah wished for an ounce of that youngster's energy. Crying was hard work, and she was totally spent.

She tore some tissue off the roll and blotted her cheeks dry. She blew her stuffy nose. What was she going to do? She didn't feel like getting on an airplane.

Her insides were hollowed out, as if a powerful bomb had exploded in her middle and all that remained was gray ash and smoldering wreckage. Why were there so many happy songs about falling in love? This was the unhappiest she had ever felt.

Her lower lip trembled, and she gutted through it. She was not going to dissolve in another puddle of tears. She could get through this.

Food. She hadn't eaten in almost twenty four hours. She had over two hours before she was supposed to board her plane. Food would be good.

She settled for chocolate yogurt and a solitary seat at an unused gate. In no time, the yogurt was gone. She hadn't really expected to finish it, hadn't known if she could keep anything down. It was down all right, and she felt less empty.

The loudspeaker announced a final boarding call at the gate directly across from where she sat. Hannah discarded her yogurt container, returning to her molded plastic seat. Clumps of people hurried past her dragging small wheeled suitcases. A golf cart beeped slowly through the crowd, scattering folks as it went.

"Hannah?"

She looked up as her name was called. A familiar balding researcher in jeans, sneakers, white dress shirt and blazer waved hello to her. Hannah rose, bracing herself for more unpleasantness. "Dr. Esteban. What are you doing here?"

He jerked his thumb towards a distant gate. "Catching a plane."

She struggled to remember the conference rotation schedule. He'd already done the conference circuit with last year's research, and this year's project was stalled until the findings of her audit were released. "Where you headed?"

"Atlanta. I called Dr. Reed and asked for a tour of their labs. Turned out, he was flattered by my request and invited me down."

He was joining forces with his nemesis? Go figure. "Have a great trip."

She turned to gather her things, but he touched her arm. She glanced down at his offending hand. "You don't want to do that."

He blanched and withdrew his hand immediately. "Don't tell your boyfriend. I want to apologize for my outburst the other day. I've been under a lot of pressure lately, and I was behaving badly. I meant no disrespect. I'm sorry if I frightened you."

Her boyfriend. If only that were true. "No problem. I really should be moving along."

She strode purposefully away, merging into the foot traffic of another concourse. At a pain in her jaw, she realized she was clenching her teeth. She rubbed her aching temples. Time. She needed time to think. If she could decipher the day's events, then she'd know what to do.

Thinking wasn't easy. A big roadblock stood between her and a clear head. Her broken heart.

How could she have been so wrong about Jake?

How could she have misjudged the stark hunger in his eyes?

She wasn't completely lacking in intuition or feminine sensibilities. When a man looked at a woman with such undisguised longing, it was more than sex. It had to be.

Her cell phone rang.

She stepped out of the throng into a gate area. Hope spiraled madly through her as she clawed through the contents of her purse to find her phone. "Hello." She winced at the tentative sound of her voice. *Let it be him. Let it be him and let this afternoon have been a very bad joke.*

"Hannah?" her mother asked.

Her heart sunk at her mother's concerned tone.

It wasn't Jake. What was she thinking? He'd dumped her. Men didn't call the women they'd just dumped. She wouldn't hear from Jake again.

A fresh wave of desolation crashed through her. Hannah clung to the phone. She was alone and hurting, and her mother had called.

Hannah sighed out her disappointment. "Hey, Mom."

"Where are you? What's that noise?"

"I'm at the airport."

"You are? I don't understand. You're taking a trip?"

Hannah closed her eyes to the hustle and bustle. "It seems that way."

"Shouldn't you have decided before you arrived at the airport?"

"It's a long story, Mom. Is everything okay out there?"

"No, everything is not all right."

Hannah's eyes opened wide in alarm. Her equilibrium settled down, and she didn't feel quite so disoriented. Her mother needed her. "What happened?"

"Did you ever have a day when the scales fell from your eyes? When you looked at what you were doing and flat out asked why?"

"Yeah." Like today, for instance.

"I've been thinking about the things you said. About why I want to make a yoga video. I examined my motives, and there's no altruism there. My yoga video won't be so different from the ones that are already commercially available."

"How do you know that until you make it?"

"The truth is, I just wanted to be the star for a change. I came out here with that intention and everyone has bent over backward to be nice to me. That's pretty heady stuff."

"You don't have to make a movie to be a star, Mom. You've always been a star in my book."

"Thank you, dear, for saying that. I've never had that ready self-assurance that you and your father share. Once I meditated on the big picture, I realized making this video wouldn't bring me peace and harmony."

"Why not? Three weeks ago, making this video was what you wanted more than anything in the world. More than air, as I recall."

"You would bring that up. I'm not saying I won't make the video, I just don't want to do it right now."

"So, you're coming home?"

"Soon."

"Oh?"

"I realize truth is very cut and dried for you, but I've always thought truth was relative. I'm really sorry I didn't tell you the truth about your father earlier. I feel bad that our efforts to keep you safe caused you such pain."

Was it only a few hours ago that she'd been irate at

her parents' deception? Funny how events changed one's perspective.

"I'm sorry I came down on you so hard," Hannah said. "You were doing what you thought was right at the time. That's all anyone can do."

"There's more."

"More?"

"Your father would have my head for telling you, but I can't keep it to myself. Do you remember the troll under the bed when you were a kid?"

Hannah drew in a quick breath. "I've never forgotten it."

"Your father either. There really was someone under your bed that night. A bad person from your father's spy life. That's why D.C. left us, Hannah. He couldn't put us at risk. He loved us too much."

Hannah's blood ran cold with shock. She couldn't take any more bad news today. "Dear God."

"I begged D.C. to quit that job, but he was furious his home had been invaded. He had to even the score."

"Did he ever catch the troll?"

"No. That's why he never walked away from the job. Until he caught your troll, he wouldn't risk our safety again."

Hannah reeled from the news. Some bad person had been creepy-crawling through her childhood bedroom? No wonder her father was incensed. "Why didn't anyone tell me this? Do you know how scared of the dark I've been ever since that night?"

"Your father wouldn't let me tell. He said fear was healthy. It would keep you alive knowing there were things that go bump in the night. I agreed with him, dear."

"It's a wonder I didn't spend my entire adolescence in a shrink's chair."

"You're a strong woman, Hannah. Both of us are proud of you."

"God, Mom. How can you tell me these things over

the phone?"

"Because I'm not strong like you. I couldn't bear to see the hurt in your eyes when I told you. And I figured I had to tell you before I came home. Especially since your father had already told you the biggest secret of all."

"I hate secrets," Hannah said.

Libby held her silence for a long moment. "You were right about Doug."

"How so?"

"He kept secrets from me."

Hannah leaned into the phone. "What kind of secrets?"

"Nothing monumental like your father's secrets, but secrets nonetheless. His brother's car accident was because of an epileptic seizure. Doug has epilepsy too, only his is controlled with medication. He doesn't drive because he doesn't want to ever take a chance of hurting himself or anyone else. Isn't that the noblest thing you've ever heard in your life?"

Epilepsy should have shown up during her investigation of Doug's background. Was it possible that some records were sealed from the CIA's prying eyes? If not, she should fire her investigator.

Too late. He'd already 'fired' her. "And you believe his story?"

"It's no story. It's true. And of course I believe him."

"Uh huh." Her mother had loved the patron saint of lies. Of course she'd believe a minor league liar like Doug.

"I hope this doesn't come as a surprise. Hannah, I've invited Doug to come home with me."

A spurt of alarm shot through Hannah. "For a visit or for real?"

"We're playing that part by ear."

It sounded like Doug would stay in the picture for a while. Her Mom wasn't the type to give up easily on a man, and Doug wasn't the type to walk away from a rich widow. It aggravated Hannah that her mother couldn't see that. "How do you do it, Mom? How do you believe in someone even when you know they've lied to you?"

"Haven't you heard a word I've said? Dealing with men means dealing with shades of the truth. Doug didn't lie to me about anything important. He just withheld some personal information. We haven't been dating very long, if you recall."

"You're not afraid that he's using you?"

Hannah's mother laughed softly. "Honey, that's how it is. All of us use each other. We call it different things, but we demand the most from the people closest to us."

If that was true, then she'd used Jake for sex just as he'd used her. But it didn't feel true. It felt prickly and wrong. There had to be more to her and Jake than the physical act of mating.

"Tell me again," Hannah's mother asked, "Why are you at the airport? I thought you were opening up to this Jake of yours."

"He's not my anything."

"Do tell."

"It's humiliating."

"Don't keep me in suspense. What did he do? Four hours ago all systems were go."

"He hiked out in the woods where I was meditating and marched me back to the cottage. Then he drove me to the Baltimore airport and dumped me out. With a first class ticket to LA."

"No point in coming out here when I'll be coming home in a few days."

"I get that. Believe me, I get that. What I don't get is why he got rid of me. It's making me crazy trying to figure him out."

"I wish I was there. I'd put him through his paces. Want me to call him at your father's house?"

"No. Don't do that." Hannah cast around for another, less painful, subject. "When are you heading home?"

"Two more days. Doug has projects to wrap up, and I've got places I want to visit."

Loose ends again. Is that all she'd been to Jake? A

loose end? "That's great. Do you want me to meet your plane?"

"Is that convenient for you? What about your trip?"

"I've changed my mind. I'm not going anywhere."

Tears blurred Hannah's vision. She blinked rapidly. She wasn't going to cry again. She was a Montgomery. She had starch in her spine.

"Your Jake should be strung up by his heels for hurting you. Doesn't he realize the stress you've had to deal with recently? He shouldn't be putting any additional pressure on you in this precarious stage of your relationship."

"Mom, he dumped me. We don't have a relationship."

"He'll come around. He knows a good thing when he sees it."

Hannah didn't share her mother's optimism. "Do you want me to meet your plane or not?"

"Definitely. Doug and I need a ride home from the airport."

"Call me when you have your flight information. Bye."

Now what? She definitely wasn't boarding the plane to LA. Jake was at the cottage. Her choices were to go to her mother's house, crash at a friend's place, or get a hotel room.

She didn't want to face the questions a friend might have. Or the additional tears sympathy might bring. No point in crying anymore about what wasn't going to be. But she didn't want to be alone right now. Indecision paralyzed her.

Another clump of fast moving people thronged the passageway. How nice it must be to know your destination, Hannah thought. She had to make a decision. She couldn't stay at the airport indefinitely.

What to do?

In the past, she'd been guided by her inner voice. She'd assessed people by their actions, not on their words or appearance. That's what was bugging her now. Jake's actions didn't match up with what her instincts said.

She'd never been in love before. Emotional instability could have obscured her sound judgment. Had she been so blinded by lust that she'd misread Jake's behavior?

He'd worked with her father for years, so he had personal integrity. Her father had never tolerated idiots, so Jake had above average intelligence. Jake had spoken of her father's death with respect and regret. He hadn't seemed cold-hearted.

Except where she was concerned. Wait. That wasn't entirely true.

Jake hadn't been cold last night. He'd set them both on fire. There had been nothing cold about his lovemaking.

Nor had Jake been cold this morning as he drank his coffee. The heat in his gaze had her thinking of jumping him in the kitchen. In fact, were she to make an educated guess, she would have said it was impossible for Jake to be cold where she was concerned.

He definitely hadn't been cold during the reading of her father's letter. He'd taken her hand and reassured her with his warmth and touch.

He'd been reserved, cautious even, as if he were gauging her reaction to the information. Even when she said she wanted time to analyze the letter's contents, he hadn't been cold. And he'd made a point out of saying that her father's letter changed nothing.

But he'd definitely been cold when he'd limped out to the meadow to get her.

Hmm.

Hannah's fingers tapped the armrest of her molded plastic seat. Something must have happened between when she left him for her walk this morning and when he came to get her.

What could it have been?

What would have made him gather up her belongings, put them in his truck, and then walk all the way down to the meadow to fetch her?

For him to willingly put so much strain on his injured leg, there must have been an inciting event. What would have driven him to push his physical limits? She was intelligent. She could puzzle this out.

Crowds of people filled the center aisle of the airport as another plane unloaded. The airwaves buzzed with excited conversations, the hallways thronged with folks hurrying to make their connecting flights. Rush, rush, rush.

That's all folks did anymore.

Everyone but Jake.

Hmm.

This was good. Her head was clearer now. If it was uncharacteristic for him to rush, then whatever had happened to make him rush around wasn't a good thing. Which left a whole realm of bad things.

Dangerous things.

Hannah shivered.

Was danger close at hand?

The thought stole her breath away.

Jake's injured leg limited his mobility and muddied his brain with pain. No matter how macho he acted, Jake wasn't in any condition to defend himself. Dangerous people carried guns. Dangerous people killed for a living.

Hannah shoved her fingers through her hair. Oh, Lord. It all made sense now. Jake had hustled her out of there because danger was afoot. Just like her father had hustled out of her life after the troll incident.

Jake's life was in danger.

Air whooshed out of her lungs. The fluorescent lights overhead seemed garish, the space around her too crowded with loud people. Her skin burned with heat and dampened with perspiration.

Hannah sucked in a great gulp of air and vaulted to her feet. The time for sitting still was past. She had to take action. Now.

Hannah plunged into the throng of humanity hurrying through the airport. Even if her revised assessment was false and he sent her away again, she wouldn't be any worse off than she was right now. All she stood to lose was another half day of her precious vacation and the rest of her tattered pride.

A small price to pay for the man she loved.

On the other hand, if she was right, she would protect him. Thanks to her father, she knew basic self defense. She'd never handled a gun before, but if it was shoot or be shot, she could fire a gun.

Especially if Jake's life was on the line.

****

A hundred thirty dollars a day for this rental car. Hannah smoothed over the leather seating of the deluxe interior. The airport rental agency had this Mercury Grand Marquis or a mini-van left. She'd been leaning toward the mini-van, but the V-8 under the sedan's hood cinched the deal.

If there was trouble, she wanted lots of power. They'd nagged her to take the insurance, and she'd signed everything to get out of there as soon as possible. Her intuition about Jake better be right, or this was going to be the most expensive, embarrassing disaster ever.

It had been a major deal to cancel her airline ticket. Then they'd had to pull her luggage, and they acted all huffy about it. She thought about telling the airline officials she wasn't a terrorist, but she kept her mouth shut, keenly aware of the minutes ticking away.

She drove fast through the dark roads, catching the Baltimore beltway to I-70, and then turning up U.S. 15 to go to the cottage. On one straightaway the traffic thinned, and Hannah noticed a car behind her. She told herself it was nerves, that many cars traveled these through roads. But just in case, she purposefully slowed down fifteen miles per hour.

The car held its position the same relative distance back. Odd but not conclusive. She exited the highway in Frederick, catching two stop lights before she returned to the highway. As she waited at the last light, a dark sedan eased off the exit ramp and queued up behind her in the turn lane four cars back.

Hannah bit her lip. She wasn't making something out of nothing. That car was following her. She called the cops, checking her rearview mirror every few seconds. It took an eternity for the light to turn green. She floored it, scooting back on the highway.

"I'm being followed," she told the dispatcher, giving her heading and car description. "A similar car tried to run me off the road less than a week ago. Can a State Patrolman intercept us in Thurmont?"

"We have no record of an earlier incident."

"I didn't report it at the time, but I'm reporting it now." She hastily gave the details. "Look, I need to concentrate on driving. I'll leave my phone on, but I'm putting it down on the console."

Hannah drove faster and ignored the squawking coming from her phone. The sedan accelerated to match her pace.

She chewed her lip.

God, this was scary. The person in that sedan might be her troll from all those years ago. The man who'd given her a lifetime of nightmares. Her stomach clenched.

Only one good thing about this situation. If the sedan was after her, at least Jake was safe.

Chapter 17

Jake stared at his computer screen. The house was too quiet. Not that this place had ever been noisy, but without Hannah the place had a tomb-like quality.

Longing for her sweet smile knifed through him. His arms ached to hold her close, to bask in her sunny warmth and gentle compassion. Echoes of her subtle floral fragrance haunted him. As soon as he returned, he'd gone straight to her room and buried his face in her fluffy pillow.

She made him weak.

She was his Achilles heel.

Which was why he'd sent her away. So that he could deal with Ursula. He needed all of his wits against such a deadly opponent.

Hannah was safe. He had to remember that. He had to focus on Ursula. If his concentration was off, she'd kill him outright.

Ursula didn't play fair. She had outmaneuvered him before. That wasn't going to happen this time. She had to have had inside information, which meant there was an information trail.

He scrolled through his database of accumulated information on Ursula. Then he checked the dates and locations of places Ursula had been against agency missions he'd either been on or had known about. He added in data he'd gleaned from prior conversations with other CIA agents.

The computer massaged the data.

As the minutes passed, no exact matches were found. Jake dug deeper, cross referencing credit card purchases.

The information had to be here, it was a matter of asking the right question to find the answer he wanted. At last, a pattern emerged. One person had parallel expenditures to Ursula's in the same cities on the same days. One particular CIA agent had shadowed Ursula's location.

Graham Grafton.

Grafton. Jake's mouth puckered with distaste. Grafton was the double agent?

Like D.C., Grafton was a senior operative. Grafton's success rate had been good, but D.C.'s had been near legendary. It was well known within the agency that D.C. was the agency's 'go to' man. Had Grafton resented D.C.'s success?

Jake leaned back in his chair, massaging his aching thigh. How sure was he of this data? If he was wrong about Grafton, his life wouldn't be worth living. But if he was right, Grafton was rotten to the core. Which meant Grafton would continue to sell other agents short.

It was a risk Jake was willing to take. He uploaded the facts to a secure email server and arranged for them to be remotely mailed in twenty-four hours. Others would know what had to be done.

Grafton had had means, motive, and opportunity to eliminate D.C. Grafton knew how D.C. operated, what places he liked for meetings. Grafton also knew about Jake's tendency to find female companionship.

Hence Ursula's remarkable friendliness towards Jake. How had Grafton persuaded Ursula to help him? What was Ursula's weak point? She had to have one.

Darkness fell unnoticed as Jake scoured through databases, looking for Ursula's family members, for large debts, for anything out of the ordinary. Once he knew what Grafton knew, he'd know what he was up against. Knowledge was power.

Jake rubbed his stiff neck, ignoring the rumble in his empty stomach. Twice now he'd come across references to a jailed terrorist named Pieter Andress. There was something familiar about the man's eye shape and jaw line. According to the file, Andress was six years older than Ursula.

A brother? Jake's pulse quickened. This could be the link he was looking for. If Ursula had a brother in federal prison, Grafton could dangle his accelerated release as leverage.

He lounged back in his chair, remembering those last few days in the Middle East. D.C. had been doing recon of a terrorist sleeper cell. Old business, D.C. had said. D.C. must have been closing in on Ursula and Grafton.

Meanwhile, Ursula had done a number on Jake. He'd accepted her rules of separation during the course of their steamy affair. They had suited him perfectly. She wanted no strings and no involvement during the daylight hours.

The sex had been good, so good that he'd been rethinking her no strings policy. He'd wanted her to meet D.C. On the night before D.C. was killed, Jake had pressed her to keep a lunch commitment with him and D.C. the next day.

He shivered. Had he unwittingly hastened D.C.'s demise?

"Interesting reading?" a familiar sultry voice asked.

Jake whirled in his seat, his computer screen illuminating his dark bedroom. He took in the tall, darkly clad blonde female standing just outside the door in a quick glance. "I've been expecting you," he said.

Ursula waggled the gun she had pointed at Jake's chest towards the computer screen and back. "Keep your hands where I can see them, lover boy."

His gun.

Where the hell was his gun?

His brain kicked along at warp speed, processing and analyzing his situation. The last time he'd seen his gun was when he'd stuffed it under the driver's seat before he drove Hannah to the airport. If he'd been thinking clearly, he should have retrieved it when he got home.

Only he hadn't been thinking clearly.

"The thing I don't understand is why you came after

me." Jake assessed the potential weapons close at hand. He had a knife under his pillow, a second gun in his duffle bag. Neither of them was within reach. "If you wanted me dead, why not kill me at the same time as my partner? Why wait all this time?"

Ursula shook her head rapidly, her eyes darting efficiently about the small room. "I don't owe you anything, Jake. I'm calling the shots here. You're in no position to bargain. I'm in control of the game this go around."

"What game? I'm retired from my former occupation."

"Then how did you know I was coming after you?"

"The sunglasses. Clever of you to leave your calling card, Ursula. Or should I call you Joan?"

"I wondered if you would put it together."

"I suppose you took note of the security here when you pretended to be a renter for this property."

Ursula strode briskly across the room and trailed the cold metal gun barrel down Jake's face from temple to jaw. Her overpowering perfume turned his stomach. "Right again," she said.

The muscles in Jake's jaw contracted. Death had stared him in the face before. That wasn't new. He wasn't afraid of dying. What was new was his fierce desire to live.

****

The Maryland State Patrol didn't meet her at the ramp. There was no sign of anyone official. No sirens blaring. No lights flashing. She was on her own.

Time took on a surreal quality. She reached down and grabbed the phone. "Hello? You still there?"

The line was dead.

She was really on her own.

The sedan pulled off the ramp and accelerated briskly behind her. In moments, the sedan closed on her, ramming her in the trunk.

Hannah jolted forward, her head smacking into the head rest. This guy meant business. She coasted a moment to gain control of her skid, reviewing her options at lighting speed.

Her father had taught her to drive in all sorts of bad weather. She could navigate a dirt road, a snow drift, an ice storm. She could turn on a dime, even at high speeds. But she'd had no training on being rammed from behind.

The invasion of her space made her mad. This faceless enemy was a bully. Bullies succeeded because people were scared of them. Though she was scared, she wouldn't bolt. She would take this bully on.

She knew this road intimately. A cluster of mailboxes was coming up on the right, an intersection on the left. She'd played enough pool to know about banked angles. Her foot hovered above the brake pedal. In morbid fascination, she watched the sedan close on her again.

Timing was everything. She stomped the brake, turned the wheel slightly to the left and braced herself deep in the seat. The sedan smacked into her and she went left. Her rear wheels lost traction. Just as she'd done in those driving lessons of long ago, she kept her head and rode out the skid.

The dark sedan wasn't so lucky. It careened out of control, clipping the mailboxes, flipping upside down, and coming to rest in the ditch.

The screeching sound of tires and broken glass rang in Hannah's ears. With trembling hands she dialed the emergency number. "There's been an accident on Whiteside Road." She gave the particulars then hung up.

She opened her car door and slid stealthily into the night, creeping toward the overturned sedan. Her heart raced as she approached. The driver's window was busted out. She peered inside. The driver was missing.

The hair on her arms stood on end. Her blood chilled. She glanced around. Where was the driver? She found him twenty yards away, impaled on a mailbox post. Her breath hitched in recognition. The driver was Graham Grafton!

He was supposed to be her friend. Why was he trying

to kill her?

Was he dead? She didn't want to touch him. She used a metal mail box to poke him.

His eyes flickered open. He coughed out a gurgle of blood. "Damn you, Montgomery spawn."

Hannah stepped back in the shadows. "Why did you try to kill me?"

"You know too much."

"I don't know anything. Did you kill my father?"

"D.C. knew too much. He was coming after me."

Hannah took a wild guess. "Was it you in my bedroom all those years ago?"

Grafton coughed again. As he rasped in a breath, his arm twitched. "Yeah. Not my best work. Thought D.C. was on to our smuggling operation."

"What did that have to do with me?"

"Nothing. Except D.C. bought the doll meant for me. Naturally I had to get it back."

Hannah was conscious of the continued movement of his arm. Did he have a gun? She shifted position in the shadows as she spoke. "The doll?"

"We transferred technology around the globe in toys. That was the good old days before heightened airport security. Nowadays the transfers are electronic. I'd have gotten away with it if it wasn't for D.C. He never let up."

"He couldn't. Not until he found the person who'd been in my room."

"He had a blind spot when it came to you. No doubt about that." Grafton managed an evil smile. "But I took you away from him. I got to do things with you and your mother while he cowered. I took his strength."

"Why couldn't you just leave us alone?"

"Because you belonged to D.C. And now you belong to Jake, but his end is near."

Her chilly blood iced over. "What?"

"I sent a trained assassin to kill him."

Hannah screamed. "No." She ran to her rental car. She had to save Jake.

Behind her a shot rang out. In the distance flashing lights sparkled and sirens wailed. The police would take care of whatever was left of Grafton. She had to save the man she loved.

****

Ursula straddled Jake's lap, pushing her breasts against him as she planted the cold gun barrel on the center of his forehead. This intimate position was one they'd employed in the past, but it did nothing for Jake now. He wouldn't make love to Ursula if he was the last man alive in the universe.

Disgust rolled through him. "Get off me."

"Kiss me, Jake, for old time's sake."

"I don't kiss traitors. Did you think I wouldn't find out about you and Grafton?"

Ursula visibly startled. The gun barrel jerked to the right. "You are good. Graffie said D.C. was the brains of your operation, but I wondered why he overlooked your many talents."

Jake did not feel comforted by her backhanded compliment. If anything, her presence here showed that he was a threat. "Why did you come after me?" he repeated.

"Because you were coming after me."

"This is a preemptive strike?"

"You men and your spy talk." Ursula sighed, the sharp bones of her hips digging into his thighs. "I'm here because you've become a problem. Why didn't you let it go? I gave you a chance at life. Instead you chose to keep coming after me."

His injured leg spasmed under the unrelenting pressure of her weight. "You killed my partner. I couldn't forget that."

"Your partner knew things he shouldn't. He had to die."

"Things like Grafton taking money from your side? Is that what you're talking about? Or did D.C. know about the brother you're trying to ransom from federal prison?"

Ursula paled. "How do you know those things?"

"I'm not stupid."

Just then the driveway alarm sounded. Someone was driving up the mountain? Talk about bad timing.

"What's that?" Ursula asked.

No point in lying about the alarm. The vehicle would be here soon. "Driveway alarm. Someone's coming."

There was only one person he didn't want to see coming through that door. As long as it wasn't Hannah, he could deal with this.

He wasn't a man given to prayer, but he sent up a silent plea anyway. *Don't let it be Hannah. Please God, let her be on that plane.*

"Okay, lover boy. We're going to play this my way," Ursula said, drawing the gun down to his pounding heart and continuing down to his crotch. "If this person is stupid enough to come inside and find us, we are lovers. That shouldn't be too much of a stretch, should it, lover boy?"

"You used me." Jake's voice shook with cold fury.

Ursula laughed. The harsh rat-a-tat-tat reminded him of the woodpecker that pounded on the side of the cottage. It wasn't the soft tinkling laughter she'd affected in the Middle East.

"Get over it," Ursula said. "I should have killed you when I shot your partner. Now I have to correct my error. You've cost me a lot of time and money and that pisses me off."

Unrelenting pain shot up his leg. Even if he could overpower Ursula in hand to hand combat, his chances of sustaining another wound were high. Plus the person coming up the drive would be a secondary target for Ursula. His best bet was to sit still until he had a better chance at taking the gun without being shot. Ursula wouldn't hesitate to kill. She had done it before, but she'd also spared him before. Did she have residual feelings for him?

Outside he heard a car door close. One door. One

person. Not Hannah. Please, not Hannah.

He needed a distraction. He tried to play on Ursula's emotions. "Didn't what happened between us have any meaning to you?"

"Ah, Jake. Just because I slept with you doesn't mean you are the love of my life. Our time together was the greatest acting performance of my life. Now it's your turn. Get rid of this person, or you'll have their blood on your hands."

Jake mentally reeled. She'd been acting the whole time they slept together? He didn't believe it. No one was that good of an actress. He struggled to regain his equilibrium.

Ursula jammed the gun into his testicles and whispered thickly in his ear. "Put your arms around me. Make it good or you're both dead."

Jake lowered his arms and settled them around Ursula's narrow hips. Hips that he'd once caressed in wonder, not knowing the evil that lurked within. It was all he could do not to physically recoil at touching her.

"Jake?" Hannah said, flipping on lights as she walked through the dark house.

All the blood drained from Jake's head. His lungs locked in mid-breath. He screamed a silent warning. *No. Go away.* But the tension in Hannah's voice ate at his frozen heart. She was hurting. He'd done that to her.

He'd brought so much pain to her door. She didn't deserve any of it. And now this. She would see him with another woman in his lap. His frustration imploded.

His dreams of making things right with Hannah vanished in the blink of an eye. Infidelity was not something a woman ever forgot or forgave. He had no future, but he would make sure Hannah had one. This would be the most important role of his life.

"Answer her," Ursula said. "Make her leave. Or, I'll kill her."

In his former career, Jake had pretended to be many things, but he had never pretended in his private life.

There had been no need. His relationships had been superficial. Now his warm blood ran as cold as an Artic glacier.

Hannah was in danger. He had to protect her, and to do that he had to break her heart. Loss shot through him at the thought of never seeing her again. There was no other way. Jake steeled himself to the task.

This was her fault, of course. She should be winging her way to the safety of California. Instead she was walking into a deadly trap.

She wasn't good at taking direction. He used his anger at that to harden his features. He could not allow either Hannah or Ursula to guess his true feelings for Hannah or his sacrifice would be in vain.

When Hannah walked in his bedroom, he glared at her. "What a surprise."

Hannah's mouth dropped open. "Who's she?"

"His lover," Ursula said, rubbing up against him and purring. Her gun jabbed painfully into him as she ground her bony hips against him.

Helpless rage tore through him. He stared pointedly at the Zeiss binoculars slung over Hannah's chest, afraid that if he met her razor sharp gaze his composure would slip. "Aren't you supposed to be on a plane?" he asked.

Hannah's unspoken questions charged the air, seared his skin. "Plans change."

The hair on the back of his neck stood on end. He had to get Hannah out of here. Ursula had a short fuse. "I don't want you here," he said.

"Tough. This is my house."

His gaze rose and locked on hers. From deep within, he summoned words he didn't want to say. Her safety depended on him delivering the right message. "There's nothing here for you, Hannah."

Hannah heard the words Jake said, but the banked heat in his eyes revealed his lie. Fury filled her veins, flooding every pore with outrage. He knew she hated lying. Hated it with a passion. It made no sense that he was lying now.

She detested liars.

Hot tears burned her cheeks. She'd come back here to save him from an assassin, but the joke had been on her. Grafton had lied to her too. There was no assassin, just another woman climbing on the man she loved.

No wonder Jake had hustled her out of town. He wasn't in danger. He was horny. This woman must have called while Hannah was walking in the woods this morning. He wanted this sleek blonde in his bed, not dumpy old Hannah.

Only twelve hours ago she had been in Jake's bed. She had given him everything she had to give: her virginity, her heart, her soul. Her love. He'd taken them greedily without making any promises.

What a fool she'd been. He'd played her from start to finish. He must have thought of Hannah as amateur hour. A diversion to occupy him until this hot blonde number was available.

White hot pain sliced through her heart leaving her fragmented and empty. She'd been so naïve. Jake didn't need her. He had this blonde to see to his needs.

Her brain whirred in useless circles as she stared at the woman sitting on Jake's lap. Details filtered through her anger. His hands weren't touching the woman. His arms crossed the legs of the blonde straddling his lap, but his hands dangled towards the ground.

In her experience, Jake wasn't one to keep his hands to himself. Her intuition told her this was an important detail. Something wasn't right here.

Her self-confidence came roaring back. If Jake wasn't having a tryst with this blonde bimbo, then what was going on? Though it was hard to believe the woman was a threat, Hannah wanted to believe the blonde was dangerous.

She shivered. If the blonde was a threat, what could Hannah do? How could she protect Jake?

She had no weapon, only her father's binoculars,

which were still slung over her shoulder bandolier fashion. Zeiss field glasses were heavy. Her father had taught her to use whatever was at hand for defense. She'd surprised Grafton earlier by taking the offensive, and she'd surprise this woman. The blonde woman wouldn't expect Hannah to attack.

As inconspicuously as possible, she moved her left hand to rest on the binoculars so that she could unlatch the leather strap. She prayed she wasn't about to make an even bigger fool of herself. Then again, what did she have to lose?

She wanted Jake, and she believed Jake wanted her, despite his hurtful words to the contrary. It was time to peel away the lies and find the truth. Montgomery's did not walk away from a challenge. They dug in and conquered.

Marshalling her courage, Hannah crossed the room and leaned down into Jake's face. When she had his attention, she asked heatedly, "Why is this woman pretending to be your girlfriend?"

Alarm flared Jake's eyes. He recovered quickly, but that burst of truth filled Hannah with soaring hope. She was on the right track here.

"Hannah -" Jake said.

"Forget it, Jake." The blonde uncoiled from his lap and pointed a gun at Hannah. "She's not as stupid as she looks. Where did you find her, Jake? Oh yeah, I remember, she's your dead partner's daughter."

Hannah tried to back up but her legs didn't respond. This was the second time she'd seen a gun in this house, and it was two times too many for her peace of mind.

Jake surged to his feet, but the woman anticipated his move and jammed her gun up against the side of Hannah's head. "Move and I'll kill her," the woman said.

The hard metal barrel of the gun pressing into her temple was warm. Odd. She'd always thought guns were cold. Would she hear the gun roar? Or would she suddenly see her brains splatter on the wall? How quick did death come once a bullet plowed through your skull?

Hannah's stomach heaved. Dizzying nausea whirled through her like a funnel cloud. A cloying acrid scent emanated from the nameless blonde. Hannah gripped her binoculars, her fragile tether to reality. If she so much as moved a finger wrong, she would be at the mercy of the swirling winds of fate.

Oh God.

There was a gun to her head.

She couldn't breathe.

She was going to die.

She'd forgotten to tell her mother that she loved her.

And Jake.

She loved him.

Some help she was.

The blonde had been holding the gun on Jake when Hannah appeared. This was no lover's tryst. This was a very deadly situation. This woman was the assassin.

Were they both going to die?

Chapter 18

Hannah fixed her gaze on Jake. If she was going out, his precious face would be the last image she saw.

Ice radiated from Jake's taut face. "Leave her out of this, Ursula," he warned.

"Not a chance," Ursula said. "Her being here makes things much easier for me. Your deaths will look like a murder/suicide. Two star-crossed lovers going out in a blaze of glory."

"Hannah has nothing to do with this."

Ursula's harsh grating laugh startled Hannah. "Not your call, hotshot. She can identify me."

Jake's face blanched. Hannah realized her legs were trembling. Sweat dripped down the channel of her spine. There was something she should be remembering, something she should be doing.

"You're too late," Jake said. "I've already forwarded proof about your working both sides of the street to the authorities. Your intelligence career is finished."

"I don't believe you."

Jake shrugged and leaned over his chair. "See for yourself." He tapped a couple of keys on the keyboard, and a new window opened on his computer screen.

Hannah couldn't believe Jake could calmly type on his computer. Her fingers were so thick and clumsy with fear that she couldn't even do something as simple as unhook her binoculars.

Her brain whirred. Self defense. She wasn't helpless. She had a weapon. Her binoculars.

That's what she'd been trying to remember. Her binoculars. If she could forget about the gun pointed at her head, she could finish unhooking her binoculars. Easier said than done.

Ursula shoved Hannah closer to the computer screen with the barrel of her gun. "I don't trust you. Get away from that computer, Jake."

Hannah stumbled forward, reaching out to steady herself on the corner of the desk. In that topsy-turvy moment, the buckle on the strap of her binoculars released. This was what she'd been waiting for, a window of opportunity.

If she didn't act now, this crazy woman would kill them. Hannah wasn't ready to die. She flung her binoculars upward at the woman's wrist, hard. At the same time, she dropped to the floor, her hands cradling her head.

The roar of the gun blocked out all other sound except the rapid pounding of her heart. Hannah wanted to close her eyes and have this bad dream go away. Only this nightmare was as real as they came. A real live troll with a gun.

Hannah was afraid to look up, afraid of what she might see. She was even more afraid that the woman would shoot her while she was cowering on the floor. She didn't come back here to die a coward's death.

She was here for a reason.

Jake needed her.

She couldn't fail him now. Hannah took a deep breath, gathered her scattered wits, opened her eyes, and assessed the situation. Less than two feet away Jake sprawled on top of Ursula. He was alive. Thank God.

Jake couldn't remember when he'd last taken a breath. His lungs demanded air. He inhaled shakily, the influx of air burning his oxygen-starved lungs.

He'd almost died twice in one day.

Once when Ursula put the gun to Hannah's head, and again when Hannah smashed her heavy binoculars into Ursula's gun arm. He'd had more stress in the last thirty minutes than he had in eight years of being a spy, with the notable exception of the day D.C. died in his arms.

He glanced overhead at the bullet hole in the ceiling. It had been close. Too damn close.

He'd been waiting for the right moment to disarm Ursula. He'd counted on her absorption in the contents of his computer screen. That's when he planned to take Ursula out. But Hannah had taken matters into her own hands and nearly gotten herself killed.

His blood jack-hammered through his ears.

She'd almost gotten herself killed.

He couldn't stand to think of anything happening to her. One night with Hannah hadn't been nearly enough. He wanted a lifetime of nights with her.

That realization rocked him. He'd never been so invested in the welfare of any other woman, but Hannah was different. She made the sun shine brighter, the sky bluer, the grass greener.

He loved her.

He'd been willing to step in front of Ursula's bullet so that Hannah wouldn't die.

Hannah had nearly ruined everything with her brainless stunt. Ursula squirmed underneath him, but he paid no attention to her restless movements. "You okay?" he asked Hannah.

Hannah sat up slowly, rubbing her shoulder where it had hit the desk. "I think so. How about you?"

"Fair." Jake allowed himself a full breath. His leg ached like a son of a gun, but that was no surprise. "There's a roll of duct tape on the back porch. Get it for me."

"What about the gun?" Hannah rose in stages, as if she were assessing which joints worked. He understood her tentativeness. He wasn't sure he could stand without crumpling. Between walking to the meadow at noon, driving Hannah to the airport, sitting in his computer chair for hours, and then supporting Ursula's weight, his left leg was overdone.

Jake nodded towards the door. "Don't worry about the gun. Our top priority is securing Ursula." Not that he had the energy for many other priorities, but at least he sounded authoritative.

Hannah bolted out the door like a frightened rabbit. He couldn't fault her for running. Who would want to hang around a place where they'd almost been murdered?

D.C. had shielded his family from this part of his life, so this had to be another first for Hannah. A very unpleasant first. Not a first Jake wanted her to have. Clearly he wasn't doing such a hot job of looking after her if guns were being pointed at her head.

This mess was his fault. Because of him, Hannah had almost died. To her credit, she had handled the situation like a seasoned pro. She'd stayed calm when things were dicey and acted courageously when she had the chance.

He was proud of her.

But she had probably changed her opinion about him. The way she'd skirted around him before she ran out of the room said more about her true feelings than words could ever say.

He'd put that fear in her storm blue eyes. It made him feel small and empty to think of her walking away from him. Is that what would happen next? The upshot of the whole deal would be them going their separate ways?

He didn't like that answer. He wanted more, an entire lifetime with the woman he loved.

Ursula squirmed underneath him. "You're hurting me."

He gripped her arm tighter. There wasn't a chance in hell of Ursula getting away from him. He had so much fury pumping through his body that he was beyond sympathy. "Too bad."

He heard Hannah open and close the door to the porch. He'd been meaning to oil those hinges, but he hadn't gotten around to it. For a moment he worried Ursula might have brought along Grafton for backup, but then he heard the door again and the sound of Hannah's rapid footsteps. He knew it was Hannah because of that little hitch in her stride, the one where her right foot scuffed the floor on its forward movement.

"What's your price?" Ursula asked caustically.

"Forget it." When he'd punched up Ursula's info on the computer a moment ago, he'd also keyed in a silent alarm. Help would be arriving shortly.

"I'll give you whatever you want if you let me walk out of here. Money, women, drugs. Anything."

Disgust curled his stomach. "You have nothing I want."

Hannah returned with the duct tape. In silence, he wrapped the tape tightly around Ursula's wrists and ankles. He sealed her mouth with another piece.

Then he picked up the gun, set the safety, and stuck the gun in the back of his waistband. When the weapon was secure, he turned to Hannah. Could she see that she held his heart in her hands? What could he say to her that would make up for what she'd just been through?

Keep it simple, he thought as he rose to his feet. "I'm sorry," he said to Hannah.

She flew into his arms. "Jake. I've never been so scared in my life."

Jake reached deep for another burst of energy. He wanted to take her clothes off and reassure himself that she was whole, that Ursula hadn't tainted her.

His arms closed around her. Deep relief filled him. She wasn't repulsed by his touch. She wanted him. He hadn't lost her.

She trembled like a broken branch in a wind storm. Jake stroked her tousled cap of hair. Its silky texture made his fingertips tingle with need. "It's all right," he said.

"It's *not* all right." Hannah pounded on his chest. "You could have been killed. You would have been killed if I hadn't come back to rescue you."

Jake scowled at the top of her head. "You shouldn't have come back. I had everything under control."

"I had to come back. I had to know why you were acting so strangely."

"I didn't want you involved in this. That's why I sent you away."

Hannah leveled a shaking finger at Ursula. "Shouldn't we call the cops so they can come arrest her?"

"I took care of that when I accessed the computer. Help is already on the way. Why don't we wait in the kitchen? She's not going anywhere."

Hannah didn't budge. "Why did she come here, Jake? Why?"

"She killed your father."

Hannah glared at the bound woman on the floor. "Give me the gun. I'll shoot her."

"You'll do no such thing. She isn't worth it."

"Is she the one who hurt you?"

"Yes."

"She said she was your lover."

"Was. Past tense."

"Why did you sleep with her?"

Jake rubbed his aching thigh. He wanted to pick Hannah up and carry her to the kitchen, but with all the exercise he'd gotten today, he was spent. He sank wearily on the bed, propping his leg up on the bed pillow. Hannah sat next to him.

"She pursued me," Jake said. "I was flattered by her interest. I didn't know she was using me to get to D.C. Between her efforts and the mole in the CIA, our mission was compromised before it began."

"I could have told you she was trouble."

Jake smoothed a silky strand of hair behind Hannah's ear. She was safe now. If he kept repeating that, maybe he'd start believing it.

"I'm actually a shrewd judge of character," Hannah said. "I knew you were lying to me earlier too."

Jake had seen the narrowing of her perceptive eyes when she first walked in. Hannah's father had had the same inner eye. D.C. never would have bought his phony act, not for one second.

"You've got the Montgomery eye," Jake said. "Your father had the same gift. That's what made him so successful in the field. He could size up a situation and make the right decision every time. D.C. would have been very proud of you for what you pulled off here tonight. Weren't you scared?"

Hannah nodded. "Absolutely."

"Why didn't you sit tight until I had things under control? I promised your father I would look after you. That includes keeping you out of danger."

She grabbed two fistfuls of T-shirt. "You did a lot more than that, buddy boy. Surely you haven't forgotten last night."

"I'll never forget last night. It was the highlight of my life." Jake brushed his lips over hers. Heat flared down his body.

Maybe he wasn't so tired after all. Maybe he could summon the energy to make love to the woman in his arms.

Hannah reached around him for her binoculars on the floor. As she examined them, a frown filled her face. "Dang. I shattered one of the optics in my father's binoculars."

Busted binoculars were the least of their worries. "I'll buy you a brand new pair if you promise to never, ever do anything so foolish again." At the sight of the small object on the strap, his gaze narrowed. "Damn."

Hannah sighed. "What now? Haven't we been through enough today?"

"These binoculars. This little gizmo. It's a bug. That's how they knew what we were doing. Grafton planted a bug on the binoculars."

"That sneak." Hannah chewed her lip. "About Grafton—"

Jake caressed her mouth with his hand. "Grafton was the mole. I've already turned him in. He'll never bother us again."

"You're right about that. I think he's dead. He followed me from the airport. When he tried to run me off the road again, I did some defensive driving. He wrecked his car and impaled himself on a mailbox post."

Jake hugged her close. How many times would the universe try to take her away? "I'm sorry. I wanted you to be safe."

Hannah pushed away and looked up at him. The serious expression on her face tugged at his heart. "He was the troll in my bedroom, Jake. He terrorized me as a kid to get some doll with smuggled electronics in it. He's the reason my parent's divorced. He's the reason my father lived such a lonely life."

"I never knew Grafton hated D.C. so much. He never let on."

"Before he shot himself, he bragged about how he'd taken my dad's power away."

"Not for long. I'll bet D.C. has plenty to say to him right about now." He hugged her again. "Why'd you come back, Hannah?"

When Hannah's head nestled on his chest, he felt powerful enough to leap tall buildings in a single bound. "Like you, I believe in going after what I want. Once I figured out that you sent me away to keep me safe, I couldn't sit idly by. I wanted to make sure we had a future."

Joy flooded Jake's senses as he hugged Hannah close. Hannah thought they had a future together. Life didn't get any better than that.

****

Later that evening, after the house emptied of folks with badges and handcuffs, Jake followed Hannah to her bedroom, the gentle sway of her hips working their usual sensual magic on him. By all rights, he should be exhausted, but during the briefing of the authorities he'd gotten his second wind.

Hannah had come back to him today. Knowing that she believed in their strong connection warmed him from the inside out. She wanted him. Incredible but true.

He closed the bedroom door until he heard the snick of the door latch. Moonlight flooded the room, illuminating Hannah's shapely curves. There was one thing on his mind right now. Making love to Hannah. After that, he planned to sleep with her in his arms.

His eyes locked with hers as he limped across the room. The heat he saw in her eyes further fueled his desire for her. Oh yeah. This was going to be good, very good.

Keeping his gaze on her, he unbuckled his belt and let his pants slide to the floor. His leg ached fiercely, but nothing ached as much as the urgency to make love with her.

"Are you sure you're up to more physical activity?" she asked as she shimmied out of her jeans. "Your leg must be killing you."

Jake stilled. "Hannah, I need you."

Her arms slid around him, her hands nestled in his hair. "I need you too. I was so scared today. I could have lost you."

"If you ever try to disarm a cold blooded killer again, I won't be held accountable for my actions." Jake kissed Hannah, running his hands down her slender back, lowering her to the bed. His body covered hers, molding her curves into his hard angles.

"If you ever entertain cold blooded killers in the bedroom, I won't be held accountable for my actions," Hannah muttered when they came up for air.

His hand cupped one rosy breast and then the other. "We have to have a serious talk about your tendency to disobey orders."

Hannah cocked her head. "What about your tendency to boss me around? That's the real problem."

Jake nuzzled her breast. "Can't fault me for that. Not when your safety is at risk."

"Don't..." Hannah nearly came off the bed when he touched the steamy juncture of her legs. "Don't stop," she finished breathlessly.

When they were both glassy-eyed with need, he surged into her welcoming recesses with deep satisfaction. Hannah was his. He was certain of it.

But later, as he hovered in that warm afterglow he worried about the nebulous future. He had Hannah, but for how long?

He wasn't poor, not by a long shot, but he had no job lined up. Her job was in the city, two hours away from this cozy cottage in the woods. Living in the fairy tale cottage with Hannah was the future he wanted, but he didn't know how to make it happen.

He still couldn't believe his good luck. Hannah wanted a future with him, Jake Sutherland. The kid from the wrong side of the tracks. He envisioned spending the next fifty or so years with Hannah at his side. They'd get a dog that loved birds. There would be children in that future.

Children.

The word made his stomach flip flop. Would his children have Hannah's beautiful eyes? Her creamy complexion? Her endearing spunk?

Whoa. He was getting ahead of himself here. Children implied a commitment they hadn't made. He'd always been commitment averse with other women. Being with Hannah had changed him. Now he wanted things that were previously out of his field of interest. Things like a wife and a home.

Would Hannah marry him? Women like Hannah came along once in a lifetime. If he was smart, he'd assure his success by making sure she couldn't refuse. He'd think of something in the morning.

He dozed off, holding her snug against him. Her gentle exhalations stirred the mat of hair on his chest. She wasn't getting away from him again, not if he could help it.

****

Hannah awoke warmly cocooned in a sunny room.

Jake's arm was draped across her breasts, pinning her to his side. She smiled as the memory of last night's lovemaking replayed in her mind. That was one happy ending that she'd never forget in a million years.

She'd taken a chance on Jake and it had paid off, big time.

In his arms was exactly where she wanted to be. All she had to do was convince Jake that he couldn't live without her.

She had a plan.

A secret that gave her an edge.

In all the excitement last night, she'd forgotten to tell Jake she loved him. She'd get to that, but first she had to impress on him why they were so good together. She didn't want to go through another emotional low like she hit at the airport yesterday.

It was time that she laid down the law and set Jake Sutherland straight. He loved her. She was sure of it.

She stretched and his hand reflexively closed over her breast, anchoring her to him. "Morning," she said.

Jake's lean hardness made itself known. In spite of her plans to set him straight, Hannah wiggled against him, delighted that she had this effect on him.

Jake had freed her from a bleak future where the most exciting thing in her life was erroneous data. She wanted to wake up every morning with him beside her. Two nights of loving didn't fill the years of loneliness in her heart. She needed a lifetime of loving and Jake was just the man for the job.

"Thought you'd never wake up," Jake mouthed between the honeyed kisses he feathered along her neck.

Hannah shivered with anticipation. She yearned for the pleasure Jake could give, but she had to look at the big picture here. Long term planning was important. She rolled over to face him.

Jake looked rested and ready to go. Molten heat steamed from his smiling brown eyes. Hannah felt her cheeks flush in response. She fanned the heat away from her face with her hand. "Time out."

He raised his eyebrows suggestively and tweaked the tip of her breast. "Time in."

She delighted in his smiling, playful mood. This was a side of Jake she'd never seen before. He seemed freer, easier. As she returned his smile, his fingers feathered down her belly causing her nervous system to short circuit.

Goosebumps broke out on Hannah's flesh. She had to remember the big picture. She could be strong. Her fingers closed firmly around his questing hand. "We need to clear the air," she said, ignoring the tingling sensation originating from her palm. "I have things to say to you, and I expect you to listen."

She tried to read his expression, but all she got was lust in spades. Jake tended to be a very focused individual, and she was the current target of his focus. "I won't tolerate you lying to me," she said. "I saw my mother fold in on herself after being devastated by my father's lies. I don't want to relive her life. You will tell me the truth. No more lies, got it?"

"Sure. No more lies." Jake folded the sheet down to his hips and leaned back into the pillows, bracketing his head with his hands.

Hannah sat up and covered herself with the patchwork quilt. "We're a good match because we both seek the truth. We're trustworthy, resilient, and tenacious. Both of us have a history of sitting back and watching the world, so we're good at reading people. Do you agree?"

"I agree. Come here. I've got something to show you."

Hannah sat up straighter. "This is serious. I need to get these details ironed out. I have to know how our arrangement is going to work."

"Our arrangement?"

"Don't go getting testy on me. You're a detail person too. I need to know what's going to happen after my vacation is over. I should think you'd want to know too, seeing as how we're such a good match."

"Hannah, I already know you want to sleep with me. What more is there?"

"What more is there?" Hannah picked up her pillow and whacked him over the head with it. "You stupid man, I'm trying to tell you I love you."

Jake blinked. "Don't tease me about this."

Hannah realized her breasts were exposed. She hugged the pillow to her chest. "I've never been more serious in my life."

Jake's eyes blazed with strong emotion. Hannah hoped it was love. She prayed it was love.

She strained to hear his response, leaning forward just in case he whispered of his love for her. Time ticked past with agonizing slowness. Why didn't he say he loved her? Wasn't that how it was supposed to go? When one person said I love you, then the other person said it right back?

"I'm not going anywhere without you," he said, scooping her up in his arms. Her pillow tumbled to the floor. "But, we'll have to continue this discussion later. I always thought I was a leg man, but it seems I'm a breast man. I can't concentrate when you're flaunting your nakedness before me."

Hannah inhaled deeply of the intriguing bouquet that was pure Jake. She loved him, and he wouldn't leave her. It was a good place to start. The big picture could wait a few more minutes.

****

"Come for a walk with me," Jake said after they'd showered and dressed. He hadn't wanted to get up at all, but he couldn't afford to lounge in bed the entire day.

Now that Ursula and Grafton were out of the picture, he was free to pursue his own happiness. He'd learned something important during this last separation from Hannah. He'd learned he never wanted to go through that ever again. He wasn't a man to sit around and bemoan his fate. Action suited him. Action and goal setting.

His new goal was acquiring Hannah.

"Aren't you hungry?" Hannah's damp hair curled about her head. "What about breakfast?"

He wanted to take her in his arms right now. She would melt for him. He knew because she'd been melting against him since midnight. He'd never get enough of Hannah's special loving. "Breakfast can wait. I have something to ask you."

"So, ask."

No way was Jake going to ask a life or death question in such a casual manner. For this particular question, he needed to set the stage. Someplace where she was very comfortable, someplace where she would be predisposed to provide the right answer. "All in good time. Why don't we take some food with us?"

Jake ignored the enigmatic look Hannah shot him. He waited patiently as Hannah collected fruit, cheese, bread, and bottled water in a plastic bag. Jake picked the bag up and ushered her out the front door.

Hannah's beautiful eyes danced with questions. "Are we going far? You shouldn't push that leg too much today. You know you overdid it yesterday."

"My leg is fine," Jake said, locking the front door behind them. His terse statement came out sharper than he intended. He didn't want her sympathy.

"Are you always so grumpy in the morning?" she asked.

Jake pointed his cane westward towards the sun. "It's afternoon, and I'm not grumpy. I'm determined. There's a big difference. You're the grumpy one. Didn't you get enough sleep last night? Or maybe you got up on the wrong side of the bed?"

Hannah had been insatiable, and he'd been very willing to accommodate her. Consequently neither of them had gotten much sleep last night.

"I slept late this morning because you kept me awake most of the night." She tilted her head to look at him in that special inquiring way she had.

"Are you complaining?" he asked.

"Bragging actually."

To his delight, Hannah blushed bright red. Satisfaction hummed through his veins. All he had to do was convince Hannah that they were meant to be together.

"Are we going to the meadow?" Hannah asked as they picked up the narrow trail through the trees.

"I can't slip anything past you."

But he was counting on slipping a marriage proposal right past her. He'd never been a betting man, but he wished he knew what the odds were of her saying yes to his proposal. He'd give anything to know her answer before he popped the question.

Because if she didn't say yes, he'd wither up and die. Without Hannah, his life had no meaning.

Chapter 19

Asking a woman to marry him was a first for Jake, and it scared him senseless. Those four words, *will you marry me*, were as huge as any mountain range. If she said no, would he beg?

Jake's stomach twisted like the furry vines growing up the rough bark of the trees beside the narrow winding path. Practice makes perfect, he thought. He mouthed the words silently as he walked. Will you marry me? His stomach knotted with each successive iteration.

His mouth went dry. How was he going to do this without sounding like a complete idiot? Fear gripped him tighter than any clinging vine. Though it was a mild spring day, sweat trickled down his spine and beaded on his brow.

She was the woman he wanted to spend the rest of his life with. She would say yes. She had to.

It was important to him that they get this settled right away. He wished he'd had time to buy her a ring, but he'd only decided to propose this morning. Right after she announced that she loved him. He didn't waste time when an objective was within reach. He'd propose first, buy the ring second. She could even select the ring she wanted, as long as she said yes.

As he walked out of the dark tunnel of trees, the sunny meadow inspired him with hope. The bright green meadow grass and the cheerful blue flowers were vibrant testaments to nature's yearly rebirth. Birdsong filled the air.

He'd lived in the shadows for a long time. Would he fit in Hannah's vibrant Technicolor world? His fingers tightened around the grip of his cane until his knuckles stood out in stark relief. Nerves. He had to harness his nerves.

Hannah cocked her head and listened intently.

Jake automatically scanned the area for threats and found none. He forced air into his lungs and mopped his brow. He needed to rest his leg for a moment, so he headed for the wooden bench by the spring. "What do you hear?" he asked.

"Nuthatches, ovenbirds, towhees, chickadees, and Carolina wrens. That flute-like call is a veery. I'm sure if we stay here long enough we'll hear a ruffed grouse drumming. I heard one last time I was in the meadow."

Hannah sat beside him on the bench and reached for the food bag. "I'm famished. How about you?"

Eating was the last thing on his mind, but if it made Hannah happy to fuss with the food, he was all for that. "You go ahead. I'll get something in a bit."

Jake studied Hannah covertly. She seemed at ease, relaxed even. It had been a good idea to come here. A proposal should be special, and this place was special.

It occurred to him that the reason he'd been restless for so many years was because he hadn't known what he was looking for, he just knew he was looking. A future settled down in one place no longer sounded like a fate worse than death. It sounded like paradise.

Home, even.

The place he'd been longing for all of his life.

And home meant Hannah.

Why did he have to *ask* her to marry him? Why couldn't he just tell her that's how it was going to be? Asking her took him out of the driver's seat. And the uncertainty was hell on his frayed nerves.

"Here," Hannah said.

Jake accepted the miniature fruit and cheese sandwich Hannah handed him. He tried a small bite, but his nervous stomach rebelled. He set the sandwich down on the bench.

"Don't you want it?" Hannah asked.

He loved the way her hair shimmered in the sunlight. So many reds and blondes and browns, his fingers itched to explore every silky strand. Soon, he promised himself. Once his future was decided.

"Later maybe. I have too much on my mind right now."

"Your loss." Hannah scooped up the sandwich and swallowed it whole. "I'm famished."

Jake closed his eyes for a moment to gather his wits. He should have bought the ring first. A lady expected a ring when a gentleman proposed. He was no gentleman. He was a washed up, unemployed, injured man.

But Hannah loved him. And she wasn't the type of woman to be impressed with glittery trappings. She was very much no nonsense and goal oriented, like himself. She wouldn't blame him for doing things out of order.

He took a shaky breath. His jittery stomach turned and twisted and inverted with every beat of his racing heart. She might refuse. She might accept. He'd never know if he didn't get on with it.

Jake edged forward off the bench to kneel in the lush grass at Hannah's feet. On the way down, he got tangled up on his cane and spilled awkwardly on the ground, his injured leg catching underneath him. He grimaced at the pain.

"Jake! Are you all right?" Hannah slid off the bench and knelt beside him. Her comforting hand rested lightly on his shoulder.

"Fine," Jake said through clenched teeth. It was a wonder she hadn't run screaming from the meadow. "Get back up on the bench, Hannah."

Hannah's lips thinned. "Don't order me around. I'm not your employee."

Her curt response irritated him. His throbbing leg irritated him. Nothing was going as he had planned. But he couldn't stop now. This was the only plan he had. "Don't fight me on this. Sit on the damn bench."

Damn. He hadn't meant to cuss at her. That wasn't the way to soften her up. Jake blinked his eyes shut momentarily, embarrassment heating his face and neck. "I'm sorry. I didn't mean to snap at you. Please. Sit on the bench."

Hannah sat. She scowled at him.

Jake took her delicate hand in his. Her skin was warm and soft, but her fingers lay unresponsive in his hand. Though water flowed in a soothing rhythm next to the bench, his nerves wouldn't settle. They couldn't. Not until he popped the all-important question.

He'd never wanted anything in his whole life as much as he wanted Hannah to be his wife. He met her trusting gaze with all the love in his heart.

"Hannah, I want us to be together," Jake said. "Will you marry me?"

Hannah cocked her head in that considering way she had. Was she evaluating his proposal? Jake's stomach went through another series of gymnastic gyrations. On the plus side, she hadn't rejected him outright. He still had a chance.

Seconds ticked by, seconds that Jake knew he could never get back. With each second he felt himself free falling through space, tumbling out of control into a bottomless void. Why didn't she answer? Didn't she know the agony he was going through?

"Why?" she finally asked.

Her question floored him. "Why? You love me, that's why."

She shook her head quickly, her bright eyes glassy. "Why do you want to marry me?"

Moisture from the ground wicked up into the fabric of his jeans, and weary numbness spread up his trunk into his heart. Despair clouded his vision. Was she stalling to prolong his agony? "Is that a no?"

Hannah leaned down into his face. She didn't appear to be ecstatic about his proposal. Jake's heart sunk. He'd screwed up all right. His first and only marriage proposal, and he'd blown it.

"Don't you put words in my mouth, Jacob Sutherland. I didn't say no. I'm waiting to hear your answer."

Jake couldn't take another second of this agonizing uncertainty. "Hannah, I'll answer any question you have if you'll just say yes."

"Why do you want to marry me?"

With great effort, Jake swallowed around the giant lump blocking his throat. "You're not making this easy for me."

Concern immediately etched her features. "Why don't you sit on the bench? Kneeling in the damp grass can't be good for your hurt leg."

No kidding.

But he was used to the throbbing in his leg. His aching leg was a fact of life. If she said no, would his heart also pain him for the rest of his days? "Would you knock it off about the leg? My leg is damaged, just like me. I'm not perfect by any means. I'm just a man. A man foolishly, passionately in love with a beautiful woman."

Hannah's face lit up, and she jumped him. "Yes. Yes. Yes. I'll marry you."

The weight in his heart lifted. Jake's arms closed reflexively around her as her momentum carried them backward into the soft meadow grass. He rolled to take the brunt of the fall, cradling her on his chest, protecting her from harm.

He smiled.

She'd said yes.

Joy flooded through him in great crashing waves. He kissed her with exquisite care. His hands shook with relief, and his pulse danced a merry rhythm.

She was going to marry him.

He had a home, and that home was Hannah Montgomery.

Not bad for a drifter like him.

He lay on the ground and looked up. Brilliant blue sky formed a captivating frame around the woman he loved. Her beautiful eyes sparkled like the rarest of jewels.

If a bolt of lightning were to strike him dead right at this moment, he'd die a happy man. The most wonderful woman in the world had agreed to marry him. He could hardly believe his good fortune.

He'd been given a rare gift, the love of a good woman, and he would treasure her for the rest of his days.

Hannah exhaled slowly, allowing the breath she'd been holding to go free. Jake's curt proposal had taken her by surprise. She wanted to marry him, that wasn't the problem.

The problem was that Jake hadn't known why he wanted to marry her. Or at least, she thought he didn't know why. But he did.

He loved her.

He was foolishly, passionately in love with her.

A happy smile bubbled out of her center, renewing and recharging her, even as she held Jake tight. With her ear on his chest, she could hear the rapid beating of his heart.

She wanted to marry Jake. To have his children. To make a home with him.

She trusted him. With her life and with her heart. Jake would be there for her. She'd seen firsthand that he didn't run from danger or conflict. He was the type to go toe to toe with someone until an issue was resolved.

He'd said he was damaged, but she was damaged too. Heck, no one was perfect. Everyone came with baggage and preconceived ideas. The trick about life and marriage was to stay the course.

He had waited here for her for months. He wouldn't cut and run at the first disagreement they had. He was solid. And she loved him.

She'd never known such pleasure could exist until she'd fallen in love with Jake. He'd opened up a whole new sensual realm to her, and she couldn't wait to explore it again. The gentle murmur of the spring and the rich earthy smell of the moist earth would forever be linked in her mind to this happy occasion.

A question bubbled through her happiness and she raised up to ask him, "Why did you choose to propose out here?"

"Because this meadow makes you happy." Jake's fingers gently caressed her forearms. "I've been thinking. I want us to keep this place, Hannah. To live here."

Hannah blinked rapidly. Living here in the woods was fine and grand, but it didn't pay the rent. Of the two of them, she was the only one who was employed fulltime. "But my job. It's too far to commute from out here. Living way out here isn't practical."

"You belong here. I've known it from the start. Besides, this is the first place that ever felt like home to me. I wouldn't ask you to stay here if I didn't think it was important. In a perfect world, would you live here?"

She liked this place a lot. Was Jake thinking they would ask her mother for money to live on? Not going to happen. But it wouldn't hurt to humor him. "Of course."

"What would you do here, in a perfect world, that is?"

Why did he insist on talking about things that weren't possible? The grim reality was that they needed income. Love wouldn't put food on the table. "The things I talked about before. I'd make this meadow a sanctuary. For people or for animals, or maybe both."

He smoothed back an errant strand of her hair. Hannah couldn't keep herself from arching into his touch. She'd never thought of herself as poor before. If they lived here, they would definitely be poor.

"I've got some money set aside," Jake said slowly. "And I'm good at investing. That's how come D.C. had such a nice nest egg for your mother. He trusted me to handle his investments."

Jake had savings? Better yet, Jake had a marketable skill that didn't involve guns?

Hannah envisioned Jake managing investments out of a home office. The idea had great appeal. "Investments, eh? I like it. It's safe. And it's a service people need. People want a good return on their money."

Hannah's mind raced ahead, trying to fit these new details into the shifting matrix of her life. Marriage. Living here in the woods. Jake working in a safe job from a home office. That led to the question of her career. "I suppose I could ask my company if I can telecommute."

"Only if that's what you want to do," Jake paused momentarily. "What I'm trying to say is that I have enough money set aside that neither of us has to work a nine-to-five job if we don't want to. We can do what we like with our lives."

Hannah shrank back in mock horror. His arms only let her go so far before she met with stiff resistance. "You want me to become a kept woman?"

"I'd love to keep you here in my arms for the rest of our lives. You fill up all my empty spaces, Hannah."

"Oh, Jake. You say the sweetest things. How did I get so lucky?" Hannah stroked the side of his face. She never wanted to wake up from this wonderful fairy tale of a day.

"I've been asking myself that question ever since you walked into my life," Jake said, his eyes brimming with love.

"That's so sweet." Hannah rested her cheek in his palm and felt stirrings so deep she trembled. This was real. She loved Jake more than anything. He was no big bad wolf. He was her very own prince come to rescue her.

Without warning, Jake went rigid beneath her.

"What is it?" Hannah asked in alarm, lifting her head from his broad chest. "Jake, are you all right?"

He had to be all right. She had been waiting for him her entire life. Fate couldn't be so cruel as to take him right at this moment, could it? The thought took her breath away.

"Look." Jake pointed at the underside of the bench.

Hannah glanced in the direction he was pointing. A plastic encased sheet of paper was stapled securely to the bottom of the wooden bench. Whatever this was, it wasn't a threat to Jake's physical existence. She could relax. Air rushed into her lungs. Her heart resumed beating. "What is that?"

On her hands and knees, she crawled over to retrieve the packet. Soft meadow grass tickled her palms, but she barely noticed. Her attention was focused on the note. She plucked the packet off the underside of the bench and read her name on the paper.

The familiar scrawling handwriting gave her cold chills. Ice crystallized in her veins. "It's from my father."

She couldn't believe how calm she sounded. Every time she'd found one of these notes from her father, her life had changed. Her life was perfect right now, thank you very much. She didn't want another change.

Jake sat up and motioned her back over to him. Hannah scrambled back to the safety of Jake's arms. Jake spread his legs so that Hannah sat in the vee of his legs. His arms encircled her tensed shoulders.

His calm presence reassured her. Whatever was in this letter, they would deal with it together. She wasn't alone anymore. Jake would be there for her, for better or for worse. With a deep breath, she opened the note and began to read aloud.

Dearest Hannah,

I have always wanted the best for you, and I'm hoping that you've discovered that life isn't always straightforward. There are twists and turns that life throws at you, and it's best to endure them with someone you love and trust by your side. I hope you'll find happiness and if you haven't already found happiness, I'm taking this opportunity to recommend my partner, Jake Sutherland. He's had some experience in the school of hard knocks, but he is true blue. He's got what you need and he's my wish for your personal "Happily Ever After." Tell Jake to retrieve the Banana Fund. It's a little something I set aside for you. I love you, now and forever. Your father, Dean Christian Montgomery

ps Jake, look out for Grafton. I believe he's the one

who scared Hannah years ago.

Hannah closed her eyes to the tears that blurred her vision, grateful to the warm sunshine that was thawing the chill in her veins. Her whole life, she'd been trying to earn her father's love, only she'd had it all along.

She'd had it all along.

But, her efforts hadn't been in vain. There was a strength in her that most women her age didn't have. She was stronger for it, stronger and better equipped to go after her heart's desire.

Because of that, she'd found her future, and she even had her father's blessing. It didn't get much better than that.

"D.C.'s instincts were right on the mark with Grafton," Jake said.

"Yeah, but it took him twenty-two years to flush the man out," Hannah complained. "Do you think Grafton would have killed my family if my father had stayed with us?"

Jake's eyes went all narrow and squinty. "I think D.C. believed it was very possible. He couldn't accept that risk."

Jake was a lot like her father. He'd already tried to send her away when the going got tough. "Would you have reacted the same way?"

"I would do anything and everything to protect you. You have my word on that."

Hannah's heart sunk. "You are not sending me away again. I won't stand for it. If we have an outside threat, we face it together."

"For someone who doesn't like being told what to do, you sure give your share of orders."

"I guess that's because deep down where it counts I am my father's daughter."

"I wouldn't have it any other way."

Happiness sang through Hannah as she listened to the steady rhythm of Jake's heart. She wouldn't lose her independence by marrying Jake. Instead, she'd be gaining a valuable teammate.

"What's this Banana Fund?" Hannah asked.

Jake grinned. "Just what he said. An investment account. I set it up for him."

"I thought my Mom inherited all his investment accounts."

"Not this one. It was structured to be under the radar. Your father put your name on the account. It was his nest egg for a rainy day."

Hannah considered that. "Is it illegal?"

"Nope."

"How many bananas are we talking about?"

"Not as many bananas as your mother inherited, but respectable nonetheless."

"Why didn't I hear about this account before?" Hannah's gaze narrowed in suspicion. "Are you marrying me for my money?"

Jake's brown eyes gleamed. "Not a chance. I invested my windfalls too." Jake paused. "I may be unemployed, but I'm not a pauper."

Sounded like Jake was being modest. "Dang. I hardly know what to say."

"Say that the money doesn't change anything. That you'll still marry me."

"Of course I'll still marry you. I love you, remember?"

"I'm not likely to forget." Jake stroked his fingers down her arms. "D.C.'s middle name was Christian? He told me it was Colin."

A smile tugged at the corners of Hannah's mouth. She'd forgotten about her father's aversion to his given name. "Dad liked to say it was Colin. He thought Christian wasn't manly enough. That's why he went by his initials."

Jake's laughter warmed her even more. "He was something else, wasn't he?"

Hannah craned her neck around to look up at Jake. "Did you know he meant for us to be a couple?"

"All I knew was that he wanted me to make sure you

got settled after his death."

Suddenly, it wasn't enough to look at Jake over her shoulder. Hannah turned in Jake's arms and cupped his precious face. The coarse stubble of beard rubbed against the smoothness of her fingers. "I feel settled. The future feels special because you're sharing it with me."

Jake's knowing look turned her insides to mush. "One thing you should know right up front. I won't walk away from what we have, not for any reason. At heart, I'm not a person who changes course easily."

"You haven't met my Mom yet," Hannah teased.

"Sweetheart, I haven't met a woman I can't charm."

"About that," Hannah said, stiffening her spine. "I expect you to curtail your woman charming if we're getting married."

"No 'if' about it. We are getting married. Soon."

"What's the rush? Putting on a wedding takes at least a year to do it right. It probably takes that long to find just the right ball gown."

Jake turned green and Hannah laughed. "Just kidding. I'm not the ball gown type or hadn't you figured that out yet?"

"Don't tease me about this," Jake said. "It's important to me that we get married as soon as possible."

Hannah's eyebrows rose as her forehead furrowed. "Are we talking about a tacky Vegas wedding?"

Jake shrugged. "Why not? You're still on vacation and the world is temporarily safe from terrorists. This is the perfect time to get married. I can book us a flight to Vegas tonight."

"Whoa. My luggage got bashed when Grafton rammed my car. The police took my clothes as evidence. I don't have any underwear other than what I have on. I can't go to Vegas with no underwear."

"No underwear works for me," Jake said with a rakish grin, his hands skimming over her curves.

Hannah shivered with excitement. "It would."

"I promise to buy whatever you need if you'll marry

me right away."

"Gosh, that's so romantic." Hannah's voice dripped with sarcasm.

Jake looked like he'd swallowed a bug and she took pity on him. It really didn't matter to her where they got married, or even when they got married. As far as she was concerned, her new life had already begun.

"Don't fret," she said. "I'll do it, as long as we include my Mom. I can't get married without my mother. And what about your foster parents? Shouldn't they be invited too?"

"You can invite whoever you want as long as you understand one thing. No one else is welcome on our honeymoon," Jake cautioned.

"Our honeymoon," Hannah repeated. She hadn't even considered that aspect of getting married. "Where are we going for that?"

"Your choice."

Hannah eyed him expectantly. Was Jake's leg well enough for one of her birding adventures? "I've never seen the birds in Greenland."

"Greenland?" Jake choked out, his robust color graying.

"Teasing. How does the Arizona desert sound? I'd love to see the west, and it will be convenient since we'll already be in Vegas."

Jake hugged her and kissed her lightly. "Done. Let's go home and make the arrangements."

"Home. I like the way that sounds."

"Me too."

Hannah gathered up the remains of their breakfast picnic. "I love you, Jake. I'm planning on loving you for a very long time."

"Even though I'm secretive, obstinate, and occasionally stuck in the past?"

"Especially then."

About the author...

Maggie Toussaint is a scientist by training, a romanticist at heart. She's fascinated by how things work, whether it's complex machinery, a Sudoku puzzle, or the male female subtext of a conversation. She's married, has two children, and lives in coastal Georgia. Contact Maggie at Maggie@maggietoussaint.com. Visit Maggie at www.maggietoussaint.com.